FOREST OF THE MORNING

BY

EMMYLOU KOTZÉ

Book 1
Forest of the Morning

PINK HYDRA PRESS

2024

Copyright

Forest of the Morning
Book 1 of the Forest of the Morning series

© Emmylou Kotzé 2024
www.amphipolitan.com

Paperback: 978-1-0370-0596-1
e-book: 978-1-0370-0597-8

Pink Hydra Press
www.thepinkhydra.com

The Great Northern Continent
– The Old World
Religious wars wracked
this land
and so Bavarian's folk
fled to safe haven
in the south
ARVENIAN ISLES
The Western Continent
Lands of Bavarian
and the Forest
of the Morning
Middelmarkt
Bladbergen
Krokana
RIVER TROLLSDAUGHTER
SVANFELD
Sulshome
SEA OF CALMS
Pine
Ulhard
SVANLYN
Lynborder
Tenna
Quinen
Chuub
Von Dharen
RIVER GRANITE
QWU'MALLORN
Albrecol
Armour City
Wilderland
Catrool
VAILANA
Freedom
MOTHER THALE
Zarath
Cythece
Cygnath
The Eastern Empire →

PROLOGUE

The Armour Hills were brilliant with moonlight. Behind them, the city was burning.

Hiram kept a fast grip on his daughter's hand, willing her not to look back and think about the two they had left behind, willing himself not to stop. They were almost clear of the madness, the slaughter and the burning. They were at the top of the gulley. He stopped to catch his breath. Lathea's hand, slick with sweat, slid out of his. Her breathing—as it well might be, in her condition—was strained.

"They're killing everybody," she gasped.

"Only those with the Gift," Hiram insisted. "You and I, we don't have it. We'll win free."

She stared at him, huge tears beading in her amber-brown eyes. "Mother has the Mage-Gift." Her voice shook. "Karat has the Mage-

Gift." She placed a hand, protectively, on her distended stomach. "And you know as well as I do"—her voice broke—"that there's an even chance my children will have it."

"Come here." Hiram drew his daughter close, held her tightly. "They'll be all right," he breathed, trying to reassure himself as much as her. "They have magic; they're together. They'll meet us on the other side."

The face of his wife, Drailin, flashed into his memory, grey hair silvered in the light of the burning fires. The people coming for them, Hiram didn't know whether they were soldiers or denizens of Armour City itself. Whether perhaps he would know some of the faces that leered out from the formless mob, their own neighbours perhaps, or petitioners he'd once given audience, people who'd kept their hatred and their boundless spite out of sight, below the surface. Until now.

Gunshots echoed in Hiram's mind; his son-in-law, Karat, raised a hand, and they flew wide. The lead balls were vulnerable to magic.

"They can't touch *us*." His wife stood strong, in his mind's eye, before the approaching mob, though she was no warrior herself, only an artist, a maker of magical portraits and beautiful things. "Hiram, take our daughter and *go*! Save her. Save yourself. We'll stop them here, and meet you outside the city."

Back in the present moment, in the stillness of the night, the glow of the burning city seeming nothing more than a reflection of the indifferent stars, Lathea gazed at him desperately. "Father—if they're born with the Gift—"

Hiram couldn't worry about that right now. If he and Lathea got safely away—if the shock of their flight did not cause stillbirth or worse—if one or both of his grandchildren actually survived and happened to have inherited the Mage-Gift—he would worry about such things when they came to pass. Right now, the only thing that mattered was their lives. His daughter's life. He had to save Lathea. Hiram's family had splintered apart, his wife and son-in-law lost somewhere on the streets of Armour City. Lathea was all that was left to him.

"They'll meet us on the other side," he repeated. "Your mother, and Karat. They'll be there."

"Where?" she asked desperately.

"The Asmyth road." He and Drailin had discussed this, months beforehand, when the warlord Arran Sylvaissen still seemed only a distant threat to most people within the city. Not to Hiram. He was an Alderman, part of the governing structure that was meant to keep the city, and by extension the whole of the land of Vailana, safe. Arran Sylvaissen and his creed of segregation had frightened Hiram even then. If the hammer blow came, he knew, most people with the Gift would flee to the ancestral home of all those who possessed magic—the Forest of the Morning. But Hiram's little family had no ties there—both Drailin and Karat were city-born mages, their lives and livelihoods tied to *here*.

"We'll go to Svanfeld instead," he remembered saying. "This Sylvaissen's armies won't follow up there, not into the mountains. And I spent some time at a monastery there, once. The monks might help us to start anew."

Lathea was still breathing harshly. They had to move, Hiram thought. They had paused here for far too long.

"Who goes there?" came the sudden shout, and he froze like a hunted hare. A lantern glared in the darkness, moving somewhere along the riverbank above. Hiram could not make out the face of the one who held it, but he saw, as shadows, the long pointed shapes of the musket guns the group carried. Only soldiers would carry firearms. Arran Sylvaissen's soldiers.

"Go," Hiram whispered, pushing his daughter towards the mouth of the gulley.

"Stay where you are, old man!" Hiram froze in the act of following his daughter. "Yes, we see you. Stay where you are, or we'll shoot!"

"Father?" Lathea whispered. She was already halfway down, clinging to the boulders at Hiram's feet.

"Save yourself!" he whispered back, his voice low with urgency, praying that they would not hear. The troop of soldiers was making a lot of noise, coming down the dry riverbank towards where Hiram stood.

"No!" Lathea returned, fiercely. She moved, grasping for her father's hand.

A musket spoke, deafening thunder followed by the crash of a lead ball into the bushes somewhere far too close by. Hiram cringed back, and shoved Lathea away from him.

"Stay where you are!" came the shout, again.

"*Go*," he whispered, one last time. "Please."

Chapter I
Soldier

When Albryan Lana saw the panther, he crouched low in the bushes, mouth going half open, a length of wavy auburn hair escaping its knot at the back of his head to tickle his fuzzy upper lip.

The cat was beautiful, mist-and-charcoal-striped like the finest tabby silk from the weavers of Sanghui, and Albryan raised an arrow to his bow for a brief moment before deciding against it. It didn't seem right. Not at this time of year, with the woods emerging from the teeth of winter and the great cat having survived the lean season. It looked rangy, yet big-boned, probably a male. Rare enough to see one here, in the lower hillands of the sacred forest. It must have ranged down from the Svanlyn mountains, perhaps looking for food, for easy prey. Lambs from the western borderlands of Qwu'Mallorn.

The cat had come to lap at the pool which lay at the foot of a great, grey-barked ironwood tree. Albryan had been on his way to touch the great tree and kneel at its foot, to say a prayer to the goddess his people named Qwu'Kiya, mother deity of the magic-folk, or the Morgei as they were known to outsiders. Now he crouched in the undergrowth, making no sound, and watched until the panther finished drinking and slinked away into the bushes.

By the time Albryan finished paying his respects at the ironwood, the sun was westering and an icy breeze had come up, blowing straight down from the mountains. He shivered and hooked his hunting bow over his shoulder, attaching the leather cap on his quiver. It was time to head back. Even though he had caught nothing on this little trip, despite dreams of fur-lined boots and perhaps a warm pair of gloves, he still felt that it had been worthwhile.

It was two hours' walk back to the barracks near the town of Tenna. The air was cold, though at least the forest canopy kept things somewhat insulated down here. Albryan's upcoming assignment would take him into the land of Vailana, a vast plainsland that baked hard in summer and froze solid in winter. Armour City, its capital and buzzing hive, never seemed to variate its dust and dirt despite the passing of seasons. Albryan had been born there, but held few fond memories of the place. He had been about seven years old when the blood sorcerer, Arran Sylvaissen, had forced the Morgei out of Vailana and into the refuges of their ancestral home, Qwu'Mallorn, called by outsiders the Forest of the Morning.

Half ancestral for Albryan, some might say. Though he was possessed of a strong Gift, fit for war-magic, more than respectable for a son of a noble house such as his father's, Albryan was never unaware that he did not look Morgein. The reddish hair, blue-green eyes, and freckles that sprinkled his cheeks even in full adulthood came from his mother, who had been nonmage Vailanan. This wasn't that unusual; not for Vailanan-born mages, anyhow. Morgei and nonmage had once mixed freely in the bustling marketplaces of Vailana, but here, where the old mage-families still ruled the sacred forest, blood had always mattered more.

Albryan's mother was gone now; she had caught a deadly disease less than a year after their family had fled Armour City. Albryan's father, Alban Lana, had remarried into a much more profitable situation, a prosperous noblewoman from the town of Catroot. His older brother Caras had also stayed in Catroot, was now married to a Councilwoman with whom he had two young daughters and a third on the way, and Albryan had joined the army.

Though he often missed Caras, it was a huge relief to be two hundred miles away from his father, and Albryan had not returned to Catroot very often during his past nine years at the barracks of Tenna. He slowed for a moment on the narrow forest path, last year's leaves crunching under his boots, and noticed how pale his skin had become, after the winter and so many days of wearing full armour. The three white scars that striped the wrist of his right arm were barely visible these days.

Albryan shook his head, not wanting to dwell on thoughts of his family. The boughs of star chestnut and bushwillow were bare all around him, but the false olives and twisted milkwoods had weathered the winter in their thick evergreen coats. They made dark splashes of life along the way, the olives bushy as the end of a broom, the milkwoods twisting their branches against the forest floor like thick black snakes shedding skins of peat-coloured bark.

Around sunset he stopped to defuse a snare he had set earlier, and found caught in it a plump hare, still warm. Certainly not big enough for a pair of gloves, but more than adequate for dinner. He would be late, but Albryan had no fear of walking back in the moonlight. His friends and fellow officers of the Morgein army might miss him, this night just before he was due to leave, but he could say his goodbyes over breakfast tomorrow. He built a fire, skinned and spitted and roasted the hare, and enjoyed the solitude and secret noises of the evening forest.

By the time he arrived back, almost everyone else was asleep. He let himself into his private quarters, stripped off his comfortable long tunic and woollen breeches, and went to bed.

His dreams were unsettled, of blood and ash and dark magic, and the exodus of the Morgei from Armour City.

Albryan had not been there, that night nearly nineteen years ago when Arran Sylvaissen's armies had sacked the city. His family had fled for the refuge of Qwu'Mallorn some weeks beforehand. But when he was sixteen, he'd spent a while as a patient in the mind-healers' sanitorium in Catroot. Some of those who'd survived the massacre still came there for intermittent treatment, and Albryan had heard stories that chilled his blood when he was still a young boy. In the years since he'd joined the army, he'd tussled with Arran's non-mage armies often enough in the ongoing war, and seen more than a few blood-chilling things for himself.

He dreamed of the musket guns and cannons that Arran's soldiers carried, the thunderclap when they discharged, the crash and shatter of lead all around the battlefield. Magic could nullify the devastating effects of these weapons, but only when the magician was quick and focused enough. And the backscatter could be dangerous. Albryan had lost enough horses from under him whilst protecting his men.

He dreamed of all he feared: armies invading Qwu'Mallorn, breaking the magical barrier, overrunning the sacred woodland. He dreamed of a dark shadow that engulfed all the earth, more terrible than anything he'd ever imagined. He dreamed of the death of gods, the desolation of all civilization.

"Put some backbone into it, you lazy lot! I've seen better lines at the marketplace! Perhaps I should go and find your little brothers back home and put them into formation! They couldn't be worse than you! By the Goddess's tits, there's been too much slacking off around here! Now get your lazy arses to the top of the hill, and best hope I don't catch up with you!"

He came conscious with a start, heart thundering in his chest, chilled in the breeze that wafted through his half-open window-shutter. It was morning, and the barracks had come to life around him. A drill-sergeant was shouting at a group of recruits outside, loud enough so that Albryan could hear every word as if he were standing right over the bed.

Slowly, Albryan made himself breathe deeper, calmed his racing heart. He was no stranger to bad dreams. Seeking to settle himself, he tried to place the voice of the sergeant. Not one of his; but it had been a long time since Albryan had had a command of his own.

Far too good at being a spy, he thought, a touch sourly, and with that heaved himself out of bed. Flinging his nightshirt aside, he opened the door to his closet. Like the rest of the room, it was made of a light golden wood which looked decorative but was hard enough to sharpen and use as spear-points. It was harvested from the yellow-wood trees which grew only in Qwu'Mallorn.

Albryan cast a longing look over his standard-issue ringmail and silver-edged plate, and ran the velvet of one of the forest-green tunics between his fingers. *No uniform for you today, Captain Albryan Lana.* He reached for the rough garments that lay across the stool in the corner, the clothes of a man inured to hardship and bloodshed, the leather and steel of a nonmage mercenary. His disguise.

He ran a hand along his heavily stubbled jaw, yet another thing that set him apart from the average Morgein man. It itched already, but it was better he should look the part. He quickly dressed himself in the leather and undyed wool, and headed to the mess for breakfast.

The recruits had already been in and out, and the mess-hall was almost quiet. Albryan joined a table with his fellow officers, who welcomed him like the brothers they were. Outside the wide-open windows, the woodland encroached close to the building, threatening to embrace it back to nature. In Qwu'Mallorn, the forest was never far away.

The shouty sergeant had sent his unlucky recruits all the way up Triaan's Hill, a high rocky knoll atop which General Thinas Sovaya, the commander-in-chief of Qwu'Mallorn's armed forces, had his quarters. The road up there was long and winding. Beyond the hill to the east lay the town of Tenna, which held the dubious distinction of being the closest settlement to the Vailanan border. People said that traders from all across the continent had once come to Tenna, buying and selling fabulous goods in the marketplace. Little remained of those glory days, and Albryan had never known the town as anything other than a military outpost.

The banter of his brothers-in-arms flowed around Albryan, and when he finished eating, it ebbed expectantly. It was time to say his goodbyes.

"Good luck out there," said Gardan Féa, a young lieutenant who was on his third cup of coffee. He was only twenty, completely beardless, tawny-skinned, dark-eyed, black-haired, almost an exact average of the mage-folk. Next to him, his best friend and fellow lieutenant, Erastes Linné, nodded.

"I hear that soon the two of you will be heading out as well,"

Albryan remarked.

"Only a simple expedition. Reconnaissance," Erastes confirmed. He was a bit fairer than Gardan, with eyes that were almost green and hair more sandy than brown, but was also smaller, as the Morgei often tended to be. Albryan's mother had been both fair-skinned and unusually tall, and Albryan, correspondingly, towered over every other officer at the table.

Albryan glanced over at the youngest lieutenant, Evanos Sevelai, and to his surprise the young man saluted him. "Good luck, sir!" The hilariously forgetful gesture—Evanos had once been a sergeant under Albryan's command—broke the ice, and the table erupted into laughter.

The mirth was led by Captain Elithan Dorad, who lounged back in his chair almost like the panther Albryan had seen yesterday. Elithan was his best friend and by far the handsomest of the lot, with glossy jet-black curls that brushed his collar, a broad smile that came often and easily, and a sprinkling of acorn-brown freckles across the deep tan of his cheekbones. They were the same age, and had trained together, developing a bond almost as close as the one Albryan shared with his blood brother Caras.

Albryan stood up, and Elithan rose and came over to him, clasping his hand warmly.

"Get away with you," he said with that easy grin and a wink. "Can't wait to see the door close on your ugly face."

"And on yours, you goat."

Elithan's face became serious again. "Don't be too long out there, Bryan," he said, clasping Albryan's shoulder. "Ambry misses you, and the little ones do as well. But she has told me specifically to tell you that she hates when her 'Uncle Bry' goes away."

"And the youngest?" In contrast to Albryan's relatively chaste ways, Elithan had already produced four children in the vicinity of Tenna. He had not yet convinced any of their mothers to marry him, although Albryan often wondered if the convincing would not in fact run the other way. Elithan had his own income and plenty of personal glory as a war hero, after all.

"You will miss her naming ceremony." Elithan scowled good-naturedly. "And I will not tell you what her mother has chosen for a name, until you get back."

"Tell Ambry I will miss her too," Albryan said. "Even if she is the daughter of a goat."

Albryan was already on his way out as Elithan threw him a parting insult and a last chuckle. The general was not known to be a patient man, and he was worried he might be late already. He threw a quick salute to a few officers conversing at other tables; they gave the Morgein military salute back, their right hands going from heart to brow and out.

The path up Triaan's Hill was winding and steep, and by the time he reached the top, the sun was shining brightly and Albryan felt the first stirrings of summer. The cluster of low wooden buildings which surrounded General Thinas Sovaya's office had no forest cover, only the occasional thorn-bush growing between the bony rocks that serrated the summit of the tiny hill. Most of the open space was used for parades, exercise and inspections of the troops.

The reception area of Thinas's office was empty, as usual. The general kept finding better jobs for his secretaries. *Such as spy.* Albryan had had a brief stint as the general's secretary, and held the record for being the man who had occupied that position for the shortest amount of time.

The door to the general's office was closed, which *was* unusual. Albryan rapped at it, and heard Thinas call him in, but the door jerked open before he could lay a hand on the knob.

Albryan came face-to-face with a cinnamon-haired woman in green robes. Unfortunately, he recognized her immediately. *Mialiné Ebraskaia.* She flounced to the other side of the tiny room upon seeing him. "Is *this* truly more important than what *I* have to say, Thinas?"

The general, behind his desk, looked a good deal more careworn than Albryan had seen him lately. Thinas Sovaya was not what people expected to see in a highly-renowned military man even at the best of times, and he was getting old. He had not won his high position by prowess nor even the strength of his Mage-Gift. Thinas was a born strategist, and it was his careful planning and broad vision that had kept the Forest of the Morning safe, all these years. The general's hair had long since turned silver, but his eyes were still ageless, bright and dark brown. He was dark even by the standards of his people, and some had been known to call him "the old forest goblin" with varying degrees of affection.

The general ignored Mialiné's sally towards him. "You're late," he told Albryan, though without any true sternness.

"Please accept my apologies," Albryan said, bowing. He inclined himself very slightly in Mialiné Ebraskaia's direction. "My lady."

"I see you are dressed as befits your kind, today," Mialiné said acidly, looking Albryan up and down. She glanced at Thinas. "Are you sure you can trust this—this half-breed?"

"Fine thing for *you* to say," Albryan snapped, before the general could respond. "With your own sister sitting in Armour City beside the enemy."

Mialiné went chalk white, and for once Albryan wondered whether he might have gone too far. Arran Sylvaissen, enigmatic as he was, had no natural children of his own. Some said that the dark magic he practiced prevented it. Little was known regarding blood sorcery in Qwu'Mallorn; it had been outlawed for hundreds of years.

Regardless of the reason, Arran Sylvaissen seemed to collect foster children the way some noble ladies collected hunting dogs. Somehow—Albryan didn't know the full story—Dannine, birth daughter of the Councilwoman Tiralinna Ebraskaia and Mialiné's older sister, had become one of those children. Apparently snatched from her mother's retinue in the chaos of fleeing Armour City as a small child, she had been raised a princess of Vailana, Arran's favoured daughter. Now, nineteen years later, she was as accomplished a blood sorcerer as Arran himself. She had killed more of Albryan's comrades than anybody else. She was known amongst the men as a shadow that hunted by night, a glinting shape seen for a moment in the darkness just before you died.

"You dare speak of this?" Mialiné hissed. "Of my sister, whose memory I grieve, stolen from us by the enemy?"

"Stolen? Fine story. They tell something different, when you listen in the right places."

Before she could retort again, Thinas rose from his seat. "That is enough," he said coldly, and both of them recoiled from him. Thinas did not often need to raise his voice to express displeasure. "Mialiné, I remind you once more that I will *not* be responsible for your sorcerers. They are not enlisted in the army, and most of them are women. I have no authority over them, and I cannot stop whatever antics they dream up. You must instil discipline in them yourself."

Mialiné glared at the general with a grudging respect she had never given Albryan. "If I could, I would spank them from here to Catroot," she said. She edged around Albryan, making sure not to brush against him in the tiny enclosed space. She left with a toss of her head, without saying goodbye. Thinas immediately rounded on Albryan.

"Just what is it you think you are doing?"

"Defending myself," Albryan snapped.

"No. You are aggravating an ally whom we both badly need." Thinas glanced around his desk, which as usual was overflowing under stacks of paperwork, and snatched a map off the top of a teetering pile. "Do you think you could suppress your own sense of self-importance for a few weeks, and get your actual job done?"

Sullenly, Albryan took the map from his superior. "Sorry, sir," he said in a low voice.

"Do not be *sorry*. *Do better*." Thinas sat down again, as angrily as Albryan had ever seen anyone sit. "Leave that story about Dannine Ebraskaia alone. No-one cares *how* the girl got into the clutches of Arran Sylvaissen. The trouble she's caused—that's our problem, now. Along with the other accursed so-called children of this blood sorcerer."

Albryan let the silence sit for a moment before he asked, "Why was she here? Mialiné?"

"The usual. Trying to get me to discipline some scouts of hers." Thinas shook his head. "Mialiné, despite her fierceness, is desperately afraid of offending anybody whose birth ranks higher than hers. Since I am counted as an independent party, she thinks that I can get away with disciplining the daughters of powerful women better than she can."

Albryan shrugged. "You probably could."

"True. But why take on this extra burden unless she makes it worth my while?"

Albryan suppressed a smile. It was not often that Thinas could boast of having the upper hand against one of the highborn who moved in Council circles. Mialiné was young, subordinate to her mother, and she had been made captain of the female sorcerers who were the town's first line of defence without having any qualifications, as far as Albryan could see, apart from her high birth. Unlike the army, where men were promoted according to their skillset and prowess, the highborn females had a constantly shifting pecking order based on whose family possessed the most power and influence. And many of those families had been feuding against each other just a few generations ago.

The officers sometimes jested, amongst themselves, that the women should be made to join the army and learn proper discipline and obedience. But it was a suggestion that no-one would ever take seriously. No Morgein man, especially one who was common-born, would be permitted to issue orders to a daughter of the high houses. The camaraderie of the army, where common-born sergeants could order highborn boys around and make them scrub the latrines, could only exist amongst men, who had no political voice and no place in the ruling chambers of Qwu'Mallorn.

The general also firmly believed that the presence of women amongst them would distract most of his soldiers from their duty. Not for fear of love trysts—there were enough same-sex trysts amongst the soldiers regardless—but because of the perceived duty of all Morgein men: to protect the womenfolk, the core of the tribe, at all cost, even in battle. "Put girls in the ranks," Thinas had once said to Albryan, "and they'll never see a trace of the enemy. Our lads'll fall over themselves, just to protect them, and then who will hold the lines?"

Thinas gestured towards a chair, his anger seemingly forgotten. "Are you ready to receive your final orders?"

Albryan gathered himself together, and sat down with the curt nod of the professional soldier. "I'm ready."

CHAPTER II

THE MAGICIAN'S LABORATORY

THE NIGHT WAS SCREAMING.

An evil wind descended upon the earth, bringing destruction and misery wherever it blew. The dreamer wandered through ruined towns and burning forests, listening to the cries of women who had seen their children slain, to the shrieks of maidens ravaged in the ruins that had once been their homes.

She was diamond in this dream, and nothing could touch her. She could not help them, those shrieking, weak women who stretched out their hands to her in supplication. She could only avenge them.

A shadow rose before her, reaching out to gather her to its bosom of darkness, and she cried out. She was a child again, an infant no more than three years old, and she was afraid. Her mother was hand-ing her over to a stranger, a man whose teeth glinted like diamonds in the starlight. She began to sob, but a hand pressed down over her mouth and her nose, stifling her cries, suffocating her. She struggled, but to no avail—

The princess Dannine awoke with a scream, throwing off her silken coverlet. The gibbous moon shone through her window, its silvery light pooling on the floor of her bedroom and reflecting coldly from the silver-plated suit of armour that stood in the corner.

She was shaking, she realized, and took her body firmly in hand, reminding herself that she need be afraid of no-one. She was Dannine Sylvaissen, warrior and sorceress and daughter of the most powerful man who had ever lived. No-one would harm her whilst she was under the protection of her father.

But sometimes her body was traitorous, and did not respond the way she wished it to. She shook with the effort to keep from crying, to hold in the sob that was stuck halfway up her throat. As slowly she gained mastery over her body, took her nerves in hand and turned them rock-steady once again, smoothed the anguish on her face into her usual expression of steely calm, Dannine stepped out of bed.

The castle was pitch dark and silent. She casually glanced towards her armour, caught sight of her reflection on the breastplate, and quickly looked away, not wanting to look upon the beauty that others found so fascinating. Dannine hated reflections of herself, and always had. She always felt as though someone else were watching her from the mirror, a skinny weak girl with brimming blue eyes and unkempt golden hair.

Dannine reached for her hairbrush, making herself presentable even though there was no-one in the darkened room to see her. She slipped on a thin dressing-gown before opening the door to her balcony and stepping outside. The night air was cool on her skin, and the stones of her balcony were covered in dust. There had been a strong wind the previous day, blowing the choking red sands of the plains all through the city, but the night was perfectly still now, carrying the promise of a balmy springtime.

Dannine did not lift her eyes to the wide violet horizon nor the golden plains that lay dreaming beyond, but instead contemplated the sleeping city below. Her father's castle stood on a hill in the centre of the city, aloof from the bustling hordes who laboured daily in the crooked alleys and crowded slums of Armour City. Directly below her, the marble houses of the rich merchants and nobles could be seen, but beyond that, the city stretched on into ever filthier, more crowded boroughs. The castle itself was dwarfed by the high hills just outside the urban sprawl, where the miners daily brought the metals of industry to the surface—copper and iron for weapons and the armaments of war, arsenic and mercury for the artificers and apothecaries, and precious gold for those who had been born to better things.

She turned away from the hills, from the sunrise that was now slowly creeping over the dry plains and touching the walls of the castle that surrounded her, bringing out the sparkling micas in the sandstone bricks and warming the dreary hovels of Armour City's slums with golden rays of hope. Dannine had not been raised to dream over the future, as other noblemen's daughters were. Since she could re-member, she had walked through the fire, progressing from chil-dren's magic to war-magic to blood sorcery. She had known all her life that she was a sword to fight her father's war, as all her siblings were, and that they dared not fail him. Arran Sylvaissen had adopted them for this task: to help him win the only war that mattered. The war that would make him greater than any magician who had ever lived.

The thought of her brothers and sister reminded Dannine that she had failed to check on them the previous night; she had been too exhausted. *No matter*, she told herself. *Plenty of time to do it now.*

Her feet took her into the corridor beyond her bedroom, then along the winding passageways through the silent castle until she found the windowless room where her father kept his laboratory. There was no lock on the ebony door, but Dannine simply raised her hand, and the door swung open without her needing to touch it. She was the only one, apart from Arran Sylvaissen, who could gain entry to this room. This was the trust her father had put in her.

There was no need to light a candle in the room; as soon as Dan-nine stepped inside, an eerie blue light began to emanate from the ceiling. She walked over to a low table where four glowing jars were lined up next to each other, picked up the jar which pulsated with magenta-red light, and gazed at its surface for a long while, apparently lost in thought. But any magician would have felt the energy in the air, felt the undeniable power that radiated from the jar, and they would have known that Dannine was performing no ordinary observation.

This jar represented her sister Ceazyn, reflected her mood and whereabouts, and Dannine could feel her face flushing even as she gazed into the depths of the scarlet light. Ceazyn was abed, but not asleep. She had never been one to deny herself any kind of carnal pleasure, and the sexual embraces that still pained Dannine to think of had always excited and impassioned her older sister.

Ceazyn was far away in the jungles of the Eastern Continent, the heart of slavery and darkness, arranging for new bodies to swell her father's armies. And clearly, she was not in the least bit shy about taking her pleasure amongst the natives whilst she went about it.

Dannine set her sister's jar down with a scowl and contemplated the jars of her two brothers. Taunus, the eldest, glowed with rippling silver; he always had been a swordsman at heart, and slower than the others when it came to magic. Baukin's jar was a strange combination of blue and yellow, yet never green; the two colours swirled together, touching without mixing. Both her brothers were in the north, preparing the kingdom of Svanfeld for their father's imminent conquest. Whilst Baukin laid plans to attack the capital and dispose of the king, Taunus had been tasked with destroying the Sven monks, the most powerful religious authority on the continent. Both of them were fast asleep, though she caught the usual edge of anxiety from Baukin's jar. Being away from the city did not suit him.

Dannine passed over her own jar, which glowed with blinding silver-and-gold radiance, and on impulse reached for a fifth jar which stood apart from the others, hidden in the shadows they cast with their brilliant lights.

This jar was black and empty, and there was a draining feeling about it, as if all magic had been sucked from the space it occupied. A magician might question why Arran kept this around. Another man might have destroyed it long ago.

Dannine rubbed the cobweb-shattered surface of the jar, tried unsuccessfully to read it. There was nothing, as there had been nothing for the past eight years.

This was her little brother Deryck's jar, and he had disappeared. *No,* Dannine corrected herself. *He did not disappear. He ran away.* He had been only eleven, the youngest of Arran's adopted children.

Why, Deryck? Dannine wondered, as she did every time she thought of him. She could have protected him—no doubt he had been afraid of Taunus, who had bullied them all mercilessly as children. Dannine had surpassed Taunus in power long ago, and Deryck might have surpassed *her* if he had remained. His disappearance had vexed her father more than anything Dannine could remember.

But who would have protected him from Arran? a traitorous voice whispered in the back of her mind. Perhaps things would truly be different for her, if Deryck were still here. Perhaps he would stand where Dannine stood now, at Father's right hand, carrying all his hopes, carrying all his burdens.

She shook her head violently, almost dropping the jar. She should not be having these kinds of thoughts. She should carry her father's hopes and burdens as an honour, and do all he asked of her without hesitation. How could she not? Her father was the only person who had ever cared about her—about all of them. All five of his children had been set aside by their birth families. Dannine's mother had given her up in exchange for safe passage to the Forest of the Morning. Deryck's parents had sold him to slave traders for a handful of silver pawns. Arran had saved all of them, and more. He had given them power and rank and riches, taught them the secrets of high sorcery, and they had never wanted for anything.

And how does Deryck repay him? He leaves us. Disregards all our father's careful plans. Dannine's eyes brimmed with anger. *If I meet him again, he will not be my brother anymore.*

She could feel, once more, the call that had woken her up, the pit of uneasiness in her stomach that washed over into her soul. These were no ordinary nightmares she was having, her father said. His success was close; the nightmares came from the presence of the goddess Qwu'Horya, as she drew ever closer to the mortal world.

Dannine turned to look at her father's map of the Western Continent, pages of parchment enclosed in a glass box. She found Armour City, and followed the continent northwest to where it was bisected by the Svanlyn mountains, a vast range of high, nearly impassable peaks. Across those mountains lay the highlands of Svanfeld, where magic was unknown. But to the northeast, a thin strip of land beside the Sea of Calms enclosed the ancient home of the Morgei, the mage-folk. The Forest of the Morning. The people who opposed her father in every way, and who had fought against him since he was a youth. Dannine was not sure how old her father was, for the blood magic he dabbled in had given him eternal youth and vitality, a blessing from Qwu'Horya. But many years ago, Arran had attempted to share his revelations with the Morgei, and they had banished him from their land.

They feared his power, Dannine knew. *They feared the truth of what he was saying. The matriarchs of the Morgei would hold onto their power at any cost, even if it meant the whole world would be darker for it.*

Dannine laid a hand on the glass, blotting out the Forest of the Morning. She had asked her father to let her oversee troop movements on the border, but he had refused, leaving the job to one of his nonmage generals instead. Dannine could not understand why. She had been there before, last summer, punching holes where the magical barrier that protected the land was thin, attacking farmsteads and taking slaves, sowing terror in the hearts of the mage-soldiers who came out to face them. If Arran wanted the Forest of the Morning burned, there was no better person for the job than her.

Soon they would be waging a war on two fronts. The conflict with the Morgei had been festering for the past nineteen years, but if Baukin and Taunus succeeded, they might soon have to deal with a retaliatory attack from Svanfeld. If Dannine had not known that her father was the Goddess's chosen, that he alone could lead a new world into prosperity, she might have been afraid. There was more at stake in this war than a throne, or power over toiling peasants and shifty merchants.

She turned her head, her hair whipping across her face, as the Goddess called to her again.

There was a second door in this room, held with even stronger magic than the first. It had to be secure; it sheltered all her father's plans and dreams behind it.

Dannine was able to open this door too, and she trembled with anticipation as she ran her hand down the smooth black wood. Her skin prickled all over; even a nonmage would be able to feel this kind of magic, the way it crackled like lightning in the air and made every hair on her body stand upright.

She opened the door, and at first saw nothing but blackness. The darkness inside this room was different from any other darkness. It sucked at her eyeballs, inviting her in, promising an eternity of nothingness. There was something seductive about its relentless lack of *anything*—no shade of purple or grey to the dark, no pretence of being anything more than the void it was.

Despite the enduring blackness, after a minute or two of gazing into this room, Dannine could see movement in the dark. She entered the room fearlessly. Even Arran sometimes hesitated the tiniest bit when approaching his goddess, but Dannine felt no fear when facing the darkness and the oppressive sense of great and ancient magic.

The darkness was a sheet, she thought, and beneath the sheet, a presence moved, ever testing the fabric, looking for weaknesses, trying to tear a hole in the world. She almost fancied she could see the shape of Qwu'Horya straining against the fabric of the darkness, a protuberant head questing, looking for a way into the world; two hands stretching out, grasping for the slightest purchase.

Beneath the sheet of darkness, the goddess reached out a bony hand, and Dannine could see the shape of her palm, could see the wispy fingers clawing towards her. Transfixed, she stepped forward, lifting her own hand—

"Dannine."

Her father's voice was unmistakable, and Dannine cast her eyes downwards as the Goddess drew back.

Arran Sylvaissen was framed in the blue light of his laboratory, his pose relaxed as he gazed calmly at his daughter in the dark room. He was already dressed for the day, in a white waistcoat trimmed with thread-of-silver over a crisp white blouse, white trousers and polished white leather boots with silver trim. His white-blond hair had been skilfully combed as usual, giving him a whimsical and boyish appearance, but his eyes were as cold as two chips of blue ice. Though he was not a particularly tall man, and now that Dannine was grown she could see eye-to-eye with him if she straightened up, he filled the room with his bearing and his magical power. He was the most magnificent person Dannine had ever known, and she naturally deferred to him.

"I am sorry," she began. "The Goddess—she called to me in my dreams."

"No need to apologize," Arran said, beckoning for Dannine to come towards him. She obeyed, and he closed the door on the darkness, returning the laboratory to relative normalcy. Dannine stared at the floor.

"You still have the dreams?"

Dannine nodded.

"She gets closer and closer to us every day," Arran observed. He walked over to the map of the continent, and studied it. "The fighting must have been particularly ruinous lately. The war fuels her; the more who die, the more power she gains."

"Soon she will be free," Dannine said tentatively.

Her father shook his head. "No, sweet girl. However strong she becomes, she cannot be freed unless a very special sacrifice is made." He turned towards her. "I must find *she who has only known despair*, and I must eat her heart and offer her to the Goddess. Or so the tomes of the past say, in metaphorical language as usual."

"They could be wrong. They have been wrong on many things."

Arran shook his head. "I have tried so many other things, and still *her* divine power is not yet mine."

"Then you must find her, this maiden who has only known despair." She smiled crookedly. "Though I think you will not find it hard to extract whatever parts of her are necessary for the spell to work."

"That is the easy part," Arran agreed. "The hard part is to find this person." His expression changed quickly, a serene look replacing the frown that had been there just a moment before. Dannine expectantly awaited the change in his mood that would come.

"My servant in Qwu'Mallorn," Arran said, "has revealed that we will soon have the opportunity to capture a high-ranking soldier from one of the noble families. His identity and description have been given." He placed a hand on Dannine's shoulder, drawing her closer. "I want you to capture him and bring him to the castle, ensuring that he survives the ordeal. Go alone, and take one of the quetzals. Speed is of the utmost importance."

Dannine's heart leapt; an opportunity to engage herself in her father's fight was all she lived for, and she could not resist the lure of hunting a quarry that would no doubt challenge her powers. Even more, she loved to fly the quetzals, the feathered lizards that her father had brought from the distant Pirate Islands. "Consider it as good as done, Father," she replied eagerly.

"I can always rely on you, Dannine," her father said, caressing her glossy hair. "As I watched you grow up, I realized something. Do you know what it was?"

His mood had changed again, and Dannine had not anticipated it correctly. She shook her head numbly, biting her lower lip.

"Neither of your brothers are truly worthy of succeeding me,"

Arran said softly. "I once hoped that either of them would be able to rule this city, with you by his side." He trailed off, and Dannine said nothing, her heart suddenly beating very loudly. Though he had not uttered it, her brother Deryck's name resounded in her head as if someone had whispered it from the past, from the shadows surrounding her. Arran had always meant for Deryck to stand at his right hand. Had he not run away, Deryck would have been here with her right now.

"But I see the only solution now," Arran finally said. "*You* are my chosen heir, Dannine, and I will delegate all my power to you. I will make you my queen."

Dannine couldn't move, and her throat felt suddenly dry. "I would be queen?" she whispered. "But—"

"You will marry me, and rule by my side as the queen of my new world," her father said, taking her shoulders in his hands and bearing down upon her with all the force of his cold blue gaze.

Dannine felt as though her stomach had attained the weight of lead and fallen through the floor. "But you cannot have children," she whispered. "Neither can I," she added, even more softly. "The sacrifice required by the magic—"

"We would not need children," Arran interrupted. "We would be immortal. You would be my shining queen, my right hand." He leaned forward and kissed her forehead. "We will be married at midsummer," he said, "when the people hold the festival for the king of Armour City."

Dannine could not tell why she wanted to burst into tears; she knew from experience that such a display would only harden her father's heart, not move it to pity. "But we would be,"—she hesitated—"husband and wife? In truth?"

"Of course."

Dannine said nothing. She could not disobey her father, and she never had. Part of the process of blood sorcery involved sexual ritual, and she had nearly failed. She had been twelve at the time, and her father had refused to postpone the ritual until she was any older. She had found some boy to perform the sex act with, but when it had come down to the ritual, she could not find the strength to go through with it. She remembered vividly the jeers of Taunus and the others, and the curiosity of Deryck, who had only been eight.

She had gone to her bedroom in tears, wondering if her father would cast her out for failing the ritual. But a few hours later, Arran had come to her, holding out his hand.

"I will not let you fail," he had said. "I was wrong to expect you to behave like your sister, Dannine. You have greater power, and you should not have to mingle with someone unworthy of you." She remembered how she had gone limp in her father's arms. "You will complete the ritual with me, Dannine. Tonight."

Those rituals were Dannine's only experience with sex, and she had always thought that she would never have to endure those things in her day-to-day life. She was shivering, and drew her dressing-gown closer around her body.

"You are quiet, Dannine," her father observed, his face still pressed close to hers. "Are you still my obedient daughter?"

"Yes. Yes, I am." Dannine lifted her eyes to his, trying to put all her love and devotion for him into her face. Maybe he would realize how hard this was for her. Maybe he would take pity, and change his mind.

"Then you will be my queen," Arran said, smiling upon her. "But for now, there is work to be done. Get dressed, and join me in the courtyard."

He briefly caressed her hand before striding away. Slowly, Dannine moved away from the presence of the Goddess and followed him. Behind her, Qwu'Horya clawed at the fabric of reality, screaming to rip into the material world and rage and despoil it until there was nothing left, but no-one could hear her.

Chapter III
Partners in Crime

The assassin moved with deadly purpose down the lane.

Ülhard was silent. The capital city of Svanfeld did not truly sleep for long, but Nicolas Klavbert, the youngest established assassin in the milieu of its underworld, never failed to choose the opportune time to carry out his deadly work.

Here, in one of the nouveau-rich suburbs outside the limits of the northern city's white marble walls, the silence was deep enough to be eerie. Isolated street-lamps did very little to illuminate the shadows. Nico was dressed to match them: not in black, but in patchy shades of grey that rendered him virtually invisible whenever he stood still. A floppy hat typically worn by labourers in the city obscured half his forehead, covering his light blond hair. The rest of his face was shadowed by the growth of a new beard. Men of Svanfeld, even those who lived in the city, set great store by their luxuriant beards; not only did growing one help Nico to fit in and remain unremarkable, but it also made him look a bit older than he really was, a good move when you wanted hardened men to take you seriously. Nico was only twenty-two, but anyone who had hired him could attest to his skill.

This past year, he had become indisputably better. Nico paused for a moment, getting his bearings, looking up to the palatial mansion where his victim dwelt. As he set off, he knew that his partner, a lithe young man known as Benjamin Fisher, or more commonly just Fish, was somewhere off in the shadows, watching his back.

He had not seen so much as a fleeting shadow, heard not even the slightest whisper to suggest that another person was abroad tonight. That was as it should be: Nico was good at moving secretly, but Fish was a master none could match. Shorter even than many women, he was built to be light and fast, and to move like an acrobat. Nico, on the other hand, had always been tall, and was now starting to shed the adolescent leanness that had usually put him in good stead for his job. Another year or two, and he would look more like a mercenary soldier than an assassin. He might be better served hiring out his sword for honest fighting . . .

Nico shoved that thought to the back of his mind, along with every single other repressed desire, and focused on the matter at hand. It was no different from any other job: a man too arrogant to flee the city, too short-sighted to guess that his fellow Guildmasters were plotting to have him killed.

There were only two guardsmen at the gates of the mansion. *Hired thugs more than anything else*, Nico thought. *Does he believe that these will save him?* The two of them were deep in conversation with each other, and did not notice as Nico crept stealthily along the high wide wall that ringed the grounds. He crouched beneath the branches of a bushy evergreen that grew alongside the wall, waiting.

Fish arrived just in time, as usual. Down the far end of the gardens, somewhere amongst the manicured shrubbery and fallow flowerbeds, a twig cracked. The two guards looked up briefly, and one shook his head. They fell back into conversation.

Nico could only just make out the figure of his partner, a shadow that moved through the bushes into the wavering light cast by the moon as it passed through wisps of cloud. His knees began to ache from crouching down, and silently he shifted his position, frowning.

Down in the garden, Fish deliberately trod on a stick again, this time allowing the guards to turn and see him. One of them pointed and exclaimed, and the other went after the shadow. Fish took off immediately, flitting through the shrubbery.

Nico watched for at least ten more minutes as they played cat-and-mouse amongst the shrubbery, the guard clumsy and Fish much too good at this. Eventually, the guard remaining at the gate left his post as well. Nico waited a few more minutes, watching as his partner led both guards off in the direction of the ornamental stream that flowed through the grounds. Then he jumped lightly from the wall, landing with his weight spread evenly, a trick he had learned recently from Fish.

The assassin sauntered towards the silent house, unhooking the grapnel at his belt and winding out the long rope attached to it. The garden was so quiet that he could hear the snores of his victim echoing from the back of the house.

Several nights of reconnaissance had confirmed that Martin Erdmann, master of the Guild of Apothecaries, had taken to sleeping alone in the master bedroom of his house, wooden shutters closed securely inside windows of bubbly glass. Nico knew that Erdmann had sent his wife and children to his estate in the country, and he had to pause to admire the boldness of the man, just a little. *But it will make no difference.*

Nico would never have agreed to harm the man's family. There were some hells that were too low for even him to contemplate sinking in, some lines that were too hard to cross. Nico believed that he had never killed anyone who was truly innocent. The politics and backstabbings of the Guilds flew above his head, but men who held power like Erdmann's had never gotten it with clean hands. Nico had known this long before he came to the city, back when he had been an orphan boy out in the foothills on the northern side of the Svanlyn mountains. Svanfeld might be ruled in name by a king, but it was the Guildmasters who held the true power in the country. Nico had never seen the king nor any other member of the royal family in his entire life, but the Guilds were everywhere, buying and selling, brokering labour, building silos and factories, stockpiling gems and herbs and corn, guarding the villages from raiders and slavers with their private armies.

Nico was not as silent as he would have liked as he secured the grapnel on the mansion roof and swung up to the shuttered window; he was definitely getting heavier, more muscular, shedding his youth. *One day soon, you must find a different profession*, he told himself. His lambskin boots scraped against the window-sill with a soft sound. The snoring from within did not falter.

Nico took a deep breath, braced himself against the wall, and swung inwards, shielding himself with the steel vambrace and pauldron he wore on his wrist and shoulder. The thick cloudy glass shattered, and the wooden shutters were thrown open with a violent crash. The Guildsman sat up in bed, yelling.

Not my most subtle moment, Nico reflected, but there was no way he was going to try and kill the man in the city in broad daylight, with city guards crawling everywhere, and he was *not* going to try and enter a house via the chimney again. Erdmann kept no servants in his mansion save a very deaf old woman who slept in a detached cottage. *You can yell all you want, no one is around to hear.*

He swung feet-first through the window, landing lightly on the floor and recovering in just a moment. There was glass everywhere, and the Guildsman was out of bed. He took one look at Nico and ran for the door. He was nowhere near fast enough.

Nico's dagger flashed silver in his hand. It was over in a matter of seconds, the Guildsman sprawled on the floor, choking in a pool of his own blood. Nico took some time to make sure that he was dead, wiping the blade of his silver-edged dagger on the man's nightshirt. The rasping gasps died slowly away, and the twitching hands came to rest. Nico checked for any movement of breath, double-checked the man's pulse, and turned away in satisfaction.

Back in the gloom of the garden, Fish came sidling up as Nico was securing his rope and grapnel on his belt again. The chestnut-skinned youth had not even broken a sweat. His imp's face with its too-large nose was lit up with its usual crooked grin. His curly coffee-brown hair flopped over his forehead, his golden eyes amber-dark in the light of the moon.

"What did you do with the guards?" Nico asked softly.

"I didn't kill them." Fish brushed the dishevelled curls out of his face. "I led them to believe I jumped in the stream to escape. They'll probably be coming back this way soon."

"In that case, we had better leave."

The pair wound their way back through the silent yard, skirted the stone wall, and were swallowed up by the forest that grew around the northwestern walls of the city. Nico let out a silent sigh, relieved of the tension that had gripped him. It was all over. *Another job, another death, another day.* He looked over at Fish. The boy's face was briefly lit up by a sliver of moonlight, and suddenly Nico ached to take him into his arms, to kiss him roughly on the lips, push him into the undergrowth and have him, for the first time, right there and then . . .

But the moment passed, as it always did, and Nico settled for putting his arm around the boy's shoulders, drawing him into a hug. Perhaps he squeezed him a little too tightly; perhaps his cheeks were stained with a little more colour than usual. But Fish did not notice, as he never had before.

"Am I mistaken, or is this the biggest fish we've hooked so far?" he asked eagerly.

"You're right." Nico put his longings away, even as his arm remained over Fish's shoulders. "We might not have to work for half a year after this."

"I suppose this is why you chose this line of work in the first place." The boy's smile was dazzling, even in the uncertain light of the forest path.

"Oh, I wanted to be an honest mercenary, once," Nico said lightly. "But for anyone to take you on as a trainee, you need good references. The chances of a penniless boy from the sticks being able to get the contacts . . ."

"Are not good," Fish agreed grimly.

"So the streets trained me instead." Nico considered asking Fish where *he* had gotten so good at slaughter and subterfuge, but Fish had never answered him before, only shrugged and diverted the question. There were secrets in Fish's past that were locked away from everyone, even Nico, and part of what made their partnership so easy was that Nico respected that. After all, there were things *he* would never tell Fish . . .

By the time they reached the Smuggler's Gate, a secret entrance in the city wall that allowed people of their ilk to come and go as they pleased, Nico was sombre again, his elation subsiding. It was only battle-lust, he told himself; like any kind of warrior, he found himself joyful to have survived another encounter which could have killed him. It was the same as simply wanting a woman . . .

But simply wanting a woman did not dredge up the same mixture of fear and guilt and self-hatred in Nico's gut. It did not remind him of the mountains, and the fresh-faced orphan boy who had dreamed of being a wandering hero, taking only jobs that benefitted the downtrodden and punished the evil.

Nico would have given almost anything to be that innocent orphan boy again. To have made different choices. To have been less trusting of the adults around him . . .

"You're quiet tonight," Fish remarked, and Nico only shrugged, not knowing what to say.

"I'm getting older," he said at last. "I barely made it through that window, Fish. Next time, you're going to be the one climbing up walls. I'm done with it."

"You should buy a gun. No need to get close, then." Fish's tone was mocking. Nico snorted.

"And bring down the whole damn neighbourhood on us? Do you know how loud those things are?"

Fish's reciprocating laugh was intoxicating. Nico followed him to the tiny loft apartment they shared in Schooner Street, and did not once let go of his shoulder. The cold sneaked between the linked warmth of their bodies, an insidious icy breeze creeping through the city like a mountain lynx on the prowl.

The weather had been like this the night he had met Fish at that tavern brawl in the Black Ass. That was over a year ago, Nico realized. But when had he started to covertly admire his partner from afar? When had the physical touch grown so natural between the two of them? When had he started to become infatuated with Fish?

These questions were pointless. The boy had walked into Nico's life unasked for, unannounced, and yet fitted into it so securely that Nico could not imagine relinquishing his company, despite the discomposure he often felt around him. Four years ago, before events had set him on his way to the bloody path he now trod, Nico might have welcomed these feelings. Back in the mountains, he'd never been shy about loving whomever he loved, be it boy or girl, but that was *before*.

He did not, *could* not, desire anything more from Fish than friendship. No matter what his unruly longings traitorously whispered to him.

There was a fleck of the apothecary's blood still on the hand that rested on Fish's shoulder. Nico moved it reflexively, not wanting to stain the boy's clothes. It would wash off easily enough.

CHAPTER IV
SVANLYN MOUNTAINS

HUDDLED IN HER CLOAK against the damp and cold, Velda Davidz stared out across the black mud towards the distant graves of her husband and child.

The rain beat down without mercy, turning the yard into a morass of sucking mud and manure, the grey sky mocking all her past hopes. It was supposed to be Firstmonth—the tail end of winter, the new spring—but she had seen no sun since the week the snow fever had come to the farm. The bright sun had seemed unseasonable then, and now she could not help but see it as an omen of what was to come. By the fifth day, Emmett had begun to cough. By the seventh day, the sun had gone, and her nineteen-year-old husband lay on his deathbed.

Velda would have given almost anything to be lying out there beside them, together in the ground instead of remaining here alone, but the snow-fever took only those who had never suffered it during childhood. Velda had been about seven when she survived it. But her son had been only just over a year old, not old enough and not strong enough. Infants died easily of fevers, she had heard, but she had never dreamed that death could rob her of all so quickly. It had taken no more than a week to claim them both.

Velda could not tell whether her cheeks were wet with the rain or her own tears. It had been three months, and there were some days now when she did not cry. But those were worse in a way, for she would sit at the kitchen table, alone, and gaze out at the winter land-scape for hours, not knowing what she was seeing, the silence in the house seeming to fill the whole world.

She hefted the pail and stepped out into the rain. The pigs began to grunt and squeal in anticipation when they heard her footsteps sloshing towards the pen. She managed a smile as they all jostled for the best place at the feeding trough. The big sow, which Velda suspected was pregnant, was able to keep her position of pride simply by interposing her great bulk between the younger pigs. *Emmett's prize sow,* Velda thought, and turned away. *It was so unfair!* They had done so well for themselves, worked so hard . . .

The way back to her kitchen across the mud seemed to last an eternity. Her cloak was soaked through, and she left her boots out-side to avoid bringing the mud onto the sturdy wooden floor. She looked around the kitchen, hugging herself to try and get warm.

There was more than half of yesterday's bread left; she had baked far too much. Of last year's jam, one unopened jar remained.

I cannot stay here. The thought struck Velda like a lightning bolt, and her bare feet seemed to move with a will of their own towards her bedroom. She flung open the chest that contained her clothes. During wintertime, there was nothing to do but hold on, but as soon as the rain let up, the planting season would begin. The farm was barely workable with two pairs of hands; Emmett had hired lads from down in the town to help him with the harvest last summer. It was good land, but challenging with the mountain slopes and springtime flooding. The homestead nestled in between a long finger of rock called the Witches' Horn, and the falling valleys that led down to the town of Lynborder. Fertile land, owned by the Sven Church, but barely cultivated because it was so high up and so remote. It had taken Velda three days just to get down to the monastery to fetch a monk for the last rites.

She still did not know exactly how she had made it down without giving up and lying on the freezing ground to die. They had had to wait at the monastery for nearly a week before making the ascent back up to the homestead, waiting for the snow to stop falling. By the time they had arrived to bury the bodies, the house had been cold as death . . .

Velda began to pack the chest. Clothes, shoes . . . She got up to fetch her books, which were on a shelf near the kitchen hearth. She stopped in her tracks.

What am I doing? She went back to the chest and pulled her shoes out, then sank down on the bed with them still in her hands. *Where can I go? I have no family, no-one to run to.* The closest she had to her own kin were the girls who had grown up with her at the monastery. Kilda, Liezl and even little Susie were all wives themselves now, with households of their own to manage. She could not impose on them. She had to depend on herself, and herself alone. That was a lesson she had learned when she was very young—it was one every orphaned child needed to learn.

She could not go back to the monks—as kind and generous as what they were, their charity was reserved for lost children, not grown women who were merely lost in soul. Velda rummaged through the chest until she found, at the very bottom, the box in which she kept her silver medallion. All orphans received one when they departed the monastery, a small thing of worth to help them should they fall upon hard times. She wondered whether it was worth more than the things her husband had left her: the pigs, his clothes and boots, the cradle and furniture. If someone else dared to start their own farm in this forsaken nest in the Svanlyn mountains, she could sell them everything . . .

Velda thought briefly of her husband's family, but there was no recourse there. He had been orphaned young, shunted between indifferent relatives for most of his life, and finally left them forever to seek his fortune. She was too proud to throw herself upon the goodwill of distant relatives, and why should she have to? She had no money to speak of, but all of this . . . all of her life was worth some-thing, if she could bring herself to sell it.

You must, she told herself sternly. *You must bring yourself to say goodbye to it all. Leave Emmett and little Ric, and find some place where it hurts less. Unless you want to marry again, and try a second time . . .*

"No," she said aloud. She would not marry again. Not now, per-haps not ever. As a young bride, the world had seemed full of won-drous possibilities. She had been happy at the prospect of raising her own children a stone's throw away from the place where she had grown up. But with Emmett gone, what was the point?

She wished, not for the first time, that she had some inkling where she had come from in the first place. Many of the fosterlings at the monastery were bastard-born, their mothers unmarried, their families too destitute to provide for them. People came from the mountain towns, from the farms in the valleys, to give up the chil-dren that they could not afford to have, delivering them into the arms of the monks of Svanfeld, who were sworn to succour those in need.

Velda's story was different. No weeping mother had made a se-cret pilgrimage for her; no shamed father had quietly consulted the monks about her. Nineteen years ago, the faraway stronghold of Ar-mour City had fallen to the sorcerer-king Arran Sylvaissen, and the Morgei living in Vailana had all fled, died, or been captured by slav-ers. One such band of slave-traders, seven months after the city's fall, had tried to cross the mountains here in an effort to reach the port at

Sulshome. They'd had two dozen Mage-Gifted captives in their caravan—and one who had no magic at all. That one had been the seven-month-old infant Velda.

During her childhood, Velda had talked with every monk who had been there that day, with every stout farmer who had helped ambush the slavers and even the wives who had watched from the hilltops. They all told thrilling stories of triumph: the townspeople had surprised the slavers as they were attempting to cross a narrow valley, and had wiped them out to the last man. The Mage-Gifted would-be slaves had turned around and made their way east to the Forest of the Morning, hoping to start their shattered lives anew amongst their own kind.

But none of them had known Velda's identity, not even the woman who had served as her wet nurse. According to them, the baby girl had been acquired off a pair of unscrupulous traders—obviously not her parents—somewhere near Armour City, for the price of a handful of silver pawns. She had no name; the monks had given her the name Velda Quix, after a hermit-nun who had written extensive works on the will of the gods, and a last name belonging to one of the senior brothers at the monastery.

Velda did not regret being left to the care of the monks; she had never gone hungry, never wanted for clothes or shoes, and was much better educated than the average Sven woman. The monks wished all orphaned children to be able to make something of themselves. Most village girls gave up their schooling by the time they were eleven, and had barely learned to read and write. Velda had been made to rigorously attend lessons on literature, medicine, history, and everything else the monks deemed important, until the day she left to marry.

But her questions would never let her rest. For a time they had been stilled: when she met Emmett, when she chose to love him, when motherhood and farm-work filled up her days, and he was there for her to take refuge in every night. But now, the old restlessness returned to her heart with an even greater vengeance than before.

How much would she keep, of her old life here? Where would she go? Her birth family must have been from Vailana. The people of Svanfeld were a fair-skinned race, with straight or wavy hair that was typically some shade of wheat or flax. Velda had always looked exotic, unusual enough for people to stare. She was several shades darker than anyone else she had ever met, almost as brown as the chestnuts the pigs loved to snack on. Her curly hair alternated between dark brown and black depending on the light that shone upon it, and her nose had always invited commentary. A great beak of a thing, so many boys had been wont to tell her that she would be a beauty without it that she had acquired something of a reputation for punching boys in the face when she was fourteen or so.

For a moment Velda smiled, thinking of the little feral thing she had been, running wild in the forests and hills. But the wild girl had been tamed by love, only now the love was gone, and she was alone again, with no pack to run in the wilds with her.

The road to Armour City was dangerous, Velda knew. The city itself, perhaps even more so. But it was her best chance. It was a new beginning, in the place where her story had truly begun. Perhaps there were still answers, even after nineteen years, lying dormant somewhere. Where better than the place she had been born?

Outside, the rain had begun to ease. Velda wandered into the kitchen to peer out of the top half of the doorway. The kitchen faced north, and she watched a sliver of sunlight break free from the clouds that shadowed the Witches' Horn. It would not warm the mountain, not yet, but spring was on its way.

Chapter V
Dannine Sylvaissen

THE DAY WAS STUFFY AND STICKY, and Albryan's horse seemed full as irritable as himself. The tall grey mare tossed her head over the dewy grass and only picked at the oats he offered her. The entire situation made Albryan uneasy.

The late cold had not lasted long; only a day after he had taken leave of Thinas in Tenna, rain had fallen from a leaden sky, and the day after that, the heat had settled in, growing ever worse as Albryan rode to the southeast. Back in Tenna, the breeze coming off the still-snowy peaks of Svanlyn might serve to stir up the air and lave the heat somewhat, but in the marshy dwarf forest he travelled now, there was no such relief. The trees were low and stunted here, an abundance of thorn-bushes and wild figs and long plains grass all crowding in for space on the boggy soil. The land curved downwards, forming a bowl-shaped valley with slopes so gentle you would never notice the swamps until you were right on top of them.

Albryan kept well clear of the known swampland, traversing the very edge of Morgein territory, the cool forest sometimes seeming so near that he could smell it. Yet he well knew that he was no longer in Qwu'Mallorn. He had passed the border three days ago, and had felt the comforting touch of the country-wide magical shield leave him, along with all the magic of the forest that sheltered behind it.

The swampland around here was not a friendly place to bring an army. Yet there had been skirmishes here recently, hordes of Arran's nonmage soldiers suddenly appearing out of the brushwood to challenge the patrols. Thinas did not know if they were amassing somewhere near the swamps, or whether their command lurked somewhere close by. That was what Albryan was hoping to discover.

Sweat dampened the auburn curls over his brow and trickled down his neck. The stubbly beard that he had grown since leaving Tenna prickled his skin in the heat. He was dozing in the saddle, and had to sternly shake himself awake. His horse passed a pile of dung lying in the long grass, and he bent to take a look. *More than a month old, disintegrated.* There were tracks, but they were old, and petered out after a few feet.

Albryan passed a hand through his hair, vainly hoping that some air might stir and cool his head. As yet he had found nothing to follow. A few traces, months old, faint tracks that led nowhere. The traces *had* become more numerous as he travelled south, but the men who had left them seemed long gone.

The sun was nearing its zenith, and Albryan decided to stop for lunch, allowing the mare to graze. The heat had sapped his appetite, but he forced himself to chew on a sticky nut-cake, washing it down with swallows of water. Even the wild berry bush he sheltered under seemed to have wilted with the heat. For a moment, he entertained the idea of stripping off his armour, but decided against it. *Something* made him uneasy, despite the fact that he was almost certain there was no-one else within range.

He would have dozed, but there was a prickling on the back of his neck, a feeling as if he were being watched intently. He could not shake the idea that something was lurking in the long grass, watching from the shelter of the thorn-bushes, ready to strike.

Albryan stood up. Ignoring the instinct which entreated him to glance over his shoulder, he closed his eyes and rooted his stance, letting the magic flow through him, connecting him to the earth beneath his feet and the world at his fingertips. His breath slowed and evened out. The world dimmed, the bright sunlight beating on his eyelids and the hum of miscellaneous insects in the bushes.

In this half-trance, with the physical sensations of his body muted, Albryan could pick up what his magical senses were trying to tell him.

The answer came immediately, and so strongly that he cursed himself for a fool. All through the scrubby bushes and long grasses that surrounded him, the slimy sense of an alien magic rustled.

Albryan opened his eyes and the world rushed back. Every inch of skin felt as though it were prickling with sorcery, now. This was no magic from the Forest of the Morning. He could feel the difference, the unease, whereas within his homeland the constant background of Mage-Gifted felt only normal and familiar.

Albryan had never actually faced one of Arran's brood before, never tested their magic for himself. One of the blood sorcerer's children was somewhere nearby, had walked in this bush only a few short hours ago and left their residue for anyone who had the Gift to sense.

He had time. Time to decide what to do. If the source of this magic were close enough to harm him, he would know it. And yet this uneasiness had been growing on him all day, and even now was intensifying with every moment that passed. It could only mean that this blood sorcerer was drawing closer.

Albryan walked over to the horse, unsaddled her, drew the riding bit out of her mouth. It was pointless to try and hide. Anyone with even a trace of the Gift could sense another. The stronger the Gift, the stronger the presence in the ether felt to others. This one was very strong, and Albryan was sure that they could feel *him* just as surely.

Spurred by instinct, he wandered along a narrow path that he had taken for an animal track. He had not gone far before he was jolted to a halt. Before him, stretched between two trees, a silvery spider's-web wavered and glinted in the sunlight.

Albryan drew a deep breath. No spider had spun this web, even if it were possible for a spider to have grown to that size. Magic clung to the webs like dew. *A lovely trap*, he knew. He thought of slashing at the web with his sword, which was edged with silver, but decided against it. Although magic gave way before silver, there was an edge to the magic that made him uneasy. It was more than likely that whoever had created this spell had woven some kind of failsafe into it, a trap in case he tried to break it using this simplest of resolutions.

He wandered around for another hour, during which he discovered more of the magical webs, nearly a dozen in total. He returned to the horse, paced around and wondered whether he should leave this place. Those webs were set up to catch something, and their creator was drawing closer.

But Thinas was relying on him not to flee. If he could meet one of Arran's children face-to-face—kill them—

So then it will come to a showing of strength, the magic of the blood sorcerer against the best of Qwu'Mallorn.

Albryan held no pretensions regarding his own Gift. The magic had been strong in him since birth, and had only been fine-honed during his nine years of military training and practice. He was the best soldier that Qwu'Mallorn had to offer: how would he fare against one who had augmented their natural Gift with the life-force of others, drawn through blood sacrifice?

He shaded his eyes with his hand and gazed up at the sky. Clouds were moving over the sun, damping the heat. Albryan knew that it would be past nightfall before the blood sorcerer drew close enough.

As the day drew to a close, Albryan found the tallest tree in the area and scaled it, settling himself against in a nook where three branches came together. With a commanding view of the surrounding countryside, he felt safer. After securing himself to the tree-trunk, he drifted into a doze. The air was not so clammy up here, and sleep took him quickly.

HE AWOKE WITH A START, and stared out into the night. It was pitch dark. He was anchored securely against the tree, though one foot trailed off the wide branch into space. Albryan brought that foot up, wincing slightly at the scrape it made against the branch in the night's silence.

He glanced up to find the moon. Nearly full, it had moved past its zenith some time ago, and now lay close to the horizon. It must be early morning, though the birds had not yet begun to sing.

The presence of alien magic lay thick upon the earth, so strong that Albryan could taste it in the back of his mouth. It tasted disgusting. Albryan had never felt anything but comforted by sensing magic before. Even on the occasion when he had practised duelling against others, when a sudden flare of sorcery had stood his hair on end and burned metallic in his mouth, Albryan had never felt this sense of revulsion. "What does magic taste like?" Elithan had once jested to him. "Like copper pennies."

This magic, thought Albryan, *tastes a lot more like fire and blood.*

The promise of battle beckoned. Albryan fumbled with the knot that held him to the tree. A cool breeze came up, and he shivered for a moment. He had slept in his armour, and the silver-plated steel of his breastplate was icy cold to the touch.

He lingered in the tree, making sure his sword was within reach. The bush below was pitch dark, and he could faintly hear the snoring of his horse. Any descent from the tree would be heard immediately, if anyone was down there. Albryan wished, not for the first time, that his magical senses might be more precise. He knew that the enemy was close, maybe even within his range of vision, but he could not pinpoint their exact location.

Magic, however, was not the only resource available to him, and Albryan gently chided himself for not simply using his mundane senses in the first place. He waited in the tree; watched, listened. Like any experienced scout, Albryan knew when to trust his gut, and this was one of those times.

All his senses, his gut, his eyes and ears and even his nose, were telling him that there was no-one at the foot of the tree.

Albryan dislodged himself from the branches, and hopped down from one branch to the next, making a lot more noise than he would have liked. His boots finally hit the ground with a thud, and he swivelled, scanning the uncertain shadows of the brush around, hand on the hilt of his sword.

There was no-one within sight, and Albryan relaxed infinitesimally. He tended to his most urgent morning ablutions and looked for the horse. She was sleeping under the tree where he had left her.

Albryan retrieved his saddlebags from where he'd hung them in the tree before sleeping. He took a handful of trail mix to eat, chewing as he paced in the humid air, washing it down with water from his tin flask.

This was all the preparation he could spare. It was time to find his foe at last. Albryan began to circle the stand of stunted trees, looking for any sign of an intruder, ready for whatever might come at him.

He had not gone far, only a few dozen paces, when he saw the spiderweb.

Albryan halted in his tracks, willing his racing heart to calm down. Though the entire area around was criss-crossed with these sticky magic webs, there had not been one this close to his tree last night. The sorcerer had been here whilst Albryan was sleeping, and had woven this without waking him. The idea of someone wielding such subtle magic, of moving so quietly beneath the trees, made the hair on the back of his neck stand up. His mouth went dry.

Albryan approached the web, looking carefully for any signs of the sorcerer's passage, which way they might have gone. This sorcerer was as good a woodsman as magician, however, and had cleverly concealed their tracks.

He turned away from the web. Something glittered in the corner of his eye.

Albryan's hand had already been on the hilt of his sword; now he drew it in one fluid movement. He arranged himself, instinctively, into a defensive stance as she stepped out onto the trail before him.

Her armour was beautiful, exquisitely tooled and fitted to her slim, athletic body. The silver plating dazzled him as the dawning sunlight reflected from interlocking scales that covered her from head to foot. The armour Albryan wore was well made and quite expensive, but it could not match something like this. This was the kind of armour that noblewomen on the Council commissioned for their daughters; the kind that tended to hardly see any fighting, but was sure to do its job if ever it did.

He had the feeling that *this* woman's armour had seen more fighting than its owner could rightly reckon up.

Above the gleaming mail, a face as perfect as the armour she wore peeked out from beneath a decoratively tooled, close-fitting helmet. She was grinning, and Albryan registered her beauty even as the blood in his veins turned to ice. Long hair the colour of spun gold flowed in a silky braid from underneath the helm, and slanted eyes the intense blue of sapphire regarded him with something like amusement. She was as lovely as a carefully polished and faceted diamond, and just like that diamond, there was a hard edge to her beauty. How could there not be? Albryan's breath hitched as unbidden fear caught in his throat. She was her father's most favoured child, the most ruthless killer he would ever meet. There was *nothing* tender or soft about her, no matter how deceptively feminine her beauty. She was Dannine Sylvaissen, once Dannine Ebraskaia, the shadow who hunted by night.

That she had appeared before him at the break of day only made Albryan all the more uneasy.

"You may as well put your sword away." Her voice was melodious, as lovely as the rest of her. She had not drawn her own weapon, a slim, curving sabre sheathed at her hip. A smile played around her lips.

"No thank you. I prefer to have something against your magic." Half surprised by how steady his own voice sounded, Albryan shifted his pose, wishing that the magic spiderweb were not quite so close behind him.

"As you wish." She drew her sword, the silvered blade gleaming in the early rays of waking sunrise.

Even though Albryan was tense with anticipation, he still could not believe how fast she advanced upon him. In a heartbeat, she was close enough to strike. The slim sword flashed towards his face then back again, searching for an opening, forcing him to parry wildly and fall back. She moved like a dancer. Albryan matched her, the two silvered swords clashing together like the sound of ringing bells.

She drove him back, step by step, towards the spiderweb.

There was no escaping it; her advance was too aggressive, too fast, and he could not find an opening against her.

Albryan pivoted, letting the tip of her sword nick the leather of his thigh armour, and slashed his blade in a great stroke across the tendrils of the web. As he had hoped, the magic parted, curling up into the still air and dissipating like smoke. He launched himself through the opening where the web had been, and turned to face Dannine again.

Her smile did not falter for a single moment; in the face of death, Dannine Sylvaissen reflected only joy. She came on again, pressing the attack without even pausing for breath. She drove him halfway down the trail, hammering at him, appearing in openings he couldn't anticipate.

She was driving him towards another web, he knew, and he dove to the side, landing in the long grass beside the trail. She threw a web of magic from her hand, glowing in the ether. He dodged it, but silvery tendrils snaked towards him all the same. The web made contact with his right hand, dug its tendrils into him. He could feel a numbing pain in his fingers. The web snaked up towards his wrist, clawing itself further into him, threatening to crawl beneath his armour.

Albryan dropped his sword and seized a silver-edged dagger from his belt, knowing that he must stop the web before it was able to embed itself. With a swift movement, he drew the silvered blade down his wrist, severing the tendrils of magic from his skin, flicking the web aside as if he were skinning a stubborn tropical fruit. The blade of the dagger nicked the back of his hand, and droplets of blood flicked away along with the web.

There was no time to recover, for Dannine had already sent another, larger web flying towards him. Albryan let go of the dagger and dove for his sword, rolling clear of the approaching web. As it hovered in mid-air, reaching for him, he swept the sword around and through it in a wide arc. The magic dissipated, and the web withered.

Dannine approached again, driving him back towards the trail. Albryan spared a moment to gather some energy, and threw a firebolt at her. She deflected it without even pausing in her advance.

Albryan cursed himself for a fool. That had been an unnecessary expenditure of energy, and he could already feel the drain on his resources. He was not thinking straight, he realized. She had sapped his fighting energy; she had the upper hand. Every move of his was made in desperation.

She was upon him again. He could not believe how a fully armoured fighter could be so fast.

He had gotten disoriented, Albryan realized, and he didn't know in which direction he was moving.

Albryan quickly glanced over his shoulder. A sticky spiderweb stretched out behind him, waiting close.

That one glance had cost him; there was an opening for her to strike at his face. All in half a heartbeat, Albryan steeled himself for the blow, though he knew it would probably kill him regardless.

The blow never came. She continued to press him further back. She hadn't taken the opening.

She didn't want to kill him. She wanted to capture him alive.

The idea of being taken alive was far worse.

In the last heartbeat as she drove him back towards the web, a memory flashed across Albryan's mind.

Three years ago, he had been leading a small group of scouts, most of them around nineteen, fresh out of training. It had been his first command as captain. Nothing too challenging: reconnaissance. They were to locate a contingent of Arran's soldiers, watch their movements and send word back to the senior officers. Everything had been going well until Albryan's second-in-command, a young sergeant named Niaston, had suddenly disappeared.

Albryan had never seen Dannine, nor even gotten close enough to sense her magic. Their position had been given away; they won the ensuing fight with the soldiers they had been tailing, but at the end of it, three-quarters of Albryan's brave young scouts lay dead. Afterwards, he had gone out on his own, injured and heartsick, to find out what had happened to Niaston.

Dannine had taken the young sergeant, interrogated him, then left him for dead whilst she vanished to only her dark goddess knew where. Niaston had still been alive when Albryan found him.

Albryan was no stranger to death. He had dealt death himself, in many varied and savage ways. He had buried more soldiers under his command than he cared to keep count of. What Dannine had done to Niaston—that was beyond savagery, beyond any necessity of war. Albryan had stayed with the young sergeant until the bitter end, unable to touch him, nor even to mercifully hasten that end. Watched as Niaston's own magic unravelled from him like the stinger of a bee would unravel its own viscera, just as fatal, and inevitable. It was the first time that Albryan had seen what blood magic could do. It had seared itself across his memory—what Dannine Sylvaissen did to those she took alive.

Anger boiled up inside Albryan, and with it came steel-cold determination.

Pivoting to the side, narrowly avoiding the clutches of the sticky web, he offered Dannine the same opening once more. Once more she failed to take it, and Albryan struck into the space when she hesitated, his sword raking the gleaming scales at her breast. She fell back, surprise naked in her eyes, and he struck again, sending her reeling. Her sword fell from her hand as she staggered back.

Albryan turned and brought the sword down to sever the web behind him.

In a flash of silver, Dannine interposed herself between him and the web, catching the sword blade in her gauntleted hand.

Albryan heard the crunch as the gauntlet shattered into her palm, saw blood spurt from her hand as she caught the sword. She did not even flinch.

She was a breath away from him, the end of her braid flicking close enough to touch. She was tall, for a Morgein woman, but Albryan still had several inches on her, with the corresponding weight. He let go of the sword and lunged at her, catching her on the shoulder when she dodged the heavy blow aimed at her face.

She pivoted, allowing him to bring his arm around, and landed a blow in his chest with her knee. He came on, undeterred, and she raised her hand, made a clenching motion with her fist, spoke an arcane word of command.

The magic web behind him unfurled itself from the tree and wrapped around Albryan, sinking into every inch of exposed flesh. Sudden numbness enveloped him, and he could not even scream as all feeling was sucked from his face, his arms, his legs. He collapsed, coiled in the web as securely as a fly wrapped in spidersilk.

Dannine was panting, but the brilliant grin was back on her face. "I'd won the moment you saw the web," she said. "You were only too stubborn to see it."

She peeled the shattered gauntlet off, standing over him. Blood dripped from her hand. "All that silver in your armour is hindering my spell, though. I hope you don't mind, but I'll have to do something about that."

She picked up her sword and pivoted the hilt towards his face. She crouched down, hefting it in her hand.

Albryan saw nothing but blackness, and heard only the rattling of Niaston's last breath.

WHEN HE REGAINED CONSCIOUSNESS, he was swaying. There was a hollow, sick feeling in his gut, and his head hurt. He opened his eyes and saw bushes going by beneath him. How could that be?

A wave of dizziness and disorientation washed over him, and he closed his eyes again. He was moving, he realized at last, but his hands and feet were bound. The web-spell was wearing off, and he could feel his body again. He realized, all in a rush, that he was trussed up and slung over a horse's saddle.

He opened his eyes again, and this time there was no disorientation. He was slung over the saddle of his own horse, and as he looked ahead, he could see that Dannine was leading her by the reins. He was being taken somewhere, doubtless for her to question at leisure. Albryan's gut went cold at the thought. He knew more of the army's movements and secrets than most common soldiers, although Thinas had always taken care not to trust him with too much information for this very reason.

What did she want to know? Was it possible for him to mount a defence? Albryan struggled against the chains that bound his hands. He recognized the cold-burning sensation of silver against his wrists. It was a simple yet highly effective way of preventing a sorcerer from casting any spells—simply chain his hands and feet with silver.

Dannine looked back as he squirmed, that irritating grin on her face again. "I'm sorry I had to do that," she said teasingly. "But you wear far too much armour. Think of all the weight I've saved you."

She had stripped Albryan of everything except his shirt and pants and shoes. His armour and weapons had vanished; he supposed they were back in a bush somewhere. Perhaps a passing patrol would find them and realize what had happened to him. Albryan could only hope. He was close enough to Qwu'Mallorn that they might mount a search for him. He might be rescued.

The horse gave a loud whinny of distress and jerked to a halt, half-rising onto her hind legs. Dannine gave her bridle a savage jerk and pulled her head down, glancing at Albryan mockingly as if she had overheard his private thoughts. Albryan lifted his head as far as he could, craning to see what had distressed the mare.

There was a clearing in the brush in front of them. Albryan's breath caught in his throat as he saw what lay in the clearing, and he knew all his hopes of rescue were futile.

The creature was at least twenty feet long, from its clawed hind feet to the top of its bulbous, grotesquely overlarge head. It was an oddly formed thing, covered in iridescent blue-green feathers, with two powerful hind legs and a short humped back. Its twiggy front legs supported a pair of enormous feathered wings, which fanned out ten feet to either side as it crouched on all fours before them. Its muscular, reptilian neck was as long as a great tree-snake from the jungles of Sanghui, and thick enough to have swallowed either of them down in a single gulp. The bulbous head supported a gleaming-sharp beak that added eight feet to its already impressive length. As Albryan stared, it opened that savage beak wide and gave an ear-piercing scream directed at Dannine, who stood her ground. Albryan's horse gave a panicked neigh and danced back.

Albryan knew the beast from a picture in a book: it was a quetzal, a flying lizard-bird from the faraway Pirate Islands. As he watched, it reared up on its hind legs, almost twice as tall as any of the trees in this scrub woodland, flapping its enormous, brightly-feathered wings wide against the air. The horse rolled her eyes in panic, straining to move against an unseen compulsion. Albryan realized that

Dannine was holding the mare with magic, preventing her from running.

The quetzal gazed down at Dannine and gave another insistent scream. Dannine lifted a hand. The monster flinched back, showing fear despite the fact that it could easily have lifted Dannine in its beak and snapped her in half.

Dannine released the horse's reins and strode over to where Albryan hung. The horse sweated in fear as she worked a simple magic to lift Albryan's body and set it down some distance away.

Dannine looked the feathered quetzal in the eye, making a movement that was something like a bow and something like a gesture of allowing. From his prone position on the grass, Albryan thought fleetingly that there was actually something rather beautiful about the creature. Its feathers sparkled like jewels in the midday sun, and its enormous wings folded and unfolded with a queer grace as it moved on claw-tipped feet towards Dannine.

Dannine stepped away from the horse.

The quetzal pounced with a deafening shriek, catching the horse's head in its beak, severing it with a sickening rip and crunch of bones. Blood sprayed like treacle across the grass as the dead mare collapsed. The quetzal swallowed its bite whole and moved back in. This time it went for the horse's belly, reaching in with its sharp beak to withdraw mouthfuls of ripped hide and bone and gore.

Dannine stood near him, watching the quetzal feed with folded arms, the surface of her calm demeanour completely unruffled. She looked over at him with a smirk.

Albryan found his voice at last. The effects of the web were wearing off, though he still hurt all over, especially in his head.

"Why did you do that?" he demanded. "That was a good horse. War-trained." One of Albryan's jobs as a recruit had been to groom and feed the horses of the army, and the grey mare had been born whilst he was still a skiff in the stables. Albryan had attended her dam at her birth.

She raised a pale eyebrow. "I have my reasons. And I have no use for a dumb beast of burden."

The horse's carcass was gone now; only blood-smeared grass and some ribbons of tack remained. Albryan felt queasy. If they sent a search party out for him, and came upon *that* . . . they would be baffled, but they might assume that the blood was his, and give him up for dead.

"Come on." Dannine dragged him to his feet, using magic to augment her strength. She pulled him forward by the chains around his wrists, nearly yanking his arms from their sockets.

The quetzal shrieked and cowered away from Dannine, almost as if it feared a slap. Albryan could guess that the slap the creature feared was in truth one of magic.

"Shut up," Dannine growled. The quetzal fell silent, and bowed its long neck in a gesture of submission. Albryan saw that a kind of leather riding harness had been fixed to its humped back. Handles were fixed to a ring around its lower neck, and this in turn was attached to a saddle, stirrups included, that draped over its withers. The saddle stretched out over its back with plenty of space to carry baggage.

Albryan froze, fighting Dannine's grip. Now he knew what she planned. Despair settled in his gut and rose up to suffocate him. It didn't matter if they sent a search party. They would never find him. Not when he was being taken through the air, as though snatched up by a great bird.

"Where are you taking me?" he demanded, trying to pull back. This had never happened before. Arran Sylvaissen had never shown the slightest interest in taking hostages. Whenever men disappeared, they were always found soon afterwards, dead or alive. Sometimes the blood sorcerer's armies would kidnap civilians, mostly children too young to fully control their magic, or village people whose Mage-Gifts were extremely weak, but that was a different matter.

All of Albryan's struggling availed him nothing, as he should have known. With silver encircling both his wrists and ankles, the circulation of magic through his body was cut off from both the physical world and the wellspring of the ether. Like it or not, he was going to be strapped to the back of that thing, and *this* trip would be infinitely more terrifying than the one he had just endured athwart his own horse.

"You ask too many questions." Dannine wrested his body into place like a sack of meat, strapping him down over the quetzal's back.

"Couldn't you just let me sit upright?" Panic tasted bitter in the back of Albryan's mouth.

Dannine smirked. "Why on earth would I want to do that?" She paused a moment, checking that all the straps were secure. "I suppose I could tell you where we're going, if you haven't figured it out for yourself. It should be obvious. Whom do I serve?"

Arran. She was taking him to Armour City, four hundred miles away. *As the quetzal flies, anyway.* He felt giddy with despair. He wanted to close his eyes, but they remained transfixed upon the ground.

Dannine seated herself in the flying saddle. Albryan could feel his pulse pounding against the bonds that held him.

The quetzal spread its mighty wings, tucking its bloodstained beak down in front so it sliced like a rudder through the air. It began to run. Slow at first, ponderous, then gaining speed, faster and faster. It skimmed over the ground like a destrier on a cavalry charge. Grass and mud blurred before Albryan's vision as he lay head hanging downwards. He was utterly terrified, and yet a tiny part of him was also exhilarated. The quetzal was faster than a horse, faster than anything he had ever experienced. Ten times faster. Fifty times faster.

The quetzal's great wings began to flap, beating the air before it, as if it were forcing substance into utter nothingness.

There was a moment of lifting, a great exhilarating leap into the unknown. Albryan's insides, which were hanging upside down, rushed sickeningly towards the wrong place. There was a pounding pressure upon his head, and he could see nothing but a grey blur, hear nothing but the creak and beat of the quetzal's wings. He wanted to vomit, but there was far too much pressure. It surrounded him like a great hand, squeezing the breath out of him.

Somewhere above, somewhere around, Albryan thought he heard Dannine laugh in childlike delight. But that couldn't be. Dannine was death in human form, and nothing more. The air was rushing past him, too fast for him to breathe. He was hallucinating, hearing things.

Blinded and deafened, Albryan lost consciousness as the quetzal soared into the sky.

Chapter VI
The Prisoner

IT WAS ALL ALBRYAN COULD DO to keep from bursting into hysterical laughter as Dannine's guardsmen half-carried, half-dragged him up the sandstone steps to the palace courtyard. Still thoroughly nauseated, only half conscious, he made quite a burden for the two burly individuals who had come to receive Dannine as the quetzal landed in a sheltered yard just within sight of Armour City's magnificent sandstone palace.

Once the seat of the Eight Councillors and where they lived along with their families, the palace had been built not for defence, but as a symbol of might and wisdom. The guardsmen hauled him through a wide courtyard paved with white and green veined marble before reaching the great doors, where Albryan finally lost control of his stomach and vomited right upon Arran's doorstep.

Dannine, who had been pacing proudly ahead of the guards, turned back with an exclamation of disgust. Albryan heard a loud *crack*, and to his faint surprise, as he knelt recovering, one of the burly guardsmen reeled back as if he'd been struck.

"You incompetent!" he heard Dannine yell, with not a trace of her former composure. She was upon him then, pulling Albryan forward by his wrist-chains into a dark corridor. "I shall take him to the Sylvaissen myself! You two stay here and clean that, like the servants you are!"

Albryan stumbled along behind her, feet awkwardly shuffling in the silver chains. He felt a lot better all of a sudden, and he tried to focus on the featureless passages she was leading him through, memorizing the way.

At last she stopped before a heavy ebony door on the fourth level of the palace. She was breathing hard with exertion, for she had had to exercise more and more of her magic to haul Albryan all the way up here, and it had begun to wear her down. Albryan knew that she had not eaten nor rested since catching him early that morning.

And now I know something of her reserves.

Albryan's small elation did not last long, for the room beyond the creaking ebony door sent thrills of horror coursing along his spine. The crawling feeling of dark magic lay thick as incense in here, and the dreary sorcerous light that emanated from the ceiling contributed to Albryan's disorientation, making him feel as though he had stepped into a subterranean cave.

A pale man dressed all in white was waiting in the corner of the room, his face made strangely artificial by the too-sharp light, but Albryan's eyes kept going to a second ebony door set in the wall beside a low table beyond him. He could feel Dannine's magical presence burning like a brand before him—could feel even more strongly the black fire that emanated from the pale man, who must be none other than Arran Sylvaissen himself. Still, both of these presences paled before the *something* he could sense behind that door. Albryan's mind raced as he tried to imagine what was lurking behind it. How could Arran keep a power like that contained? Was there another sorcerer, one even greater than Arran himself, waiting within that secret room?

The thought faded to the back of Albryan's mind as the pale man came forward, smiling broadly. "Captain Albryan Lana, at last," he said, making a mock salute. Albryan went cold.

How would he know my name and rank—my description—unless he had inside knowledge already? His throat constricted. *A traitor within Qwu'Mallorn. Someone sold me out. They must have.*

Dannine bowed deeply before her adoptive father, who took her by the shoulders. "Once again, you have not let me down," he said softly. His eyes slid back towards Albryan. "You will prepare him."

He gestured towards an alcove in the spacious room. This space was floored with rough stone rather than the smooth tile they were standing on, and a hook hung suspended from a chain in the ceiling. Albryan instinctively hung back as Arran reached for him, though he knew that he was not, now, in mastery of his own body.

Arran pulled him forward and attached the hook to the chains that bound Albryan's hands before of him. He winched the chain up, going until Albryan's full weight was balanced precariously on the balls of his feet. Albryan felt painfully vulnerable in this position, yet he stood motionless, trying to suppress the sick fear that welled in his gut for whatever might come next. But the blood sorcerer only smiled pleasantly as he turned his back.

"You need rest, daughter," he said to Dannine as they turned to leave the room. "Return this evening for the procedure."

HE SLEPT, HANGING THERE in the harsh light of the room, lolling his head against his arm as he hung helplessly, unable to find a position where it did not hurt. He did not know how many hours had passed, but every muscle in his body was in screaming agony when suddenly he awoke to see someone moving about the room.

It was Dannine, and she was mixing something in a large clay bowl, her unbound golden hair falling slightly over one eye. She was still dressed in armour, her left hand bound in a strip of clean cloth. She quickly noticed that Albryan was stirring, and a smile spread over her face.

Advancing upon him, she flicked out a small knife and began to cut his shirt away from his body. Albryan flinched at the touch of the cold metal, and his face burned as she tore away strips of cloth to expose his naked skin.

What in the name of the spirit guardians is she doing?

Dannine produced a paintbrush and fetched the clay bowl, bringing it over towards him. He could see that it was filled with a heavy, viscous liquid that sparkled like molten silver. She dipped the brush in the liquid, making sure the thick bristles were well coated, and began to paint his upper body.

Albryan had to clench his jaw to keep from crying out. The stuff was *cold*, and wherever the brush-strokes went, his skin tingled as though she were trailing bare ice across it. Dannine's smirk deepened as though she knew what he was thinking.

"What are you doing?" Albryan finally burst out. She ignored him. When he repeated himself, she calmly backhanded him in the face.

She was still wearing a gauntlet on her uninjured hand, and Albryan's head spun with the force of the blow. He knew she had drawn blood; he felt warm liquid drip from his nose to his chin. She ignored that as well, and fiddled with his belt.

He had done his best to remain calm thus far, to try and think his way out of here, but panic was rapidly beginning to overcome Albryan's mind. Dannine stripped him as naked as the day he was born, then continued to paint him all over, as detached as if she were basting a turkey for the midsummer feast. He was no longer in control of his reactions, and the icy touch of the silver paint upon his skin became an agony he was desperate to be rid of. He cried out and writhed against his chains, to no avail. He tried to lift himself off the floor, but found his muscles far too weak. His vision was blurring, and his heart pattered in his chest as he realized what the purpose of the silver paint was. A kind of magical sedative—designed to keep him unconscious until—until what? Unconscious prisoners could not be interrogated. What did Arran mean to do with him?

As if the thought had summoned him, the blood sorcerer appeared suddenly from a corner of the room, smiling. He spread a roll of black velvet out upon a low table, and Albryan caught a glimpse of what was inside. Saw the silvery tools, the gleaming blades which Arran lovingly caressed. Saw him pick one up, its point glint in the crazed light, saw Arran's smile deepen.

That was the last thing he saw, for just as he tried to scream, darkness rose up and sucked him down into a tunnel where everything howled together, all his pain and fear built up into an incomprehensible torrent of confusion, and he knew no more where he was, nor even his own name.

FAR AWAY, SOMEWHERE OUTSIDE, it seemed that someone was trying to reach him. Stubbornly, he held on to the numbness, the unfeeling. There was a searing memory of pain, and fear was as bitter as cyanide in the back of his throat. If he could stay here, stay where all was numb, then nothing could hurt him, surely . . .

For what seemed like an eternity, he had had no body, and yet *now* someone was shaking his body, yelling incoherent words into its ear, gripping it by the shoulder. He felt cold. He felt . . .

All in a blind rush, Albryan opened his eyes and scooted violently away from the person who was shaking him. He cried out in panic, felt his back hit a rough stone wall. A moment of nauseating disorientation was followed by sudden realization that his surroundings had changed yet again. It was much darker here, dank stone walls barely lit by a guttering oil lamp somewhere above. Nothing like the eerie brightness of the laboratory that he only vaguely remembered.

His heart beat hard in his chest. The laboratory! What had happened there? His mind was sluggish, slow to bring up the proper memories. There was the silver paint, the numbness of sleep, and the face of Arran Sylvaissen . . . and what then?

He came a little more to himself, and realized that he was not alone. Of course; someone had been attempting to wake him, and it had not been Dannine nor her cursed father. Crouching in the shadows before him was a man dressed in rags, an old, frail man, narrow-faced behind a scruffy grey beard, gesticulating with both hands as if to calm him.

Beyond the old man, Albryan saw a row of iron bars, felt dirty straw prick through his trousers, and knew precisely where he was. In the dungeons of Arran's palace.

"Easy, youngster," the old man was saying. Albryan could comprehend the words at last. "Calm down . . ."

Albryan relaxed, slumping his shoulders backwards. The man sat away from him, falling silent. Albryan tried to sit up, but there were still silver chains around his ankles and wrists, rattling whenever he moved. The old man moved over and helped steady him, as Albryan endeavoured to tuck his legs underneath himself, to sit with at least a smidgen of comfort. The rags were threadbare, he saw as the man helped him, and beneath them he was emaciated to the bone.

"Thank you," Albryan said with real gratitude, and a thin smile appeared on the old prisoner's face. "How . . . how long have I been here?"

"Couple o' hours," the old man said shortly, his voice hoarse, as if he did not speak very often. Albryan took a look around. He and the old man occupied one cell of many, and they were all well stocked, with two or three prisoners inside each one. There was the usual dungeon-stench, of human excrement and despair, and the stony floor was cold and damp despite the thin covering of straw, penetrating even through his cloak.

His cloak? Albryan started, and quickly examined himself. He was dressed, as far as he could tell, in the same clothes that Dannine had cut from him in pieces, with the addition of the cloak he had thought lost along with his weapons and armour, the thick forest-green cloak that was always a reminder of Qwu'Mallorn for him. His belt—his boots—even his smalls—all were intact, as if he'd only dreamed the scene in the laboratory. Only his weapons were missing.

He licked at his bottom lip, felt swelling and tasted blood. So *that* had been real enough. And though the cloak was undoubtedly his—Dannine must have brought it with her—the trousers and shirt were wrong. They were far too clean.

Albryan lifted his gaze and saw the old prisoner, huddled beneath a blanket as thin as a dishrag, gazing at him. The man had striking eyes, a curious golden, almost yellow, like some great birds of prey possessed. Those penetrating eyes were set above a great beak of a nose, completing the illusion of hawkishness. Were he not a ragged dungeon rat huddling beneath a threadbare piece of cloth, the man's gaze would have been authoritative and intimidating. As it was, Albryan found it somewhat unsettling.

Albryan searched for something to say, but the prisoner beat him to it. "You're a mage?" he suddenly asked with interest. His voice creaked like a pump that had sat unused for years.

Albryan nodded his assent, and the prisoner regarded him silently for another moment. Then he asked, "Are you hungry?"

"I . . ." Albryan realized that he was. He nodded his thanks as the prisoner produced a crust of extremely dry bread from a corner, and handed it to him.

"The rats haven't been at it yet," the prisoner said. He folded his bare feet beneath himself and tucked his striped nightshirt into his threadbare pants before covering himself with the thin blanket again.

Albryan nibbled at the bread, barely taking the edge off his hunger. "How long have you been here?" he asked the prisoner, for something to say.

"If it is spring already . . ." The old man squinted a little. "Nineteen years."

"Nineteen years?" Albryan repeated. "That's—you're not a mage. How did . . ." He trailed off, not certain whether his reaction had caused offence. The old convict did not move a muscle.

"I'm not a mage," he confirmed quietly. "But those bearing the Gift were not the only ones to suffer under our king." He studied Albryan intently. "You look . . . familiar to me," he said at last. "What is your name?"

Albryan hesitated. He had an alias, of course, to use whenever he donned the clothes of a nonmage mercenary and set off into Vailana to gather whatever information the army needed. But his disguise was already cracked, and secrecy made no sense whatsoever when he had already fallen into the clutches of his sworn enemy.

"Albryan Lana," he said.

The aged convict leaned forward, a gleam in his strange yellow eyes. "I never forget a face," he said breathlessly. "You were only a little lad, as I remember, but your father was one of the Court justices. Your mother—I knew her passing well. The Lady Roseanne Jarrevoy. You are the very image of her."

Albryan drew back, startled. "Who are you?" he demanded.

"My name? I was—Hiram Lynstream," the prisoner replied slowly, as if he was having a hard time remembering. "I was an Alderman; I wrote the laws your father was expected to enforce. I sat beneath the thrones of the Eight for over twenty years, dispensing justice to the people. Or at least, that which I myself believed to be just."

"It was so long ago . . ." Albryan hesitated as memory stirred, memories he'd not had occasion to dwell on for a very long time. "I think I remember you. Your hair was black then, and you were not so—so thin."

Hiram gave a tight-lipped smile. "Living in a dungeon will not do wonders for your health."

"But why were you jailed?" Albryan asked. Even as he spoke the words, realization came to him. "Your wife. You were married to a Mage-Gifted woman. I remember you telling my mother that children of mixed blood did not always have the Gift. We both did, me and my brother, but your daughter didn't." Sadness shone in the old convict's eyes, and Albryan felt a chill of apprehension. "Did they get away?" he asked softly. "Your wife and daughter?"

Hiram shook his head. "I don't know."

He seemed loath to speak of it, and Albryan fell silent. But Hiram spoke again: "You come from Qwu'Mallorn."

Albryan nodded. "I'm with the army," he said in a low voice. Reminding himself of his true profession, he realized an important truth. He needed to get back. Someone had betrayed him to Arran. There might be a traitor in the midst of the army. Could Hiram help him escape this dungeon? The old man seemed frail, yet his eyes shone with a vitality that Albryan found hard to dismiss. Albryan knew that sometimes it was not the strength and skillset of the individual which drove them to succeed, but rather the amount of willpower they possessed. There was something about Hiram that made him think that willpower was not something the old convict was in lack of.

"I need to get back," he said in a low voice.

Hiram nodded sagely. He looked around furtively, and lowered his voice. "The guards will come soon with food. We must be ready to escape."

"How?" Albryan demanded in a whisper, nonplussed.

Hiram leaned closer. His strange eyes seemed almost luminous in the gloom. "Share your magic with me."

"I'm sorry?" Albryan could not have heard right.

"You can channel magic to me," Hiram clarified.

Albryan gaped at him. *So the old convict has lost his mind after all.*

He did not give voice to his thoughts, however, and Hiram continued: "Your hands and feet are bound. You can't touch the magic in the other plane nor release it into this world. But you still have the connection to the source, the inborn link that makes you a mage in the first place. You can still channel magic into another living being."

"I can't release my magic into you," Albryan responded, aghast. "It would kill you. It's one of the first things we learn, to not let the unGifted touch us when we're spellcasting."

To his amazement, the old man shook his head, looking for all the world as though he were lecturing a pupil. "It's dangerous," he whispered, "because the unGifted do not instinctively channel magic. There are, however, techniques that one can learn, how to channel magic even if you do not naturally possess it, and I know those techniques."

Albryan could not think of anything to say. Surely the old man had gone quite mad, stuck alone in this dungeon for nineteen years, concocting only Goddess knew what kind of lunacies in his fantasies of escape. Yet Hiram's demeanour betrayed nought but calm urgency.

"We have nothing to lose," Hiram said. "I won't die, but if I do, you may be reassured that I would much rather have died in the attempt than given up all hope."

Albryan found his voice at last. "How?"

"Trust," the old man replied, simply. "My wife—magic was her art, her song, her way of life. She wanted to share all of it with me. Even then, there were not many who would trust a mage so implicitly. But I trusted her"—the old convict reached a hand out towards Albryan—"and I will give my trust to you."

There were sounds down the end of the dungeon. The clank of a door opening. Footsteps. Distant voices approaching. *Guards.* If Albryan was to escape today, he realized, it was now or never. If he delayed, there was no knowing what would happen to him. Whether Arran would have him brought up into his laboratory for another session under silver paint . . .

Albryan swallowed bile. "What do I need to do?" he asked, hoarsely.

"Whatever it is you do to share magic."

Albryan nodded his consent, pulled up his shirtsleeve to expose bare skin. All Mage-Gifted children learned to share their magic early on, with their brothers, their parents, with playmates. But *only* amongst others who also possessed the Gift.

"You should know," he said hoarsely, as Hiram laid his hand upon the unsleeved arm with a touch of apprehension, "that I have substantially more magic than most. Your wife's Gift was likely a minor one?"

The old man confirmed this with a nod. "But we should still try. I am not afeared of the danger."

The guards were approaching. Albryan could discern a food-trolley being pushed between the cells, could smell hot gruel. He suppressed a pang of hunger. The prisoners held up rough tin bowls as the guards moved past, received a ladleful of slop each.

"I'm ready," Hiram whispered.

Albryan went to the place inside himself that was connected to his magic, located somewhere in his subconsciousness, the place of dreaming. Something did not feel quite right. Perhaps it was the effect of trying to access his magic whilst being chained in silver. Like most mages, Albryan held an instinctive aversion to the metal, and right now it was physically preventing him from drawing upon his reserves. But they could make do with the magic that was circulating within him already.

Sharing magic with another mage was like two rivers meeting, mingling their separate paths into a greater current. Albryan tried to find that current in Hiram, and found only a void, a dry riverbed. He focused intently, pulling the magic through his veins, but there seemed to be a barrier between them, like a storm dyke, holding the magic back.

It was all or nothing. The guards were only yards away, and the doors at the end of the dungeon were open. Albryan pushed against the barrier with all his might, and all at once, like a torrent-fed stream breaking through a dam wall, the magic left him and streamed into the empty vessel that was Hiram.

There was no controlling it, no modulating the flow. Albryan jerked his arm from Hiram's grip, fully expecting to see the old prisoner collapsing with a scream of pain. But Hiram was standing straighter than he had been, his eyes afire though his hands were shaking violently.

"Gods!" he breathed. "I feel ready to burn this place to the ground!"

"Don't take it too far," Albryan cautioned. He felt giddy himself, and he pulled Hiram back down to the straw. Hiram was taking deep gulps of air, as if to steady himself, and Albryan could feel the magic flaring, barely held in check by the prisoner's frail form. "Hold it in," he warned. The guards were ladling gruel to the prisoners in the cell next door.

"It's too much!" Hiram cried. Albryan opened his mouth to yell as the old prisoner lurched to his feet, but anything he might have said was overpowered by the hissing flare of magic made fire, as Hiram fired off a ball of pure energy, straight in the dirrection of the food-trolley.

The fireball was gigantic. It lit up the whole gloomy space, flaring to life and exploding right through the body of the guard who stood nearest them. He vaporized instantly, vanishing into the sphere of glowing power. The fireball hit the iron pot of gruel, which exploded. Albryan put up an arm to shield his face as chunks of sheared iron, burned porridge, and dismembered body parts of the second guard, who had been standing right next to the pot, flew everywhere.

There were shouts and screams, and a crossbow bolt flew out of the gloom, directly at Hiram. Albryan saw it coming; in a flash of movement, he flung his hands out in front of the old convict. The bolt drove into a link of the chain that connected his manacles, and split it apart.

If Hiram was impressed by Albryan's skill, he did not show it. Instead, he quickly shot off another fireball into the darkness, smaller and more focused than the first one. There was a rush, impact, and then more screams. Albryan seized Hiram's arm to get his attention; he seemed in a murderous daze. There was plenty of magic there—Albryan knew that much—yet he had no more to spare should Hiram use it all up.

"Get us out of here!" Albryan gesticulated to the metal cage around them, and Hiram seemed to come to his senses. He seized the bars in front of him, and closed his eyes. The iron bars went red-hot, giving off an acrid smell, and began to hiss.

With his bare hands, Hiram tore the iron bars apart, and stepped through the hole. Holding his breath against the smoke, Albryan came after him. They broke into a trot, Albryan shuffling in his ankle-chains.

The prison was in pandemonium. Half the inmates were shrieking in fear; the others were bawling to be released. Albryan and Hiram reached the doors, and Albryan rushed past. This was clearly the guardroom, where an array of weapons hung from a shelf along with bunches of keys.

Hiram had paused just beyond the doors. Albryan seized two long swords, and yelled at him: "We must be gone!"

Hiram had turned back to face the bawling prisoners. He lifted both his hands into the air. For one horrible moment, Albryan thought that he meant to roast them all alive. But then, a great clanging resounded through the dungeon, as the gates burst from their locks, flinging themselves wide open, and a resounding cheer vibrated through the roof as the prisoners came surging out.

"We'd better go," Hiram said, taking Albryan by the arm. There was a stairwell to their left, but Albryan could hear shouting and more footsteps coming down from the upper levels. Of course, the rest of the dungeon guards must have heard the commotion.

Hiram ignored the stairwell completely, dragging Albryan straight ahead into a narrow tunnel.

"You know the way out?" Hordes of formerly imprisoned men surged around them, ready to follow whatever path Hiram chose.

"I will make a way out," Hiram shouted back.

He was as good as his word; after ten minutes of running, he turned to face the brick wall to their left. Raising his hands, he gathered the last of the magic, which Albryan felt as flickerings in the ether, and drove a hole straight through to the other side.

Clambering over pulverized bricks and scattered stones, Albryan and the rest of the dungeon's inhabitants drank in daylight on the grassy slope of the hill. Arran's palace was just visible, high above them, seemingly oblivious to their great escape. Albryan felt giddy. He clung to Hiram with a grin.

"You are the craziest convict I could ever hope to meet!" he cried as the prisoners streamed past in the golden light of a glorious new morning.

CHAPTER VII
ESCAPE

"WE NEED TO FIND SUPPLIES," Hiram whispered as Albryan divested himself of the last silver manacle, using his stolen sword as a makeshift crowbar. The two of them were huddled beside a low stone wall in the poorest quarter of the city. A group of city guardsmen tramped by noisily, their sable uniforms drinking the yellow sunlight.

"We have to get out of the city first," Albryan replied darkly, sliding the slightly bent blade into his belt. Perhaps he could find a blacksmith somewhere on the way to Qwu'Mallorn, to hammer it out again. It was not a bad sword, especially from the arsenal of a group of dungeon guards.

"You could sneak out on your own," Hiram retorted. "You pass. Meanwhile, my clothes would give me away as soon as you could say 'convict.'"

"I agree," Albryan said absently, fingering the hilt of the sword as he peered left and right down the empty lane. "You are far too conspicuous."

"Then what are we waiting for?" Hiram hissed.

"It's too easy," Albryan whispered back.

"What?"

"It's *too easy*," he repeated, turning to face Hiram. "There's hardly any response from Arran. All he's done is to send *these* buffoons." He gestured after the group of noisy guardsmen. "Where is Dannine? The rest of his children? Where are his flying quetzals, where is their *magic*?"

Hiram did not have an answer for this. Albryan turned back to scan the street.

"So what do we do?"

Albryan examined the layout of the neighbourhood. They had headed away from the palace in a straight line towards the western mining district, and now found themselves far away from the bustling centre of Armour City. This dusty borough was one of the least prosperous places Albryan had ever seen. Clotheslines flapped in the wind as the ubiquitous iron dust blew from the mines down a pockmarked road. Albryan could feel the grit settle in the corners of his eyes and in his beard, and already it coated the inside of his nose.

They were crouching in an abandoned cartmaker's yard, a relic of past glory days. Albryan's position behind the crumbling stone wall gave him a fairly good view of the street and the ramshackle wooden buildings which passed for residences on the block opposite. His main worry was for the inevitable observer, though the inhabitants of this kind of suburb likely had little love for local law enforcement or for their glittering silver king on his hill. Whether they hated Arran more than they feared him, however, that was a question Albryan could not venture an answer to.

"We have to keep moving," he said at last. Careful to keep silent, he swung himself over the low wall, quickly crossed the street, and stepped through a ruined wooden fence into an overgrown yard abutting one of the ramshackle residential blocks. A dog barked somewhere, but it was too far away to concern him. He motioned to Hiram, who was right behind him, and they moved behind a line of laundered sheets which would shield them from sight of the building.

"Take what you need," Albryan ordered.

"What? Steal from these people?"

"It's that, or risk going back to your little jail cell."

Hiram's brow furrowed over his long hooked nose, but he did as Albryan ordered, stripping a man's blouse and a pair of baggy trousers from the clothesline. The two fugitives once again took cover behind the wall stone. Their theft seemed to have gone unnoticed. The streets in this place seemed eerily quiet to Albryan, who was used to working with throngs of people surrounding him. Back home at barracks, he was never alone; though his rank entitled him to a private suite, there were always people coming and going through the rooms of a military officer.

I must get back to Thinas, he found himself thinking frantically. *Arran is clearly well-informed and planning something. We have to work out a strategy. We have to find the one who betrayed us.*

There was still an odd feeling in the back of his head, a sensation that Albryan did his level best to ignore. He still only had very fuzzy memories of being in Arran's laboratory, and he could not be quite sure whether anything he remembered was real or not.

"Do you know of any place close to here where we could sneak unnoticed from the city?" he asked Hiram.

The old man crouched motionless without answering. There was a strange look on his face. Albryan nudged him. "Hiram?"

"I—" Hiram began. He passed a hand over his face, his slender fingers shaking. "I remember," he whispered. His voice was hoarser than ever.

"What do you remember?" Albryan asked cautiously.

Hiram did not answer, but raised a hand and pointed beyond the line of slowly collapsing wooden buildings. "A dozen yards in that direction, there is a main road which leads out of the city," he said, and his voice was steady. "Just beyond the road, there is a line of scrub trees which shield the bank of a stream that runs down to the plains. That stream will be dry at this time of year, for it only flows when the summer rains come." He finally looked at Albryan, who had the strange feeling that Hiram was not truly seeing *him*, but something or someone who existed only in his memory.

"We will be safe, going that way," Hiram murmured, "if the guards don't get us."

"If they do, take cover," Albryan said grimly. His hands were free now, and his connection to the other plane was already replenishing him with quicksilver magic. "It won't be pretty."

Hiram did not acknowledge the remark. He was shivering beneath the thin garments he had just donned, even with his convict's clothes tucked underneath. Though the sun shone brightly, the hard-packed dirt of Armour City still harboured the chill of winter. There was frost on the ground in the shadows. Albryan unclasped his long cloak and handed it to the old man. "Put this on."

The cloak was made of wool from Morgein sheep, thick and soft, and Hiram took it with hesitation. "I would look . . . odd, wearing this," he protested softly.

"I would rather not have you die on me," Albryan returned. "I owe you a great favour, Hiram." He gave the man a genuine smile. "I don't need it, not for now, at any rate. How well do you remember the way to this stream?"

"I remember it very well," Hiram replied hollowly.

"Then you lead the way." Albryan got slowly to his feet, putting out a hand to help Hiram to his. No trace of the energy that Albryan's magic had imparted to him remained. He was a weary, frail old man again, and Albryan hoped that he would last to make his escape from the city that had betrayed him.

"We must move fast," Albryan said aloud, "but we must not run. Goddess knows that we will look suspicious. I do not want us to stop for anything. Is that understood?"

Hiram nodded, and Albryan stood aside to let him lead the way.

The two fugitives darted across the desolate township, cutting through windblown alleys and across dusty circles that could have passed for courtyards. They passed a group of wine-soaked men in a sunny corner, all of whom quickly averted their eyes, anticipating trouble. A few grubby children were playing in a street as they dashed past. They stopped to stare, but kept their distance.

At last they reached the main road, where Albryan paused for a moment, scanning for guards. But there was no-one around save workmen from the mines and their dusty ponies. They crossed the road without incident, and took cover under the scrubby trees that grew along the edge of the riverbank. Albryan glanced down. The dry streambed was shallow, not more than a foot or two above the surface. Water pooled here and there between worn river-pebbles. The ground was littered with rubbish that the residents of the area had tossed into the stream: rusty horseshoes, broken pots and bottles, the desiccated corpse of a dog.

Albryan and Hiram scrambled down into the streambed, taking care to avoid broken glass and nails. Albryan turned to the old man. "Where exactly will this lead us?"

"The stream leads due west," Hiram said. He stared intently downstream, as if he could see beyond the crippled trees and grey boulders flanking the way. "There are no barriers, no wall on this side of the city. The stream will lead us downhill into farmland. From there, the nearest village is but two hours' walk away."

"It occurs to me," Albryan said grimly, as they started walking, "that this is the *perfect* place for an ambush. Narrow, winding, an obvious way to sneak out of the city." He put his hand on the hilt of the sword hanging at his belt.

Hiram did not reply. *They must be planning some kind of ambush,* Albryan thought to himself. *Some kind of trick.* His heart beat fast and loud in his chest, and a feeling of wrongness nagged at the back of his mind.

The way down the dry stream was long and wearying. Hunger started to needle Albryan, making him want to quicken his footsteps. But Hiram could not walk as fast, and it was clear that his years in prison had weakened him substantially. Albryan wondered how heavy the old man would be to carry.

At last, after a long horizontal stretch, they reached a narrow gulley which led sharply downwards. Albryan ascended the riverbank to scout the way ahead, leaving Hiram to rest below for a moment. Brushwood and thorn-bushes grew thick here, narrowing the way, and the standing pools of water had become more frequent. Albryan pulled two creepers apart and emerged on the hillside.

Armour City towered above him, a sprawling labyrinth of yellow sandstone and dull brickwork. The palace was still visible from here, though dwarfed by the hill that stood behind it. Brockton Hill, it was called; the first place where precious ore had been liberated from the earth, earning the city its name.

They had come even further than Albryan had hoped. There was fresh farmland air around him, and when he gazed west over the plains, all he could see were rolling fields of winter gold, the grasslands awaiting the season of planting.

He returned to Hiram, grinning, to find the old man standing at the edge of the gulley, staring off into space.

"We've made good progress," he said cheerfully. He glanced at the sun passing overhead. "Perhaps we will even make a village before nightfall."

Hiram did not reply, nor stir in the slightest. His aquiline features were expressionless, but there was something in his eyes which reminded Albryan of his own darkest moments, the times he had wanted to cease existing.

"Hiram?" Albryan looked in the direction he was gazing, but there was nothing ahead but golden field and blue sky. A chill crept down his spine. "Is something the matter?"

"This is where I was captured," Hiram replied at last.

"Captured?"

"Nineteen years ago." Hiram clenched his fist until the knuckles went white. "It was only me and my daughter. My wife and her husband—they stayed behind and fought. We fled; we made our way down here. I have not seen her since." His voice cracked on the last syllable, but he kept talking. "They got me. She ran. I shouted at her to run. I don't know if she made it."

Oh. Albryan looked down the gulley. Hiram had nearly made it.

He fingered the hilt of his sword, glancing around. They had made it this far, but he could not trust Dannine Sylvaissen to give up the pursuit. Urgency was in him, wanting to move on.

"Hiram—"

"If she followed our plan," Hiram said, "she would have fled north on the Asmyth road to Svanfeld. On a trade caravan, perhaps. She had some money." He paused, and suddenly looked back at Albryan. "Surely she is there now."

"I'm sure she is," Albryan said gently. "Hiram, we have to go."

The old man sighed and took the arm that Albryan proffered, leaning on him. The gulley was steep, and the protruding rocks were sharp. It was a difficult journey down, but at last they found themselves down amongst the farmlands, awash in the golden plains. No-one waited for them; they found no ambush.

THE SUN WAS HANGING LOW over the fields by the time they reached the main road. There were no settlements in sight, only isolated farmsteads, and Albryan was determined to press on until they were well out of the reach of the city. In the end, Hiram had proven a lot tougher than he looked; he was still on his feet, after nearly an hour of walking.

The two men walked in silence until the main road led into the trade road, which was dead quiet in the late afternoon. The emptiness of the land around gave Albryan an uncomfortable sense of suspense. *It has all been too easy*, he thought to himself, and fretted silently.

The road forked, north and west. They took the north turning, and rutted dirt soon turned to gravel. A milestone to the side signalled that they were in a region of some traffic, and a raised stone slab indicated that a settlement was nearby. There was no writing on the stone slab, just a rough pictorial of a group of houses. The workmen and farmers of Vailana had no use for letters. So unlike Qwu'Mallorn, where a thorough knowledge of letters and ciphers was viewed as indispensable for practicing magic.

Hiram stopped in the middle of the road. Albryan turned, half expecting to see the old man collapsed upon his feet. But Hiram was still standing, his attention arrested by a grassy mound off to the side of the road.

The metalliferous hills of Armour City were behind them, and the landscape here was flat and endless, plains grass alternating with cultivated fields being readied for planting crops. The mound did not look natural to Albryan's eyes, and a wooden post had been hammered into the highest point, surrounded by three small, weathered rocks, similar to those that lay in the unworked fields.

Hiram silently made his way towards the mound. Albryan followed uncertainly.

"Someone was buried here," the old man said, walking around

and measuring the shape with his eyes.

Albryan cleared his throat softly. "These are—quite common," he said, keeping his voice low. "They date back nineteen years, when so many fled the city and the surrounding countryside. Many tried to escape with traders in their caravans, only to be betrayed. Some were taken by slavers, promised freedom in exchange for all their worldly possessions, only to discover that they themselves were the saleable commodity." He broke off in distaste.

Hiram took a deep breath, and Albryan immediately regretted telling him about the slavers. "The village is nearby," he said, trying to distract the old man from the gravesite. "We should reach it soon."

"Slavers," Hiram repeated, staring at the lonely mound. "Unscrupulous traders. Hunters collecting bounty for catching refugees. The dangers of the road." He clenched both his fists and closed his eyes. "The dangers of childbirth."

"What?" Albryan asked softly.

"I waited nineteen years," Hiram said. "Not hoping for revenge, but for reunion. And yet, I don't know where to begin. Lathea,"— his voice broke on the name—"was about to become a mother; I was to be a grandfather. I was the last one left to protect her." He turned towards Albryan, and there was beseeching in his eyes. "I only hoped that we might escape the violence. That her children might be born in a place free of it."

"Children?" Albryan repeated softly.

"Twins," Hiram whispered. "Risky to carry, even at the best of times."

Albryan did not know what to say. But as he stood there, the only witness to Hiram's grief, a hideous scream tore through the silence.

Both men crouched low beside the mound, raising their eyes up to the clear blue sky. The silence rushed back, more stifling than before, and they saw a faraway shadow soar across the sky towards the setting sun.

Flying lower than most birds, the creature hovered far above them, and Albryan felt his courage fail. The quetzal's neck was stretched out in flight, making its form appear like a long black snake winding across the sky. Its great jaws were bared to the winds, its scream triumphal.

Albryan knew the game was up, knew that Dannine had come for them at last. Perhaps she *had* simply been playing a game, biding her time until they thought themselves free, out in the open. But there was no way they could escape her. As the quetzal widened its jaws to screech again, Albryan espied the metallic glint of her armour between the flapping of its great wings. It banked slightly, swerving in an undulating wave across the land, and now he could see the splash of bright golden hair beneath her helm.

Albryan crouched lower, gripping his stolen sword, ready to spend his last in a physical attack against the beast. Perhaps he could bring both quetzal and rider down with the right cut. There would be only one chance to strike true.

Abruptly the creature banked north again, and the world rushed in upon him as Albryan realized that they were *not* heading in his direction. The quetzal righted itself in a slow-motion roll and continued heading north by northwest, following the trade road which led to the Svanlyn mountains and Svanfeld beyond.

How is she so complacent about my escape? Albryan wondered, his head reeling. What was more important than a captured spy of high rank? What was in the Svanlyn mountains?

They're not concerned with you, he answered himself, staggering with the realization, *because they wanted you to escape.*

His mouth went dry, but as he watched the flying lizard coast towards the mountains, he knew it must be true.

Albryan went quite still as memory came flooding back. Arran and his set of silver tools, delicate blades that had been forged for the most intimate of surgeries. Holding the wicked blade up to the light, moving towards Albryan even as he slipped out of consciousness. Pulling Albryan's slumping head further forward to expose the back of his neck . . .

There were no wounds upon Albryan's body. Nothing painful, anyway. Nothing he could *feel*. He moved a hand to the back of his neck, pushing his hair away, and there he felt the unmistakable line of a new scar, so fine as to hardly be felt, barely half the length of his little finger.

Albryan swallowed hard. Hiram was still staring off after the quetzal, and had noticed nothing.

Part of him was not himself, Albryan already knew. *What did they do to me?* He wanted to shriek out, to run away from it all. What was that little set of sharp blades *for*?

Instead, he closed his eyes, focused deeply, spread his hands in front of him and called forth his magic. And there it was. He went cold to discover it, and trembled when he thought of how close it had been for him. *For all of us . . .*

How Arran had accomplished it, Albryan did not know, but he could discern the result. The distinctive, dark consciousness of the blood sorcerer was there, when he looked for it. Like a hook planted securely in that part of his being where the magic was. When Arran Sylvaissen tugged on that hook, he would be able to control Albryan through his own magic. There would be nothing that Albryan could do about it, nothing that would drive the blood sorcerer out of him. For a moment, true despair threatened to take hold of him.

Arran must have known I would return home. Of course! Did he not plant that idea himself? Albryan fumed. *Insinuating that there is a traitor within our ranks! He could have found me some other way! My name, my description? This was all set up to make me return immediately!*

But surely I must bring knowledge of this to Thinas! His own voice echoed inside his head in frustration. *And perhaps, if they know what is wrong, my own people can heal or restrain me . . .*

No, that is a vain hope. For all you know, Arran already monitors your every move. Albryan shivered in the golden evening light. *I can-*

not bring this taint home with me. He felt empty, abandoned, utterly alone. *I cannot, must not, bring the taint of blood sorcery into the sacred forest.*

"Hiram," he finally said out loud. The old man turned to him, his eyes stricken.

"I thought I was going to be heading back—there . . ." he whispered.

"This is the road to Svanfeld," Albryan stated baldly, swallowing down the despair. "Lathea might have made it. She might be there. She might be in the mountains."

Hiram digested this for a moment, his face shadowed. Then he looked back towards Albryan.

"And what road will you take?" he asked softly. "Are you going back home?"

"I cannot return." His voice did not break, for which he was grateful. Albryan took a deep breath. "Our escape was easy because Arran willed it," he said bluntly. Hiram's golden eyes widened, but he did not speak. "He *wants* me to return to Qwu'Mallorn, and so I will not." He lifted his eyes to the setting sun, to where Dannine and her quetzal had vanished into the western horizon.

Thinas had never sent spies into the Svanlyn mountains. Svanfeld claimed neutrality in the conflict between Arran and Qwu'Mallorn, neither augmenting the blood sorcerer's troops nor aiding the Morgei in any way. If Dannine was flying up into those mountains, she was not likely to be doing so with the Sven king's knowledge or permission.

"Arran thought I would make straight for Tenna," he said. "North by east along the River Granite, where there are places I could have swum out of the city in secret, and then up along the Tenna Vey. He did not expect me to come out west of the city, and he did not intend for us to see where his daughter is going." He took the old man's arm. "I will go with you to Svanfeld, Hiram. You need protection along the way, and I must uncover the mystery of what Dannine is doing in the Svanlyn mountains."

A cold wind had begun to blow from the west, and Albryan shivered without his cloak. "We can rest awhile at the village," he said. "Perhaps even earn some money. But we have to get to the mountains as fast as we can." In the past, whenever he'd run low on coin whilst sojourning in Vailana, Albryan had managed to support himself as a true mercenary, doing any odd job that came along. Sometimes with his sword, sometimes with only his two hands. Despite technically being of noble birth, Albryan had never thought so highly of himself that he turned his nose up at yard-work or farm labour.

A cloud overhead moved in front of the sun, casting a deep shadow over the mound. Hiram's eyes seemed almost black as he looked back at the three rocks supporting the solitary wooden post.

"May the Goddess be with us," he intoned before turning and looking to the way ahead.

Chapter VIII
The Guilds

NICO HAD SUCCEEDED IN BACKING HIM into a corner of the yard, and was coming at him with a swordstroke aimed right at his head. There was no escape for Fish— at least, no escape that his partner could see.

Fish ducked beneath the flying broomstick handle with lightning speed, rolled, and caught Nico across the shins with his own stick on the way up again. Nico fell to the ground, swearing loudly, as Fish straightened up, grinning and leaning the stick against his shoulder.

"You've been spending too much time practicing with Siegfried," Fish told his partner smugly, one hand holding the stick, the other resting on his hips in a deliberately languid posture. "You've forgotten how a smaller opponent can trick you into spending your strength against him."

Nico glared up at him. "It's not fair," he growled, panting. "How do you beat me *every* time?"

"You're too easily distracted."

"No, I'm not," Nico insisted, and began to argue with him. Fish took the opportunity to catch his breath, feeling the cold Firstmonth air blowing through his thin shirt, drying the sweat he had worked up during the match. Nico did not know how close he had come to winning, and Fish would never admit to it.

Finally Nico stood up, and again they pursued each other around the circle of dirt that had once been their landlady's garden. Mrs Cottbus was too old to garden now, and spent most of her time sleeping or knitting in the suite of rooms below theirs. Her rooms were situated just above the level of the whitewashed brick road that meandered crookedly through the city, with five steps leading down to it from her front door.

The bottom floor of the narrow three-level house lay mostly *below* the street, with another set of steps leading from a sunken back door down to the yard in which Nico and Fish were sparring. Mrs Cottbus let out this floor too, and it was occupied by a married couple who were almost as close about their affairs as were Nico and Fish. Both of them were good fighters, and often practiced with the two assassins, though Fish had no inkling of what either of them did for a living.

This was scarcely uncommon in Schooner Street, which was

known to be the city's most wretched hive of crime and villainy. It had originally been built as a slum quarter to house the poor, but with time, the very poor had gradually been pushed out beyond the city walls, and Schooner Street and its surrounds had become a haven for those who wished to avoid polite society as well as the city guardsmen. There was a large community of brothels here, and that in turn tended to attract a great many mercenaries and sailors for their leisure time. Over the years, it had become a convenient place to find what could not be found in the better policed areas close to the city centre.

Fish himself had a queer affection for the place. Despite being surrounded by criminals and other types of people down on their luck, he had never personally worried about being victimized. The city thieves were self-preserving enough to avoid hired swords and death-dealers. And as Nico often said, carrying out criminal acts in Schooner Street was akin to taking a squat on one's own doorstep.

"Enough," Nico finally begged, when they had been at it for almost an hour, and were both covered in sweat and dust. There was a communal well close to the garden, enclosed by wooden buildings that faced out to the streets on all four sides, and they headed there. Whilst Fish sank down to lean against the cold stones of the well, Nico drew a bucket of water and proceeded to splash his face and neck. Fish gazed up at him with eyes half-closed, wondering idly if Nico had any idea of his own attractiveness. They were both wearing the same kind of outfit: a loose white blouse that normally went under a waistcoat, plain workman's trousers and dark brown, calf-length leather boots. But on Nico, with his stern blue eyes and powerful build, that simple outfit made him look like a maiden's fantasy.

Fish was no maiden, but he had long since come to terms with the fact that he was not like other men. He could not remember a time when he had ever wanted to kiss a girl; only later, when the dark shadows of his tormented childhood had started to leave him, had he started to think about kissing boys instead.

Women seemed to sense that part of Fish somehow; they always ignored him whenever they went about drooling over Nico. The hardest part of being Nico's partner was the stab of jealousy that would strike whenever Fish had to see him with a woman. But luckily, Nico's liaisons were few, and never lasted long. One day, Fish would have to watch him walk away into a happy ending with the love of his life, but that day was not come yet, thank the gods. For today, he got to watch his golden Nico in the sunlight, got to laugh with him and touch his hand, got to ignore everything and everyone else in the world. Fish had always been a great believer in enjoying the moment, and he wanted nothing to ruin his moments with Nico.

Fish had occasionally wondered whether he would be able to cure his infatuation with his partner by finding another man, and doing all the things he had never done before. After all, Schooner Street had no shortage of prostitutes, boy or girl or whatever else one might desire. But word of this sort of thing would inevitably make its way back to Nico; *someone* always talked, no matter how discreet he might try to be. And then Nico would *know*, and Fish had no idea how he might react. At best, he might simply accept it, but it would still change their rapport, set obstacles between them that could never be bridged. At worst . . .

"Hey there, you two!" called a woman's voice, and Fish surfaced from his daydreams. Striding towards them was Gudrunn, the woman who leased the ground floor of their building along with her husband, Siegfried. She was dressed as she usually was; rather than wear a skirt like most Sven women, she had leather breeches underneath a kind of extended jerkin, calf-length and divided by four slits.

"Did Fish beat you?" she asked Nico, reaching the well and grinning at them. By her mode of talking, one could easily tell that she was Arvenian, and having some difficulties with the common speech of the twin lands of Svanfeld and Vailana. Historically, the Arvenians had come out of the north as pirates, circling the continent looking for adventure and rapine. Nowadays, most of them were honest tradesmen and merchants, making their way in the world like anyone else.

Fish stood up, shielding his eyes from the sun as it flashed from behind a cloud. "I always beat him, my lady," he said airily.

Gudrunn laughed loudly, as she always did when Fish called her "my lady." "When are we two going to spar again, little Fish? A better challenge I would be, than this clumsy fellow."

Nico was far more skilled than she was, and they all knew it, but played along. "Knock on our window whenever you please," Fish said.

"It may not be for a time yet," Gudrunn sighed. "Busy, I am. Well, the reason I am here—Eric Skimmer sends you both a message. He wants you at his inn, the usual time tomorrow. You understand this, yes?"

Fish groaned loudly, and Nico gave a chuckle. The "usual time" was at daybreak, so that they could discuss business before the inn's opening hours. Nico had no problem rising at such an unholy hour, and it was one of the few things he could tease Fish effectively about.

"We understand," Nico told Gudrunn. "We'll be there."

She smiled. "Well—I must be going back. Only moments could I spare."

When she had gone, Fish turned to Nico. "They paid us yesterday," he said, in a low voice. "Why would they need to see us again?"

Nico shrugged. "Maybe it's a new patron. We can always turn them down. We have enough money for that."

"I suppose so."

"However, we should be presentable." Nico stretched languidly, flexing his shoulder muscles. "You know what that means."

"Bathhouse," Fish sighed. "Not the one down Coley Lane, please." Ülhard's public bathhouses ranged from luxurious to downright disreputable; the Coley Lane establishment was cleaner than most of the ones which doubled as brothels, and you could actually get a proper bath there without necessarily engaging any of the girls to share it with you. Since Coley Lane was but a few minutes' walk from their building, he and Nico had often gone there for that purpose alone.

But it was not the place to relax after having a dusty and wearying day, nor a good place to try and have a serious conversation with his partner. Nico seemed to fit right in there, flirting mercilessly with the girls even though he never so much as laid a hand on them, but Fish was made of different stuff, and was never so painfully aware of it as when the girls tried to flirt with *him* instead.

"Alright, we'll try a different one." Nico was grinning broadly. "If I didn't know better, I'd think you were scared of Madam Essie's girls," he teased.

Fish did not reply, only hoping that the red-hot blush he could feel working its way up his neck and face wouldn't show under the darkness of his skin.

"Worried they're going to steal your virtue?"

"Shut up," Fish growled.

The first sign of morning was, as usual, Nico waking up and rolling out of bed, yawning noisily.

Fish refused to believe that it was time to wake. Pulling his pillow half over his head, he squirmed into a ball, and resolutely closed his eyes.

Nico padded across the wooden floor and opened the squeaky window shutters. That alone would have woken Fish, if he hadn't been awake already. The room remained almost as dark as it had been before; the day was overcast. Nico snorted, and Fish heard him make his way towards the tiny washroom—an alcove, really, with a basin and chamberpot—floorboards creaking under his tread.

Fish sighed and turned over onto his back, stretching out, aware that Nico's side of the bed was still warm and smelled of fresh sweat and soap and *him*. They slept on the same straw mattress, held off the floor by a low wooden frame and a few bricks. It was Nico who had originally suggested this arrangement, and he had never given any sign that it was out of the ordinary for two men to do so. Fish supposed that was the farm boy in him; he'd heard that it was not unusual for entire families to share a single bed out in the country, or even in the houses of city labourers.

This was probably also the reason, thought Fish, sighing into his pillow, why Nico could wake up at any given time of day and be no worse the wear for it. The timing of dawn was wildly different in winter and summer, and he could see how a lad growing up in a remote farming community might learn to adapt his sleeping needs to the season.

Fish had never learned this knack. Not in his father's house, not as a wandering urchin, not even during his stint in the Townsguard of Zarath.

Nico returned from the washroom, and gave Fish's prone body a shake. "Time to wake up, sleepy-face."

Fish groaned in response and burrowed further into the pillow, trying to shut him out. There was constant noise now, as Nico was moving around the room, taking clothes from drawers and laying them on the chair in the corner. It was enough to almost make Fish wish that he had remained in his father's house, where he had had a private suite of rooms all to himself.

Almost.

"Are you going to get up, or not?" After another shake woke no more response from Fish, Nico padded away again. There were several small clinking sounds that Fish could not quite make out. Nico padded back, and something splashed on Fish's ear. Shrugging it off, he kept his eyes stubbornly closed. It was only when the cold water reached his neck that he suddenly sat bolt upright.

"What is wrong with you?" Fish demanded, trying to dry off his face with the bedclothes and only succeeding in making himself more uncomfortable. Nico had set the water jug down and was chuckling to himself as he laced up his boots.

The drifting thoughts of his unhappy childhood were driven away, and reluctantly Fish got out of bed to prepare himself for the day ahead.

Nico was already fully dressed by the time Fish came out of the washroom, every fold of his outfit immaculately brushed into place, his hair combed down and his beard neatly trimmed. He wore a sleeveless waistcoat of blue linen a few shades darker than his eyes, and he was even wearing cufflinks, brass to match the buttons of the jerkin. He took no notice as Fish stripped to the skin and wandered around looking for his own clothes, which he found on the chair.

Nico had picked out everything for him, down to his linen drawers.

Begrudgingly, Fish had to admit that Nico chose well: the charcoal-coloured woollen waistcoat added gravitas to his youthful face, and the bright gold-plated buttons drew attention away from the circles under his eyes. Fish regarded himself in the polished copper mirror. There was not much they could do about his wayward curls . . .

Nico approached, carrying two pieces of bread drizzled with honey. Setting them on the table, he picked up a comb and his nail-scissors.

"What are you going to do with that?" Fish was half nervous.

"It needs a trim," Nico insisted, the scissors hovering over his partner's head.

"All right," Fish grumbled. "But don't cut too much off!" he added anxiously, as the scissors moved in.

"Eat your breakfast," Nico retorted. "You have a bit of stubble here," he added, as Fish did as he was told and picked up the bread.

"I don't think there's any time for me to shave."

"I'd keep it. It makes you look less of a boy."

"Well, you're only about two years older than me; if I'm a boy, so are you."

"Three years, unless you've decided to change your identity again." Nico spoke lightly, but there was something heavier behind his words, and suddenly Fish wished he could speak openly to his partner. In a way it might be easier, to share the burdens of the past with someone else . . .

Nico combed out what was left of Fish's curls, and handed him the last piece of his outfit, a black linen cravat. Fish had no more time to dwell upon his half-formed longings. Donning short jackets as well as their winter cloaks, the two young men climbed down from their loft and set off into the overcast streets.

It was a cold, brooding day, and the smell of the sea was strong in the wisps of mist that clung to the muddy streets. Fish could even hear the sea in the distance, grumbling restively as if it was just as moody about early mornings as what he was.

There were no cobbles in Schooner Street, and none of the distinctive white marble buildings that Ülhard, the White City, was known for. The only true marble buildings in the city, Nico had told him once, were the royal palace, which overlooked the city from an outcrop of rock from which sprang the famous Trollen waterfall, part of the central square, including the town hall and the temple, and the old city wall—where it had not been patched. Repair work on the wall was done with white sandstone, and the fancier suburbs were made of it too; further away from the centre, the houses were built of whitewashed brick. And the buildings in Schooner Street were made of wood, and only painted white, when indeed they were painted at all.

Eric Skimmer's inn, the Black Ass, was not far. Situated on a corner convenient for sailors and other wanderers to find, its painted sign had no words, only a picture of a donkey done in black. At this time of day, the front door was locked; Nico and Fish picked their way around the back, through the stables, where Eric's brother gave them a toothless grin as he mixed a bucket of gruel for his horses.

"Master Klavbert! Master Fish! It's good to see you back."

"Stonetooth, good morning," Nico acknowledged him as he stepped through the door. "Is your brother awake?"

"He's never been one for early mornings," Stonetooth rumbled, "but he did promise to be out at the counter by the time you arrived. Careful of his crossbow, mind you."

"Your brother is a maniac, Stonetooth," Fish said to him. Uric Skimmer only chuckled. They were peas in a pod, the Skimmer brothers; Stonetooth had been so nicknamed, the story ran, when his teeth had been knocked out by a barroom tough armed with a loose brick from the city wall. Stonetooth still had the brick somewhere, it was rumoured, along with the skull of the man who had wielded it.

Stonetooth's burly brother was fast asleep in an armchair behind the bar counter. An army-duty crossbow, loaded and locked to fire, rested in front of him. Keeping well out of its line of fire, Nico approached and banged loudly on the counter with his fist.

The crossbow was up, levelled at Nico's forehead, and set apologetically down again in a movement so fluid even Fish could admire it. Eric Skimmer grinned, showing a set of fine white teeth, the like of which his brother had once sported.

"Welcome back to my establishment," he said expansively. "You two've gotten popular, I must say. We haven't even had a chance to sit and talk over an ale since—how long has it been? Must be three weeks or more! The ale has missed you especially, Master Fish." At Nico's stone-eyed look of impatience, Eric Skimmer turned sober again. "The usual room. And mind that there's no trouble."

Nico nodded, and Fish touched one of his hidden daggers.

"I'll be back to reacquaint myself with your ale, Innkeeper," Fish promised as they went upstairs. "Don't count me out yet!"

Fish carefully straightened out his jerkin as Nico thumped on the door of the "usual room," where most of their business dealings took place. The door creaked open, and Fish espied the pockmarked countenance of Hans Wyrm, their usual point of contact, behind it.

"Welcome back, Nico," Hans said greasily, giving Fish a nasty glare which he returned with interest. He had disliked Hans from the first time they'd met, when he'd pointed out that half the coins he was offering to Nico for a tricky little job in the harbour were just slightly roughened around the edges.

Hans sidled back behind the desk in the middle of the room, and the second man stood up. Both assassins stared in surprise. The man was masked; it was one of the ugly ones often seen at cheap Guild masquerades, done up with the face of what seemed to be a gargoyle, or perhaps an inexpertly painted monkey. He was dressed in a tight-fitting red jacket with white woollen gloves, and Fish could even see pin marks on the fabric at his chest, where a Guild pin might have been removed just moments ago.

"Please, sit down," the man said. His learned, formal accent jarred with his surroundings, and the company he was currently keeping. His whole manner simply screamed "rich merchant," and he seemed quite aware of that, and not making any attempt to hide it.

Nico and Fish took the two stools offered to them, and the man sat down again himself.

"No doubt you have misgivings," he began. The assassins said nothing.

"Although I cannot allow you to identify me," the man said, "I can tell you that I am the person who hired you two weeks ago, through Master Wyrm here"—Fish saw Hans practically preen at being referred to as "Master,"—"to take care of our . . . little problem."

"Have we displeased you in any way?" Nico asked neutrally.

"Oh, no!—quite the opposite, in fact. You see, your unfortunate victim was only a beginning . . . a kind of—trial run, shall we say? We had never hired an assassin before, after all, and some of us were doubtful . . . but the two of you have proven that you can be trusted to follow orders, and even to deal with challenging situations."

Fish raised his eyebrows at that, and Nico cleared his throat. "Like handling the guards quietly, and not leaving a bloody mess and the entire neighbourhood in an uproar?"

"Something like that," the Guildsman agreed. "Now, the reason why we needed to get Guildsman Erdmann out of the way—"

"Oh, I'd figured that out," Nico interrupted. "There's a war going on in your ranks, the ranks of all the Guilds. You don't like slavery."

Nico paused. The Guildsman leaned forward, his elbows on the desk. "Go on."

"Slavery may be illegal in Svanfeld," Nico continued, "but the laws are almost never enforced. The King doesn't care if the trade Guilds are undermined, just as he doesn't care if you—how shall we say?—take it upon yourselves to thin out your ranks." Nico looked as if he was enjoying himself; the Guildsman showed no expression behind his mask, but had drawn himself up in a pose of surprise. "If slave labour proliferates, the Guilds will only suffer, but that doesn't stay the greed of some of you lot." Nico folded his arms. "I know for a fact that *some* senior Guildsman was accepting bribes from slave caravans to help them smuggle people past the towns in the northern foothills of Svanlyn. I grew up there. I remember." He scowled. "It was only a matter of time before someone was called to task for it."

Nico hardly ever spoke about his own past. Fish knew that his partner had been a fosterling, raised by the Sven monks in a small town somewhere on this side of the mountains, and that was about all. Fish had glanced at a map before and made an educated guess as to which monastery it had likely been, but Nico had never appreciated any kind of prying, and Fish had never wanted to discomfit him. He was surprised, now, to hear Nico mention something so personal.

The Guildsman responded: "Yes! And now you see the extent of our problem." He took a rolled-up map from his belt and spread it out over the desk. Fish suppressed the urge to whistle under his breath; it was the most detailed map of the Svanlyn mountains he had ever seen. The great range that separated the lands of Svanfeld and Vailana was generally shown on maps as a giant no-go area, not worth annotating in any detail.

"The slavers strike in remote villages," the Guildsman said, "and they bring their captives to Ülhard." He tapped the city on the map, where it sat curled up beside a wide bay on the western coast. "Those that they cannot sell here, they put on ships—but they do not take them far." His finger travelled southwards, along the coast. "Our operatives have witnessed those same ships coming ashore near the town of Von Dharen, which is right below the highest part of the mountains. The slaves were then taken up into the wilds, where our operatives could not follow."

Nico contemplated the map. "There is only one mountain pass which the slavers can use to pass into Vailana, or even into the lower parts of Svanlyn," he said.

"A pass which is watched over day and night by the King's guardsmen," the Guildsman said soberly. "Unless the slavers have found a way to bribe each and every single one of them, they cannot use the Beerstana Pass. They must have found some way around it."

Nico snorted. "I have seen those mountains. One does not simply 'find a way' around the Peak of Beerstana. Not unless he is part wildcat. And the slavers are travelling with frightened, exhausted people who will do their best to escape if they can. There is foul play involved in this somehow." He sat back, folding his arms. "What precisely is it you want us to do here?"

"Follow the slavers into the mountains," the Guildsman said promptly. "Find out where they are hiding. Destroy them, and do it in such a way that others will see—will know."

"As brilliant as we are, myself and my associate," Nico said, tapping the edge of the desk, "we are only two men. What if your slavers have banded together, and now form a small army?"

"If that occurs, come back, and devise a strategy for our private army to move in and destroy their stronghold."

"Why not send this private army of yours in the first place?"

"As you said, Master Klavbert," the guildsman replied, "the mountains in that area are impassable if you do not know how to conquer them. Before we hired you, we had heard tell of how once you pursued a similar group of wrongdoers into the Storm Cliffs, to cut them down one by one."

Copper smugglers, Fish thought, but he held his peace; only Nico spoke when they were negotiating a contract, and he spoke for both of them. *Copper smugglers who thought they could double-cross the man they worked for. Now that I think on it, probably a Guild member who was smuggling his own product in order to create an artificial shortage.* He shook his head to himself. *Ah, does the corruption never end?*

"I'm not sure," Nico was saying. "We have never dabbled in politics before."

There was a deep silence, in which Fish could hear the Guildsman shifting in his seat. "Sir," he finally began, speaking in a low voice, "a matter of politics this may be, but it has become something all too personal for us. Some of us have family in the areas targeted by these slavers, and our pockets are bled dry hiring mercenaries to protect them. We depend on the villagers of Svanfeld to provide the raw materials for our trades. When this labour chain is disrupted, we suffer again. Some of us in the Guilds feel ourselves obliged to protect the villages, to treat them as our people. I do not want to live in a land run by slave traders. I am a craftsman, and I wish my workers to be free as I am, perhaps even with the opportunity to one day sit where I am now."

He fell silent. Fish rubbed his nose and glanced over at Nico, but his partner was intent upon the Guildsman. Nico replied, speaking slowly: "I am inclined to agree with you. There seem to be many compelling reasons to accept this contract. Fish?" He turned in his chair. Fish only nodded, as he knew Nico expected him to. His partner was not truly asking for his opinion, but giving him a signal. The Guildsman stirred expectantly in his seat.

"However," Nico continued, "a task such as this cannot be accepted too readily. My associate and I need to construct a strategy first. If we feel that it is too difficult for us to handle, we will have to turn you down."

"We will wait a few days," the figure under the mask agreed.

"And what of our reimbursement? What are you offering us?"

"You will never need to work again," the masked man said grandly. "We have agreed to deed you a country estate outside the walls of Ülhard if you succeed."

Fish nearly gasped; tightly controlling his facial expression, he took in a sharp breath. *They're willing to make us landowners? Desperate, they must be.*

Somehow, Nico had managed to not register any expression at all. "That is . . . very generous," he said, hesitating, "but I have no wish to be permanently tied to the Guilds. I would have to refuse unless an equivalent cash offer could be made."

The Guildsman turned towards Fish, for the first time. "And you? You would refuse too?"

"Nico speaks for both of us," Fish said woodenly, secretly hoping that his partner was thinking clearly.

"Very well." The Guildsman shrugged. "We shall sell the piece of land in question and pay you the proceeds of the sale."

"The proceeds, plus ten percent," Nico said.

"Done." The Guildsman did not hesitate in the slightest.

"You will find a buyer before we leave," Nico continued, "and pay us a quarter of the amount upfront."

"Very well."

"And we will need expense money." Nico ticked off items on his fingers. "Horses, if you want us to arrive there with any sort of speed. Mules or packhorses. Gear for navigating the wilds. Winter clothes and provisions, because the snow will lie on the mountains till Third-month, if we're unlucky. High-energy rations for the horses."

The Guildsman nodded behind his mask, and detached a leather bag from his belt, setting it before Nico. "Will this be sufficient?" he asked.

Fish came forward, picked up the bag and peered inside. Glinting golden coins caught the light, and Hans's squinty eyes gazed greedily from the corner he was lurking in. Fish estimated the volume of the bag, calculating quickly how many coins were likely to be in it. Finding a satisfactory total, he nodded to Nico. "That should cover it."

"Keep the gold," the Guildsman said from behind his mask. "Whether you accept the contract or not, let it be a token of . . . trust. In our friendship."

Fish hesitated, glancing towards his partner. Nico gave a slight nod, and Fish attached the bag to his own belt and returned to his chair.

"In that case," the Guildsman said, "we will meet again in three days to hear your decision."

Nico looked preoccupied. "We'd best take our leave," he said to Fish. He glanced around the room. "Until then."

THEY LEFT THE BLACK ASS under an anxious silence. Nico suggested that they make their way to a coffee-shop they frequented in one of the more respectable boroughs nearby, and said nothing further during the time it took them to get there. Even when they were finally seated, sharing a small pot of coffee between them, he did not say anything about the situation. Fish hesitantly brought it up, and he changed the subject, eyes roving across the shop towards a table in the corner.

Following Nico's gaze, Fish saw a young man in a bluish over-coat, reading a newspaper. Or at least, he had a newspaper in front of him, but his eyes were glazed over, fixed to a single point. An empty cup sat on the table before him, yet when the serving-girl came to fetch it, he waved her away.

Fish looked back at his partner, who raised his eyebrows and said nothing. Fish put his hands on the table.

"Nic," he said brightly, "I have an idea. I want to go to—to the place where we became partners. Just for a walk. What do you say?"

Nico put his empty mug down, and Fish could tell he was hold-ing back a smile. "Good idea," he said, a touch louder than he usually would have.

There was a dusty man in a dented hat lurking by the nearest lamp-post when they left the coffee-shop, smoking just a little too slowly to have been a workman on his break. There was another at the end of the street, sharp eyes peeking out from under a floppy hat as he lounged on a public bench.

So much for trusting in us, Fish thought. *Gods, how many of them do they have?*

Fish felt the strain of keeping up the appearance of unawareness all the way to the city wall. It felt as though there were following eyes in every doorway, footsteps tracking him down every alley. It took him back to memories of another life—the years before he had met Nico, the time when he had still been a frightened child running from the horrors of his past.

They passed through a foot gate on the southern edge of Ülhard, and followed a rocky footpath over the low-growing seagrass down to the beach. No-one could follow them down there without attracting due suspicion. By the time they went striding along the sand, leaving boot-prints behind where the tide was coming in, Fish felt relaxed enough to speak.

"So they're having us followed."

"Seems like it." Nico had taken one of his silver-edged daggers out, and was absent-mindedly passing it from hand to hand.

There was a moment's silence, filled with the rumble of the waves and the sound of their boots squelching in the wet sand. The wind whipped at Fish's curls and set the edge of his cloak snapping where it pulled loose from his body. The sea came up behind them and disintegrated their footprints neatly, threatening to suck the solid ground out from under them.

"So, are we going to take the job?" Fish asked. Nico seemed to be in a strange mood, even now. He was still toying with the dagger.

"I don't see that we have much of a choice," he said quietly.

"What do you mean?"

"Fish, I know you had a gut feeling. Tell me, what do you think about our Guildsman?"

Fish furrowed his brow in thought. "Well . . . I don't think that he was lying to us," he said after a while. "When he said that this was a matter of more than business to him, I believed him. But . . ." He fought to find the right words as Nico waited. "He may not have been lying, but perhaps he didn't tell us everything," he finally said. "He negotiated our price too easily. And why give us this bag of gold to keep? Why does he have his own men following us?"

"Your questions are mine," Nico said, stopping for a moment above the reach of the tide. A flat plain dotted with piebald sheep led up to a cliff by the edge of the sea, almost half a mile from where they stood. The waves crashed against the side of the distant cliff, and Fish knew that the turbulent surf concealed a reef of cruel rocks.

"I have a theory," Nico continued. Fish looked questioningly at him. "Why did this Guildsman offer to give us land—Guild land!—so easily? Because he thinks that we will never return to claim it."

"Why would he send us on a suicide mission?" Fish asked.

"Why *not* send regular mercenary soldiers on a mission like this? Why would they need a pair of assassins?"

Fish paused. "Because . . . because they have already sent mercenaries, and they failed."

A silence fell between the two of them. A ray of sunlight broke out from behind the clouds, turning the beach sands gold for a brief moment before retreating. There was an odd glitter in Nico's storm-blue eyes, and he was fidgeting with the dagger again.

"So what do we do?" Fish asked softly.

"We don't have a lot of choices." Nico looked unhappily at Fish, his eyes reflecting the greenish hue of the restless sea. "If we refuse, they will probably kill us. Doubtless they know all of our movements across the city by now."

"But if we agree, we will walk ass-first into a situation that hire-mercs couldn't handle."

Nico nodded. "Yea, but remember—they can't track us in the wilds. They admitted as much."

"We can disappear," Fish said, realization dawning. He snorted. "You know, I bet they're not even going to sell that land," he said sourly. "Likely they'll just come up with a sum that should keep us happy, and have no intention of paying us the rest." He spat into the sea. "Gods, why did we even get involved with the Guilds in the first place?"

"It's my fault," Nico said unhappily. "Fish—"

The way Nico said his name made Fish immediately turn towards him. "Yes?"

Impulsively, Nico hurled the silver-edged dagger he was holding at the sea, as if he could arrest the motion of the tide by throwing things at it. "That's it," he announced, half laughing, his eyes glittering icy-crystalline in another brief flash of sunlight. "I'm never killing anybody again."

Fish was quiet until the rising sea frothed up the beach and began to suck the sand away from under the dagger, hauling it in. Then he strode towards the blade, picked it up, and handed it back to Nico.

"Didn't you once tell me you got these from a friend?"

Nico snorted, but he took the dagger anyway. "We got them from a mercenary down on his luck," he said. "He was willing to practically give four of these away. Two matched sets." He turned away. Fish was used to Nico clamming up about his past, however, and waited until the mood passed.

"You meant that, didn't you?" he asked as soon as it was safe, when Nico sank down upon a sandbar and sullenly started turning the dagger round and around in his hand. The tide continued to come in, and Nico watched it heave and ebb for a while before he started speaking.

"I've been thinking lately," he said quietly. "I've been thinking about—about how I would never have chosen this life for myself, if it hadn't been a matter of survival. I'm getting older now." He lifted his eyes to Fish's. "I feel as if I'm standing in that sand." He pointed at the wave line. "As if the footing is constantly being sucked out from under me. One day soon, I'll lose my footing, and then I'll drown." He ran his fingers along the silvered blade of the dagger. "Fish, there's something that I—that I've never told you."

Nico stopped suddenly, interrupting himself, and put the dagger away, looking down at his hands. "No, scratch that: there are things I'll *never* tell you. If I stay here . . ." He trailed off into silence.

Fish was stunned. This was by far the most intimate speech that Nico had ever given him, and it deserved to be validated with a fitting response. But he could not ignore the repercussions of what his partner appeared to be saying.

"You don't *want* to return here," he stated, as gently as he could manage. "You want to leave this city behind. You want a fresh start."

"We've been partners for this past year," Nico said softly. "And we've worked out better than any other pair in the city, but I can't expect you to share the rest of my life based on a—a—"

"A promise?" Fish whispered.

Nico hesitated. "I don't understand."

"We're almost at the place where we came ashore that day," Fish said. "Remember? At the foot of the cliff."

"I remember," Nico said hesitantly.

"I was injured. I'd gotten us both into a pretty bad fight with those pirates, and we hardly knew each other. I'd managed to convince you that I was the Baron Vonnegüth's son, remember?"

Despite his mood, Nico chuckled.

"I told you to leave me there," Fish said. "I admitted I lied—I'm nobody's son, least of all someone so illustrious. But you didn't care. You said you were going to patch me up again, and you took my hand"—Fish reached for Nico's right hand with his own, and clasped it—"and asked me to partner up with you." Fish turned to look into his partner's eyes, and squeezed the hand he was holding. "My answer has not changed since that day. What would I do in this miserable city without you?"

A slow smile replaced the grimness of Nico's countenance, as he followed Fish's gaze out over the beach towards the cliff. Fish pretended not to see as his partner smudged away a tear with his hand.

Standing up, Nico drew him into a one-armed hug. The tide was still rising; water lapped at their boots, then withdrew again.

"Come on," Nico said at last. "We'll deal with these bastards, but we'll do it on *our* terms."

Fish turned with him, half hoping for a second hug, but Nico was already on his way home, impatient as usual, the collar of his jacket turned up against the wind. Fish sighed and cast one last look towards the cliff as he walked after his partner, clasping his cloak tightly around himself.

CHAPTER IX
LYNBORDER

VELDA AROSE WITH A NEW SENSE of purpose, fuelled by the advent of spring at last. It was well before dawn. The house was cold, but she did not rekindle the fire in the kitchen hearth.

Instead, she wrapped her best shawl around her shoulders, put away a hasty breakfast, and went out to feed the pigs several hours before she usually did. The mud was frozen solid beneath her feet, but it was easier to balance on than the usual midday sludge. She made it all the way around the yard without slipping once.

She headed back indoors and fussed with her hair, drawing it all into a tight bun which she secured with hairpins, before pulling her jacket over her shoulders. She was wearing the better of her two day dresses, dark grey wool that was only slightly faded.

On her way out, she paused in the middle of the muddy track to look back at the house Emmett had built. A mist had fallen over the Witches' Horn, but was already dispersing further down in the valley. The earliest birds were just now awaking, sending tentative chirps of song through the moisture-tinged air.

The house faded into the mist behind her as she reached the sheer cliffside with its hairpin-bending footpath, the only way down to the town of Lynborder. She paused for a moment, ascertaining that the path looked sound. A single misstep could spell doom upon the snaking way. Looking down over mist-streaked rocks, Velda could see the high town wall and sloping rooftops of Lynborder almost directly below her. If she could fly, she would be there within ten minutes. By the footpath, it was bound to take her at least two hours.

From where she stood, Velda could just see part of the monastery where she had been raised, a square fortress jutting out from where it sat against the side of yet another sheer cliff of dark grey rock. She wondered, not for the first time, what kind of force had smashed the Svanlyn mountains into such a series of fierce black angles and cliffsides.

But this was no place for daydreams, and Velda kept her attention on the path as she began her descent down the face of the cliff. Too many a fool had faltered upon these very rocks, and ended up with broken bones or worse.

As morning wore on, the sun baked upon the mountain and dried the mud on the footpath, making the going easier than Velda had expected. It was still well before midday when she reached the crossroads at the bottom of the cliff. The right-hand fork led straight down to Lynborder, and Velda could see several parties coming and going further along this road—a group of farmers on their way to town, a gang of trappers coming up.

Velda turned onto the left-hand fork, and strode down the wide, welcoming road which led to the monastery. It stood directly before her, a few hundred yards downslope of the crossroads, a great walled fortress, grim and austere. The building's sternness belied the kindhearted nature of the monks who dwelt within. It had been constructed hundreds of years ago, when incursions of Arvenians from the coast were still commonplace. Even nowadays, bandit raids on remote border towns were not unheard-of, and the older monks claimed that these had been increasing steadily during their lifetime.

The main gate was already open, welcoming all who sought the advice and healing from the holy men. A group of young children were at work in the yard under the supervision of a black-robed brother, tilling the black soil in preparation for the year's planting. Velda was recognized immediately, and she stopped to greet the excitable group. The monk, a tall, pleasant-faced man of middle age, ambled up and motioned for them to get back to work.

"Brother Viktor," Velda said with a smile.

"Velda! It is good to see you. It has been a long time." The monk grasped Velda's hand. "Why have you come?"

"I need to speak with Father Ricard," Velda said. "I am giving up the lease of my husband's land."

Viktor had never been a man of many words, and to his credit he did not ask any more questions. "The Supreme Father is in his study," he told Velda. "I trust you remember how to find it?"

Velda nodded. "Of course. Oh—and do you know where Father Stian is?"

"In his wood." Viktor nodded towards a slope leading up the hill behind the monastery. A grove of pine trees nestled in its shoulder. "He enjoys his peace away from the children, these days. He turned ninety this winter; it was quite the celebration."

Velda smiled, and went in search of the Supreme Father first. Relinquishing the lease turned out to be easier than she had expected, and soon she was outside again, climbing the trail to the pine grove. The trees seemed almost to shift around her, sombre companions to the aged monk who sat contemplatively upon an upturned trunk. She moved closer when he did not appear to notice her. "Father Stian?"

The old monk looked up with eyes still bright in his heavily lined, pale face. "Velda! Is it you?" He squinted in her direction. "My eyes grow worse with every passing year, child." She moved towards him, and at last he chuckled happily. "It *is* you!" He cocked his aged head to one side, taking her in. "Have you come to greet me one last time, before you leave this place forever?"

Velda looked down, twisting her fingers together. "Not forever," she said sheepishly.

"You wish to leave grief behind," Stian said. The words came slowly, and his creaking voice was barely audible.

"I do," Velda said. "Is that a bad thing?"

"Of course not," Stian returned, "but I will miss you, child. I am very old, after all. This could be the last time I talk with you."

Velda sat down beside him. "You have always been like a grand-father to me," she said, taking the old man's hand.

"Yet I know that, in truth, I am not enough." Stian shushed her when Velda began to protest. "There is no need to apologize, child. I have watched over you, perhaps, a little more closely than most. I understand the need for your search. I have but one thing to ask of you." His filmy, light blue eyes fixed upon her with as much fire as they were still capable of. "Velda, do not go to Armour City."

"What?" Velda hesitated. Father Stian was known for his visions of the future, yet never had she known his warnings to be this specific. He had told her, long ago, that his dreams came from the gods—and why should the gods care about *her*?

"In my youth," Stian continued steadfastly, "this continent was so peaceful that I never believed any of my visions would come to pass. Yet I dreamed the strife in Vailana seventy years ago, and as the days creep by, my dreams become darker and even more troubled. I dreamed, once, that we of this monastery were given a precious thing—a mallorn-rose. Do you know what that is?" When she shook her head, he continued, "That is the name of the wild creeper-roses which grow in the Forest of the Morning. It was given us to safeguard, yet when we held it for too long, the rose wilted in our hands. And so I advised Ricard that it would be in your best interest not to stay here."

Velda was nonplussed. "I'm not from the Forest of the Morning."

"Yet you are not truly one of us," Stian said quietly, and she turned away. "Before you leave for Armour City, Velda, please wait awhile. A different road may yet present itself."

A different road? Velda wondered briefly whether perhaps the old monk was going senile. But Stian had rarely seemed as intent and focused as he was now. Seldom had he ever discussed his visions with her.

"What else did you see?" she pressed him, but the old monk shook his head.

"My dreams are not so straightforward. Magic is a strange force, child. It flows through all of us, yet only a few can wield it for their own ends."

"Only the Morgei."

"Magic is associated with Morgein blood, yet simply possessing magic does not make one part of the Morgein people. There are many in possession of the Gift who have never even been to the Forest of the Morning. Those born in Vailana, yes, but the Sang people across the sea also commonly manifest the Gift—and Arran Sylvaissen was not born Morgein."

Velda raised her brows at this, yet it truly made no difference to her. She sat with the monk a little while longer, saying farewell.

She was not certain whether she truly believed in Stian's portents, nor indeed that the gods watched over the world as closely as the Sven brethren claimed. If Father Stian was trying to forbid her from going to Armour City, which other road could she possibly take?

Velda was deep in thought as she trudged out of the monastery grounds. Nearly too late, she noticed that she was coming face-to-face with a thin old man leading a mule, who looked like he might have been a wandering peddler.

The mule, stubborn as all of its race, refused to step aside on the narrow path, and she and the peddler danced around each other, as he muttered hasty and heartfelt apologies. The man briefly raised his face, which was half obscured by a thick hood, and suddenly he gasped. A skinny arm appeared from the depths of his faded clothing to seize her wrist.

"Who are you?" he whispered.

Velda twisted free, expecting to have to shove him away, but the man had drawn back of his own accord, staring intently at her. His eyes were a very light shade of brown, almost yellow, and the way they were set over his prominent nose made her think of an aged, brooding raptor.

"None of your business," she said, disconcerted. She turned away from him, hastening her footsteps towards town. The peddler let her go, but she felt his penetrating gaze follow her until she was out of sight.

THE BUSTLE OF LYNBORDER TOWN was a welcome distraction from Velda's grief and uncertainty. There were traders from Vailana in the marketplace, with wares of fine leather, jewels, and silver-plated blades and armour. The wood-cutters had just been paid, and were already circulating the money back into the town, buying sausages and beer from the stand in the square, inspecting the wares of local hawkers for something to take back home to their wives and daughters. As usual, there was at least one farmer trying to drive his pigs through the hubbub, and pink-cheeked farmers' daughters were hard at work selling bouquets of the first flowers of the year. Per tradition, the money they earned in this way was theirs to spend, and there was always fierce competition amongst them.

Velda skirted the edge of the marketplace and made for the stone-paved alleyways that threaded their way between the different boroughs of the town. Here, she spent several hours going from one junk-shop to another, trying her best not to be swindled. When she came out the other end, she had sold all her small valuables except her silver Sven medallion, and even the knapsack she had carried them in. The bag of money in the pocket beneath her skirt felt conspicuously heavy, and she was certain that it would be enough to buy passage to Armour City with the Vailanan traders. She could arrange that this very afternoon, if she wanted to.

Wandering through the busy marketplace, arguing back and

forth with herself over whether she should speak to the traders, Velda was suddenly distracted by a delicious smell of roasting meat. She realized, with a start, just how hungry she was, and how long it had been since breakfast. As she slowed to a halt, she realized that she was standing near Lynborder's only inn of note, a sturdy place run by the town's sternest matriarch, Zelma Friedman.

Zelma was leaning over the counter, shouting at one of her younger children—or perhaps a grandchild—when Velda walked in. There were only a few customers this early in the day, all locals.

"Velda!" The rotund woman stopped mid-rant to greet her, and the offending child ran off. She shook her head. "They drive me crazy." She stopped abruptly, as if swallowing something she had been about to say. "Sit down, sit down. I assume you're in want of something to eat?"

Velda nodded. "Something hot."

"In short order." Zelma hurried her to a table. "You haven't been seen in a long while. It must be good for you to get away from that lonely cliff-side, especially after the winter." She paused. "I heard what happened. I'm so sorry. Emmett was a good lad."

"Thank you," Velda said automatically, seating herself in the cosiest corner she could find.

"I'll be along with the food shortly. Have some ale in the meantime." The woman set down a clean mug and poured from the jug in her hand. She hurried behind the counter and into the kitchen, and Velda took a sip of ale, surveying the room. The inn was relaxed and bucolic as always.

Two of Zelma's daughters appeared from the stairwell, brooms and a laundry basket in hand. "Where did that carrot-seller say he was from?" one of them was asking as they went behind the counter.

"From Palace," the other said, reaching for a chair and sitting down heavily. Their conversation was just loud enough to reach Velda in her corner. "And that story he told me was no joke. Three others have told me the same already."

"What *story*?" Zelma emerged from the kitchen, hands on her ample hips. "What nonsense are you two making up again?"

"It's not nonsense, mama!" the girl insisted. "The people from the other towns say there's a monster in the mountains."

"A monster! Likely story! And what are they saying about this monster?"

"It's true, mama! People have been disappearing during the winter. And they've seen strange things in the woods."

"People disappear every winter," Zelma said impatiently.

"They say the monster is a ghost," the other girl piped up, "the ghost of a golden-haired girl who died on her wedding night. Murdered."

"A ghost, you say? I thought monsters were flesh-and-blood, no?"

"A ghost who commands monsters," the first girl returned, wide-eyed. "In the winter cold, she came for a dozen men in the wood-cutters' camp near Palace. I heard it from a lad who was with the search party. Saw it all with his own eyes. The cuttings were abandoned, and they found nought but bloody footsteps leading to a dead end in the woods. Apart from that, nothing."

"A bear attack, or a mountain cat," Zelma said, but she sounded less convinced than before.

"They couldn't find *any* remains," the girl said.

Zelma's sharp eye caught the laundry basket. "Get back to your chores," she grumbled. "You're only wasting time with this nonsense."

She disappeared into the kitchen again, and emerged with a bowl of stew alongside a plate of crusty bread, still hot from the oven, which she set in front of Velda. She bustled off as Velda thanked her and set to with gusto. There were bits of bacon and mushroom in the stew, and butter to go with the bread. Velda devoured everything faster than she would have thought possible, and was working on finishing her ale when the strange man strode into the inn.

He dressed well, she noticed at once; his loose tunic was of white wool, and almost as thick as the short jacket she wore for warmth. But it had seen hard wear recently, and she doubted he'd washed it in the last two weeks. His dark trousers were equally grimy, and though his boots were made of expensive leather, they looked as though he'd just walked a hundred miles in them. A thick cloak of forest-green wool hung from his shoulders, the hood drawn up. What she could see of the face beneath looked unshaven and careworn. He was taller than most of the men Velda knew, and broader in the shoulder. And he carried a sword.

"I need food," the man said urgently, spotting Zelma behind the counter. She had frozen in the act of wiping out a mug, her eyes fixed upon him. "A meal for two, and something to go. Bread, cheese, dried fruit."

Zelma swallowed, and carefully placed the mug she had been wiping upon the counter. Though her head barely reached the level of this man's armpit, she looked him directly in the eyes. "I don't allow weapons in my inn," she said quietly.

"What?" The man put his hand on his sword. The entire inn went silent, men looking up from their afternoon ale to see what was happening. "Oh. All right." He unbuckled the sword from his belt, and put it down on the counter. "Here, I'll leave it with you." He shoved the sword towards Zelma, and she gingerly put her hand on it. "Can I have that food? My friend will be along shortly."

Zelma did not take her eyes off him. "That'll be forty pence for the meal," she said.

The stranger reached into a pocket and withdrew a single coin, which he placed in Zelma's hand. "That should pay for everything I need," he said. Velda could see Zelma's eyes go wide at the sight of the coin. "I want supplies as well. Road-food. Bread and dried fruit and anything else that will last, and I want as much as I can carry."

"I—I'll fetch your meal in a minute, sir," Zelma stuttered. "Take a seat, do." She quickly pocketed the wondrous coin and fumbled with the long sword. "I'll just put this under the counter, shall I? Lizbeth!" She called one of her daughters closer, who had been watching the scene wide-eyed. "Watch this, and don't let anyone near." She hurried off into the kitchen.

The stranger looked around the room, where every man was now attempting to hide behind his ale-mug. Sauntering towards the same corner Velda had chosen, he nodded at her and took a seat at the other end of the long table. Velda tried not to stare, but her curiosity was barely containable. Mercenaries were not an uncommon sight in Lynborder, for the town lay on the road to the port at Sulshome, but they seldom travelled alone, and were generally a lot less scruffy than this man. Were it not for the quality of the clothes he was wearing, Velda might have imagined that he'd stolen that sword.

The stranger lifted his hood from his face and stared into the shadows, passing a grimy hand over his eyes. Velda was surprised to see how young he was; he looked about twenty-five. She had envisaged an older, rougher man beneath that hood. Long, wavy auburn hair was swept into a knot behind his head, and his unkempt beard was a lighter shade of ginger.

Zelma Friedman appeared suddenly at the stranger's side, making him glance in Velda's direction. Velda hastily looked away. "Ale, sir?" Zelma asked.

Velda shook herself. She had to be on her way soon, or risk making the climb back up to the homestead in the dark. She stood up and thanked Zelma, who seemed all in a dither, then took herself back to the main thoroughfare of Lynborder.

I wonder where he came from, though? And why he looks as if he hasn't slept in a week . . . The stranger could not be of the king's militia; they moved in groups, wore armour, and were very seldom seen outside the capital city of Ülhard. *That coin he gave Zelma . . . I've never seen her goggle over anything like that before. Was it a golden piece?* Velda had to suppress the urge to turn back towards the inn and corner Zelma to ask. That would be ridiculous.

The marketplace was quieter now, and Velda quickly skirted it and made for the road that would lead her out of town and back to the mountains. But she slowed and came to a standstill when a newly-painted building to the left caught her eye.

She moved closer, staring at the colourful sign. It was done up in yellow and brown, with bold golden letters spelling out: *Coffee Shop.* Beneath the sign, a diminutive grey-haired man, with skin so dark he seemed almost black, was reclining at a wooden bench, smoking a pipe. As her eyes travelled downwards, he caught them and grinned at her.

"Lovely lady, you are welcome to come in."

Velda moved onto the raised patio beneath the sign. "A coffee shop?" she asked, her eyes shining. "I thought they only existed in the city!"

"Indeed they do, lady, but I have thought to myself: why remain where there are already so many? Do the people in the little villages not need a relaxing drink now and then? And you see,"—he took the pipe from his mouth and gestured with it—"here, I have no competition! Every wandering customer will belong to me!" He laughed, and replaced his pipe. "Would you like a cup? I use only the finest beans from the East, for the alluring price of twenty pence per serving."

"Twenty pence?" Velda exclaimed. "I could buy myself—why—four mugs of ale for that price!"

"Ale? Ale is like water here; it flows just as freely, and tastes just so—of nothing. To taste coffee is to taste luxury, the leisure drink of the Emperor beneath the eternal sun in Bassah. Very well," he said, regarding her, "for your beauty, I will subtract from the price two pence. Eighteen."

"Tuppence?" Velda laughed. "Is my beauty worth so little to you?"

"Five pence, then. Your eyes are like topaz, your face is the pearl of the oceans."

"Enough flattery," Velda turned towards the door. "That is the most heavenly smell." She turned back towards the coffee merchant. "You have convinced me. I have *always* wanted to try coffee."

"Then I am happy to provide," he said with a broad smile as he showed her into the little shop. Velda looked around excitedly as he stepped behind the counter and measured a quantity of glossy brown beans from a cloth bag. "Forgive my lack of preparation," he continued as he began to grind the beans fine, "but you are, in fact, my first customer of the day, bold lady. May I inquire your name?"

"Velda," she said, leaning over the counter as he worked. "Velda

Davidz. And yours?"

"Sefo of Bassah," he replied. "May I call you by your first name?"

"Certainly."

"Forgive my curiosity," Sefo said, "but I have not seen your face in town before. I am sure that I would have remembered you, for not since I plied my trade in Sanghui have I seen a beauty such as yours."

Velda laughed out loud. Sanghui was the place of silk and chocolate, impossibly exotic, a jungle land on the neighbouring continent that lay across the sea to the east. "I'm no exotic beauty," she said. "I have lived here all my life. I've never even been to Vailana."

The beans were ground fine at last, and Sefo transferred the powerfully aromatic powder to a small pot boiling water on his stove. "I look forward to many more meetings with you."

Velda's smile faded. "I'm afraid I will be leaving soon. My—my husband passed away, and I can't continue to work our farm on my own." This was the first time that she had said it out loud, and she was surprised how ordinary it sounded. To sum up something so life-shattering in one simple sentence seemed wrong, and she fell silent.

Sefo's face drew into his abundant wrinkles. "I am truly sorry to hear that. My wife, she has been with the spirits these past ten years now." He paused. "Where will you be going?"

He was carefully pouring out the rich brown liquid into two stone mugs now, and Velda kept her eyes on what he was doing. "I thought—perhaps, Armour City. There are merchants that regularly go between here and there. I saw them in the marketplace today."

Sefo snorted. "Do not go with those rogues, I implore you." He reached across the counter and touched her hand. "Sweet lady, if you seek passage to Vailana, *I* can arrange it for you. Those traders would sell you as soon as look at you. They cannot be trusted." He turned, and handed her one of the hot mugs. "Vailana is a dangerous place, nowadays." He tapped his nose. "But I have ways, and the means to operate under the nose of our king."

Velda laughed nervously, feeling a sudden chill in her stomach. It was a pair of traders who had apparently sold her into slavery as an infant, she remembered. "I haven't decided anything yet."

The coffee merchant gave her another smile as he reached under the counter and came up with a jug of frothy cream. "This will cool the strong flavour," he said, indicating her mug. "In Bassah, we have great herds of cows, but these mountains cannot support such. So this is from my own goat." He added a liberal dose of cream to his own mug, and for a while they sat together, drinking. The coffee had a richer flavour than Velda had ever imagined, and she savoured every sip.

"I must be gone soon," she said, checking the position of the sun from the window, and Sefo's bright eyes found hers.

"So? You live in the mountains?" She nodded, and the coffee merchant looked concerned yet again.

"Have you seen aught up there this winter that—should not be? Anything . . . monstrous?"

"You have been listening to superstitious townsfolk," Velda

laughed. "There is nothing in the mountains except bears, and maybe mountain cats, and the occasional storm. The only danger, if I return too late, is that perhaps I will slip on a rock." She placed down her empty mug. "And so I must be on my way."

Chapter X
Going Back

VELDA HASTENED UPHILL, KNOWING that the path ahead was only going to get steeper. Lynborder lay well behind her, and she was all alone when she reached the crossroads. She paused there, frowning down at the muddy and rutted track.

Her own footprints from this morning were clearly outlined in the mud, coming down. But there were other prints alongside hers now, heading the opposite way. A whole mess of prints, as if a large group had gone up to the mountain.

She shook herself. *Don't be silly.* The superstitious old coffee merchant must have unsettled her mind. She was not the only one who held land up near the Witches' Horn. Some other family could have been to town and back already, the Stein children perhaps. There were a good nine of them.

Still, she couldn't help feeling a twinge of unease as she strode up the path. It began to climb almost immediately, twisting up to the cliffside. The woods pressed close on both sides, sombre evergreens towering over the birch and star chestnut that had just begun to unfurl their new leaves. The mountain's silence hung over all, birds asleep in the late noon heat, no wind stirring in the branches.

She had not gone more than a couple of paces when suddenly there was a loud rustling in the bushes behind her. Velda whipped around, her heart racing, but there was nothing. She scanned the muddy path, and noticed the swaying of a large wormwood bush to her left. Slowly the leaves on the bush came to rest, and silence fell all around her.

Velda slowly let out the breath she had been holding. She had never carried a weapon in the mountains. There had been a bandit attack on the town one winter, when she was about eleven, and they had warded themselves with crossbows set upon the high walls of the monastery. Emmett had kept a cudgel in the kitchen and sometimes taken it with him on late errands, but had never needed to use it. Lynborder was a remote place, and its people were not so rich as to tempt burglars or highwaymen. As for monsters . . .

If there was anything there, it would have attacked me by now, she told herself, and turned her back upon the slope. Doggedly she trudged up the familiar path, yet she could not shake a prickling feeling at the back of her neck, as though something *else* were out there in the woods.

Velda slowed in the mud as she approached a sharp, steep bend in the path. The top of the bend loomed before her, and she did not lift her eyes from her feet as she struggled up, concentrating on where she put them so as not to slip in the mud. The path led on ahead, levelling out over a steep, wooded bank.

She stopped dead in her tracks. In the middle of the muddy path, there were two men. Velda recognized them both: the peddler who had grabbed her at the monastery this morning, and the rough-looking auburn-haired man who had come into Zelma's inn. The younger man was kneeling in the middle of the path, examining the footprints in the mud, whilst the peddler looked on.

In the cold light of approaching evening, Velda became uncomfortably aware that neither of these strangers was what you'd call respectable in appearance. She would normally be the first to insist that a scruffy exterior could belie what lay in one's heart—after all, Emmett had been the most honest and kind of men, yet more often than not, visitors to their farm would find him unshaven and shirtless in the fields, crusted with a full week's worth of dirt and sweat. He had always joked that he would have a decent wash when the work was all done, but of course the work on a farm like theirs was never done.

Neither of these two reminded her in any way of her late husband, however, and the younger man was armed. Theirs was not the scruff of hard, honest work, but of long travel, and Velda found herself wondering where they had come from, and why they had left. She remained where she was, irresolute, half thinking of darting back the way she had come, half annoyed at herself for being this fearful.

The young man raised his head, and saw her. The peddler, following his gaze as he looked up, saw her too, and started as if in fear or excitement. Velda glanced over her shoulder, wondering if she would have much of a head start. The young man called down to her.

"Lady." His voice was clear and calm, and his right hand rested casually on his knee, well away from the sword. "Do you live around here?"

Neither of the two had changed position, and Velda relaxed enough to walk a few paces towards them, keeping to the far edge of the bank. "I do," she replied tersely. "What of it?"

The young man pushed himself upright and glanced towards the woods, his brow creasing. "It isn't safe here," he said. "How far do you have to go?"

Velda resisted the urge to glance over her shoulder again. She kept her eyes trained upon him. Hedged in by the silent forest, he cut an intimidating figure, the old peddler remaining in his shadow. She gathered her courage, taking note of where the sword was. From its position on his belt, he must be left-handed.

"Not far," she replied offhandedly. She took several steps forward, bringing herself past the two men, slightly higher on the path. They both turned to face her as she walked, neither of them making any move to block the way.

The young man sighed. "I know there is no reason for you to trust me," he said, "but there is danger here. Please, let us—"

"What kind of danger?"

"It's difficult to explain." He moved towards her. She recoiled, and he halted. "I think you should step away from the edge—"

There was a sudden thud and a rush behind Velda, as if something had leapt down from a tree and was making right for her. The young man, moving faster than Velda would have believed possible, sprang towards her at the same time. With one hand, he shoved her hard, sending her sideways into the mud. In his other hand, his sword was a flash of silver.

Something heavy barrelled into him; Velda had fallen, and could not see what was going on, but there was a grunt, an impact, and the thud of his sword dropping on the packed surface of the path. Velda scrambled to her feet and backed away, pulling her hair out of her eyes. She was just in time to see the young man struggling with some sort of humanoid creature at the edge of the bank. She stared, trying to comprehend what her eyes were taking in.

Naked but for a few rags and bits of cheap armour, the creature was grey-skinned, completely bald, yet possessed the face and eyes of a man. Its limbs were muscled hard as iron, and inexorably it held its ground even as the tall young man attempted to gain advantage against it. His right arm was fast against its neck, and close to his face, it snapped at him with jagged teeth from a grey, foaming mouth.

Velda had only a moment to take this all in, as the young man managed to shove the creature away, sending it to the edge of the bank. Both combatants lost their balance; the creature fell first and the man was pulled behind, uprooting a hand-sized, angular piece of rock from the bank's edge as he went.

Velda and the old peddler both rushed to the edge. She was trembling; the peddler was in no better state, his eyes goggling and his breath coming in short gasps. The man and the grey-skinned creature both rolled to the bottom of the bank, scuffing up moss and undergrowth. The young man was still holding the rock, and he came to his feet a bare breath before the creature was upon him again. Swinging his left hand back, he struck it in the side of its face. The creature staggered back a step, then continued to advance, its cheekbone half caved in, showing no sign of pain or distress. Again the rock struck true, and again the creature came on, unaffected by the gaping hole the rock had made of its face.

Run! Velda wanted to shriek. Her voice was stuck somewhere halfway up her throat, and could not get free. But the young man showed no sign of fear, even though the thing was still advancing, snapping its broken teeth together like a mad dog, and frothing from the corners of its mouth. He charged towards it, seizing it by the throat. Its hands scrabbled at him, fingernails like claws raking across the front of his shirt, tearing off strips of fabric stained with blood. Kicking its feet out from under its body, he bore it to the ground, raised the rock again, and this time struck a blow that caved in its nose and jawbone. Still it kept moving, and the rock descended once more, burying itself in the black ruin of the creature's skull. Its limbs fell limp at last, and the young man got to his feet and staggered away, breathing heavily, spattered with pitch black drops of blood. His hand was clamped over his neck, where the thing had clawed at him, and as Velda watched, his feet faltered, his face contorting in pain.

"What's wrong with him?" she demanded. The peddler shook his head, his face ashen.

The young man sank to the ground, one hand half-cushioning his fall. His gaze was desperate and disoriented, as if he were falling into unconsciousness.

Compelled by an instinct she barely understood, Velda slid down the bank to crouch at his side, followed closely by the peddler. "Look at me," she commanded, though her mouth was dry with fear. She was no stranger to deathly injury, and had stitched men up after many a terrible accident with farm equipment or animals. Yet she could not see how a series of admittedly nasty scratches could suddenly affect him so. "What is it?" she demanded, moving his hand away and seeing only red scratches and welts of black blood. "Where does it hurt?"

"Burns—" he croaked, his head lolling, eyes filming over. Reaching for her hand, he clasped it in his, holding on as if for dear life. "Help me—"

"There must be something in here that will help him," the peddler said, frantically searching in a sackcloth bag he had brought with him.

The man was dying, Velda realized, and she did not even know his name. He had been braver than anyone else would have been, had fought off the dreadful creature with a courage and strength she had never seen before. Now he was close to death, and she could not figure out why.

"I'm sorry," she told him. *You saved my life.* She cradled his head and looked into his eyes, hoping against hope to see life flare behind the unfocused filminess of near death. Young eyes, she saw, lovely even in disorientation, the aquamarine blue of the sky during the build-up to a storm on a hot day. Anger welled up inside her, a shadow of the helpless rage and frustration she had felt when her son died. *This isn't fair! Gods, if you truly watch over us, why would you allow this to happen?*

The creature's nails had drawn blood from the young man's chest and neck, crimson as life's fire, yet its own blood was completely black. It had spattered in thick gobs, as if already congealed within its veins, across the scratches. There was an acrid smell, and pink welts forming on the man's fair skin where the gobs of black had landed. The creature's blood was poison, Velda realized, deadly enough to kill its erstwhile opponent even as the thing itself now lay dead.

She caressed his face, trying to see if there was still life in the blue-green eyes. The peddler produced a waterskin from his bag at last. Velda seized it and carefully poured water over the wounds, wiping away the congealed black strings of blood with his ruined shirt, careful not to touch any of it herself. There was no sign of further life, no response, no realization in the vacant eyes. "Come on," she whispered. Her hands hovered over his body, beckoning as if she could call him back from the brink of death. "Please. Wake up."

A strange, intense sensation suddenly rose up in her, and the whole world tilted sideways. She spun away, dizzy, half collapsing over the dying man. Strange warmth caressed her spine the wrong way around, and the air seethed with confusion. She gave a small cry, unsure what was happening to her, and briefly afraid. But just as quickly as it had been upended, the world righted again. The man gave a grunt, and moved under her hands.

Whatever had overcome her, perhaps some sort of physical reaction from strain and sorrow, was unimportant. The man took a deep, shuddering breath, winced in pain, blinked rapidly as if to clear bleariness from his eyes. The effects of the poison seemed to recede all at once, and he tried to get up. She helped him to a sitting position, still holding his hand, then released it awkwardly as the blue-green eyes met hers. There was a look of intense wonder on his face, and he gaped as if seeing her for the first time.

"What happened?" the peddler demanded, next to Velda.

"I don't know." The young man broke his gaze, and Velda breathed again. "One moment, I was sinking into blackness, the next—" He broke off, faltering, and his eyes turned back towards her. "I felt you," he finished in wonder. "I heard you call."

"Can you stand up?" the peddler asked. "Can you walk?"

"I—I think so." He looked again at Velda, as if trying to comprehend something that contradicted the evidence of his eyes. She turned her face away. She was trembling, suddenly on the verge of tears. It was all too much.

"Are you all right?" the young man asked.

"I—I don't know." Velda blinked away the tears that threatened to fall. "What—what was that thing? Who are you? What—what just happened? What happened to *you*?" She ran short of breath, and broke off, panting.

"I can understand your shock," he said soothingly. "Even I am not entirely sure what that—that thing is. I can tell you, it is a magical construct; we commonly call them necromes."

"A—what?" *Magical construct?*

"My name is Albryan Lana," he continued. "I come from Qwu'Mallorn."

Velda was speechless. *Qwu'Mallorn? The Forest of the Morning?*

"I was tracking a foe," he explained. "I followed their trail here, into the mountains. But until now, I did not truly know what it was I was tracking. We are all in danger." Seeming fully recovered now, he slowly got to his feet and held out a hand to help Velda to hers. "As you saw, these creatures are not easily overpowered, and more of them are loose in the countryside around."

Velda was unable to take it all in. Both men were looking at her with odd, quizzical expressions on their faces. She focused on the peddler, who had remained silent whilst his companion spoke. "And *your* part in all this?" she asked.

"I came here searching for family at the monastery," the peddler replied. "We are but travelling companions. However, I have nowhere else to go." His voice was soft.

"Family?" she repeated. "What is your name?"

"Hiram Lynstream."

"You nearly walked into me there," Velda said, remembering. Somehow, none of it felt real.

"I'm sorry. You reminded me of someone." The man's unsettling, golden-yellow eyes fixed upon her.

"There are more of these necromes about." Albryan drew the tatters of his tunic over the raw scratches on his neck as best he could, wincing in pain. "I do not know how fast they can travel, but they are a threat to whomever they might encounter. Especially to unsuspecting farmers."

"Farmers." Velda's stomach felt icy; she now wondered what would have become of her had she left Lynborder earlier in the day, or had she not stopped at Sefo's coffee shop for that long chat. "Their tracks led towards—towards my land."

"We have to follow them," Albryan said decisively.

"And what will you do against them?" Velda demanded. "It took all your strength just to best this one!"

"We were taken by surprise," he returned. "If we can get to a vantage point somewhere above them—if we know where they are, and can stay hidden—I can do much more." He flexed his left hand, closing the fingers into a fist.

There did not seem to be anything else to do; Velda was certainly not returning home alone, and the townspeople of Lynborder could hardly be well-equipped for this kind of fight. She eyed the tall Morgein man covertly. *He must have magical powers—perhaps that is how he recovered. The Morgei are magic folk, after all.* She had no idea, herself, what magic could possibly entail.

"We have to go," she said aloud. "It will soon be dusk."

"Agreed." Albryan looked up at the bank he had rolled down, sighed, and began to scale it back up, half crawling and half climbing. Velda, a foot shorter than he was, headed under the low trees towards a place where the slope gentled enough to walk back up to the path. The peddler came close upon her heels.

THE WALK UP TO THE FARM was silent. Velda's mouth was dry with fear, her worry only intensifying as they followed the mess of tracks on the muddy road. The knot of dread in her stomach did not ease as they drew near to the cliffside path. The sun had begun to set behind the Witches' Horn, and the winding path was starkly outlined in black, treacherous and full of deep shadows.

Albryan came to a halt and stared up at the path, chewing on his lower lip. "You live up *there*?"

"Yes."

"Is there anyone up at your home right now?"

Velda shook her head, and the tall man gave a sigh that sounded as though it were born of relief. "Well, there's nothing else for it," he said out loud. "You two"—he took Velda and Hiram in with his unwavering gaze—"stay at least a dozen paces behind me." He shaded his eyes with his hand, and squinted up against the setting sun. "I can't make out anything in the shadows. I don't believe that these necromes possess the ability to think or plan by themselves, but I could be mistaken. When I reach the top of the cliff, wait for my signal before coming up."

Their ascent was laced with tension, yet nothing happened. The light was fast fading, making their footing uncertain, and their way up was very slow. Heavy footprints marked the path, all intermingling with one another, and Velda felt cold all over to see how many there were. Here and there, the path was scuffed along the edges, as if the climbers had slipped in their haste.

At last Albryan reached the top, and beckoned without hesitation for Velda and Hiram to join him. They hurried the last few paces, reaching the little footpath from which they could see the farmhouse outlined in the last light. There were footprints in the fallow fields, sunken in the short mountain grass. There was no sign of Velda's pigs. When finally they reached the house, Velda saw that a wall of the sty had been broken from the inside. The pigs were nowhere to be seen. The door to the farmhouse hung by a hinge, shattered into two pieces.

Velda's feet froze under her. A deathly cold seemed to emanate from within the house, where it was too dark to see. She felt as though something waited inside, something she didn't want to witness again. She had felt the same way, that day three months ago, when she had led Brother Viktor and the gravedigger here to take care of the bodies that lay inside the homestead. It was too much the same. She was trembling, and she knew that she could not move from the spot no matter what. She could not go inside again. She could not see them again.

"Velda?" Hiram, the aged peddler, was beside her, and lightly touched her arm. She turned towards him, swallowing down hysterical tears, unable to calm her frantic heartbeat.

"I can't," she whispered. "I can't go in there."

"It's all right."

Hiram stayed beside her in the yard, as Albryan went inside the house alone. He emerged shaking his head. "No sign of them." Velda was beginning to recompose herself, feeling a little embarrassed at her sudden terror, and he asked: "How many people live near here?"

"On this side of the cliff, only me and one other family." Velda shivered. What if they had found the Stein homestead already? The gentle farmer and his family were no match for murderous magical creatures hell-bent on doing them violence . . . "There is a short cut," she said. "Instead of following the road, we can cut through the fields."

"The necrome we met was a straggler," Albryan said. "We may just have enough time to stop the main horde before they reach your neighbours. We can only hope."

"There there is no time to lose," Velda said, suddenly resolute.

She turned away from the empty homestead and strode across the fields, feeling almost as though she were being moved by some force outside of herself. There was a brief, hurried conversation between Albryan and Hiram, and then Albryan came trotting up to her side, alone.

Velda looked back. "What is Hiram doing?"

"He is more infirm than you or I," Albryan replied. "He will stay. The necromes are unlikely to look back if they expect to find fresh prey ahead."

They went in silence. The land here rose and fell in gentle curves, and Velda hastened past her dear ones' graves, through a marshy pine copse, and led Albryan out onto the Stein fields. They were at the bottom of a valley, and the farmstead lay on a small bluff at the end of a winding path. The sun had all but disappeared behind the distant mountain peaks, leaving the landscape grey and morose, the brooding pines outlined in black and the barren fields bleached bone-white.

"No sign of them," Albryan muttered. The land was empty all about.

Velda was about to suggest that they make their way towards the farmstead, when Albryan stiffened and nudged her. A gesture from him drew her eyes eastwards, where in the deepening shadow of the dusk she could just make out a horde of black walkers on a far-off footpath. Watching them for a moment, she could make out that they were not men. Their walking pace was slower, their footsteps heavier, and they hunched over forwards as they shuffled ahead, as though their heads were too heavy for their torsos to support properly.

"What are you going to do?" she asked Albryan.

A dangerous grin crept over the young Morgein man's face. "Watch and see." He stepped forward, holding his hands out from his body. Velda felt the hair on her arms and on the back of her neck stand on end. Escaped curls from her bun began to flutter upwards as if pulled by a strong breeze.

The air around Albryan began to shimmer, like the air above a pond on a scorching hot summer's day. He drew his hands together, and encased a shimmering, red-hot ball of roiling light within them.

Velda stepped backwards in fright, and right at that moment, a necrome leapt from the cover of the trees behind and ran at him.

Albryan reacted a bare moment before the creature hit him. He released the flaming ball, and it flew wide, hitting the ground several hundred yards ahead, sending mud and grass foaming up into the air. Albryan's sword flashed blue in the light of the silent detonation. This time, he struck true on the first try, severing the attacking necrome's head from its body and sending it crumpling to the ground. But the fireball had been wasted. The horde had turned and seen the two of them, and now the necromes were coming on across the field, shuffling faster than Velda would have thought likely. There were over two dozen of them, making directly for Albryan in a headlong charge.

Velda stood rooted to the spot, frozen with indecision. Albryan showed no hesitation nor any desire to flee. Hefting his sword, he strode forward to meet the horde.

The creatures bore down upon him, snarling hate and death, and at last Velda found the will to move. Something outside herself seemed to take control, making her seize a nearby stone, making her run to Albryan's side even though she was no fighter.

One of the necromes was holding a crudely fashioned club, a tree branch with a heavy, bulbous end. As Albryan laid about him with his sword, opening gaping wounds to no real avail, it came up behind him. Velda cried out, but it was too late. The club found its target, cracking Albryan a hard blow on the back of the head, sending him to his knees. He was still conscious, but his sword dropped from nerveless fingers, as he scrabbled to right himself in the dirt.

Velda pressed forward with a cry. She threw the stone in her hand; it bounced harmlessly from a grey, leathery hide. She grabbed Albryan's sword from the ground and stabbed out wildly in front of her. To her amazement, the necrome sprang backwards and hissed.

"Get away!" Velda could not believe that they would obey her, but as one man, the creatures were all backing away like frightened dogs, their dead eyes following her as she stepped protectively in front of Albryan.

They cannot be afraid of the sword, Velda realized. She lowered the point of the blade. The necromes were still retreating. She cast the sword to the ground. Still, they kept moving back.

They were retreating from her. They were afraid of *her*.

Her only wish was to defend Albryan, to keep these monsters away from him and away from the other farmers and innocents of Lynborder.

As soon as this thought crystallized in her mind, Velda felt the presence of something *other*, something unassailable, something that was not herself yet moved in concert with her own desires. She wanted to defend Albryan, and the *something* wanted to help her do it. Warmth and the sensation of immeasurable power spread outwards through her body from her heart, radiating from her outstretched hands as a pale mist that settled over the necrome horde. The feeling grew stronger, rising to a peak, wind racing through her blood, an unbridled natural force making its way through her unresisting body. Then slowly, falling from the peak, everything receded. The pale mist began to dissipate.

The features of the necromes turned human, broken fangs receding behind soft lips, grey skin loosening and bruising to a pallid corpse hue, limbs bowing as iron-hard muscles softened and long claws reduced to simple fingernails. The creatures fell, all as one, to the ground, remaining motionless, dead eyes turned to the sky, nothing more than a pile of harmless human corpses.

Velda turned towards Albryan. To her surprise, he was on his knees staring up at her, his eyes filled with awe and something that was almost like fear. He whispered a strange word that sounded like a woman's name.

"Albryan!" Velda knelt down before him, and a cloud seemed to pass in front of his eyes. He blinked and rubbed them, and gaped back at her.

"What happened?" he whispered. Slowly, he got to his feet and looked around at the corpses, his eyes and mouth both wide in amazement. "How did you do this?" he whispered, staring at her, swaying visibly.

"I don't know," Velda said, taking his arm, aware that he had been dealt a nasty blow to the head. "I think—I think I must have done some kind of magic." She giggled nervously, almost hysterically, and realized that there were tears in her eyes. A moment ago, she had been facing certain death with an incredibly handsome man at her side. Now, the danger was gone, and she wanted to laugh, to dance, to take the man's hands in hers—

Albryan shook his head. "This is not magic," he said. "This is—this is the undoing of magic. This is *light.*" He swayed again, and then gasped as if he had just remembered something. "We have to get out of here."

"Why? I think they're done for."

Albryan looked closely at her, and took her by the shoulders. "We're still in danger. These creatures don't act on their own—they have a master. She will know what happened. She will know that I have done magic. And if she finds the two of us . . ." Albryan's voice stilled as though forced into silence. "We must find some place to lay low for the night, and get some rest," he finished at last, hoarsely.

Some part of Velda's hysteria receded. "I know a cave," she said, after a moment's pause. "It's not far. Are you alright walking?"

Albryan released her, and took a few steps forward. "Yes."

"Then follow me."

THE CAVE WAS LOCATED on a footpath that wound up the southern face of the Witches' Horn, a stiff half hour's walk at the best of times. The dusk was growing deeper, and the evening mist was descending, but Velda knew these fields as well as did the antelope that lived wild on the mountain. She led the way unerringly. Before of them, the ground angled upwards steeply, dotted with patches of wild thyme and rhododendron. To their left, the ground fell away in a series of jagged cliffs. The cave was set in the cliff face at a slight angle to the path. Below the entrance of the cave, the ground fell steeply away. There was a single jutting rock, Velda knew, that served as a stepping-stone to the cave's entrance; a misstep there, and the distant abyss waited a hundred feet below.

It was almost too dark to see the cave entrance and the foothold by which it could be reached, but Albryan refused to turn back. Velda threw a stone into the cave before them, to ensure that no mountain-cat had made its den there. Then she led Albryan over the stepping-stone and into the cave, supporting him against the side of the cliff. When finally they both settled down inside, the last of the light faded as if it had been waiting for this moment.

The cave was too dark to see much, and the descending mist hid the light of the stars. The rocky lip of the cave was about a foot higher than the floor, which was smooth and hollow as though it had been scoured out by flowing water. But the cave had been dry for as long as any oldster could remember, and had served as a nighttime shelter for shepherds when flocks of sheep had roamed these hills, a few generations back. Velda settled herself against a jutting rock, with the strange young man close by in the darkness. She could hear him fidgeting as he tried to get comfortable on the hard stone floor.

"Do you feel all right?" she asked, remembering the crack he had taken on the head and the way he had overbalanced afterwards.

"I've a splitting headache," Albryan responded.

"That doesn't surprise me." Velda sighed. "All you can do up here is wait for it to pass."

"It was all such a blur," Albryan said, the words coming slowly. "I think I remember what happened. I lost consciousness for just a moment. When I raised my head, I saw you—and something outside of you, facing down the necromes. It was like I was looking at the Goddess come to life."

"*The* goddess?" Velda asked curiously.

"Qwu'Kiya," he said. "The mother goddess of the Morgei. You know—I did not even ask your name."

"Velda Davidz."

"And who are you?"

"What do you mean?"

"You have a power," he returned, "a gift. I have never seen anything like it, neither in Qwu'Mallorn nor outside." He paused. "Please forgive my curiosity, but you don't look like a Sven farmer."

Velda gave a little laugh. "So I've heard all my life." She paused. "The monks at the monastery here in Lynborder raised me, but I'm an orphan, probably from Armour City when it got sacked by Arran Sylvaissen nineteen years ago." She heard Albryan shift in the darkness. "I was only a babe, so I don't remember anything, least of all who my parents were. Somehow I ended up being taken by a band of slavers." She hesitated, suddenly remembering what the fall of Armour City would mean to this man, who was of the persecuted magical race who had suffered such great losses that night. "These slavers had captured about two dozen of—of your folk. But the villagers of Lynborder ambushed the slavers, wiped them out, and the two dozen went to live in the Forest of the Morning."

"But you—you had no Mage-Gift."

"No."

"Your land," he began. "You're a farmer?"

"I was . . . married."

There was nothing but silence from Albryan's corner for a long moment. At last he stirred. "I am sorry. It was not my place to ask."

She couldn't see his face in the darkness, and somehow that made it easier for her to speak. "My husband and I—we got this land on a lease from the monks. Everything was going well. We had a son, about a year old." Albryan did not reply, but she could sense his tension, coiled around him like the darkness itself. "This winter past, they had the snow fever come to Lynborder. It is common up here, and most of us get it when we're children. But it can be deadly to infants. I had it, years ago, so I didn't even get sick, but my son was so young that the fever . . . it consumed him. And my husband—he'd never had the illness before."

There was nothing but silence from Albryan's corner for a long moment. Then suddenly, he began to speak in a low voice. "When I was eight years old, a plague struck the town where we lived in Qwu'Mallorn. The disease was brought on a trader's ship that sailed from the Eastern Empire, maybe carried by rats in its hold, I don't know. It was so deadly that even magical healing could do little against it. My mother fell ill. For fear of contagion, my brother and I were not allowed to see her." He paused. "It all happened so fast. One day life was normal, and she was laughing with us. The next, she was shut up in her room and we never saw her again."

Albryan's voice, now that she had heard him speak for a while, was clearly accented differently to hers or anyone she knew. It threw common words in a way she was unused to hearing, making music out of the tongue she had spoken all her life.

"You are planning to leave this place, are you not?" he asked, changing the course of the conversation.

"I am not sure where I will go." The words came unbidden, borne from the confusion she had struggled with all day, now thrown into even deeper turmoil by what had happened tonight.

What she had done tonight.

"You could come with me to Qwu'Mallorn." Albryan spoke far too quickly for the idea to have been a casual notion. "I have to go back home. Hiram has nowhere else to go, either. I planned to take him with me. The Forest of the Morning is not reserved for the Mage-Gifted, and Hiram lost everything in Armour City nineteen years ago."

"Hiram spoke of finding family here," Velda said, deferring an answer.

"He lost his daughter, at the fall of Armour City." Albryan seemed to be choosing his words carefully. "She might have fled here, and she was pregnant. Hiram went to the monastery to find out what he could, but all they could tell him—"

"Was about *me*." Velda felt an odd swooping in her gut, as if it had just dropped somewhere down the side of the mountain. *Could it be?* She remembered how the old peddler had gaped at her, the odd look in his eyes. Eyes of a lighter golden-brown than hers, and a nose just as prominent . . .

"Where did you meet him?" she asked breathlessly.

"That's a long story." Albryan sounded weary. "In short, we met in Arran Sylvaissen's dungeon."

Velda shifted in surprise, and realized suddenly that she had not even wondered how it was that Albryan Lana came to be here, in the mountains of Svanfeld at least a hundred miles away from his homeland.

"These necromes," Albryan continued, "these magical constructs, they were created by dark sorcery. This magic is different from what we use in Qwu'Mallorn. Only Arran—and his children, to whom he taught his secrets—can wield it."

Velda felt more confused than ever. "What has the king in Armour City got to do with us on the border of Svanfeld?"

"A good question." Albryan sounded as nonplussed as she was, and he paused thoughtfully. "My guess is that he wishes to expand his kingdom." Velda could hear him shaking his head. "These creatures have not been seen for almost four hundred years. The sorcerers who created them were exiled, some of them executed. The method by which they are created has become legend."

"How are they created?"

Albryan drew a deep breath. "The legends say that first, you must have the corpse of a person. Any person. The sorcerer then summons a handful of black magic, a kind of essence of his will, and plants it inside the body. If it is done correctly, magic will spread through the cadaver and begin to animate it and to twist it, turning it from a mere dead body into a murderous creature, a puppet. It has no will of its own, but always possesses the desire to kill, to create copies of itself. Its blood and spit both contain poison in the form of dark magic. When its blood is introduced, or when it bites, the poison enters the victim's body and kills them, and after death they become necromes themselves. In this way, the dark magic is replicated without the sorcerer even needing to be present."

Velda was silent in horror, taking this in. "That necrome—its blood was mingled with yours," she began.

"It was your touch that healed me," Albryan said softly. "I suspected something of the sort, but at the time, I believed it to be impossible. But now that I have seen what you can do . . ." He paused again, and Velda could hear him breathe softly in the darkness. "I owe you a great deal, Velda Davidz," he finished in a low voice.

"I don't know what I did," Velda admitted. "I don't know if I could do it again."

"We could help you," Albryan said. "The Morgei, I mean. Undoing magic is, in itself, a type of magic. If you came with me, perhaps we could figure out the answers together."

I'm no exotic beauty. Gods knew, Velda had never thought herself anything special. She was just an orphan of war, blessed in some ways and unlucky in others, trying to make her own way in the world. This was the first time she had tasted adventure, and she wasn't sure she liked the flavour. Everything seemed impossibly complicated, this handsome young man with abilities beyond what she could ever achieve, telling her that *she* was something special, and the old man who might in fact be her—

"Is your headache better?" Velda asked. Her mouth was dry. Perhaps it was all a dream in truth. Perhaps she would wake tomorrow in her lonely bed without Emmett—

"It is."

"Then you should sleep." Velda drew her jacket tighter, and tried her best to get comfortable. "I will think about—about what you have offered."

"Thank you," Albryan said. Silence fell over the mountain. Velda closed her eyes, but sleep was the furthest thing from her mind. She found herself thinking of Father Stian, his cryptic words about Arran Sylvaissen, his plea for her not to go to Armour City. *A different road*, he had said to her. Yet she could not understand what any of it meant. She felt smaller than ever, helpless in the face of a vast world that did not follow the rules she had been taught as a child. Her plan to leave, to create a new life for herself, seemed hopeless, almost childish, and yet it was all that she had to cling to.

The waning moon rose over the valley, shining directly into the cave through the wisps of mist that blanketed the mountain. Albryan had fallen asleep, worn out, snoring softly. He was illumined by the moon's ghostly light as it rose. There were lines on his face that were absent now, in sleep, and Velda was surprised to feel a sudden stab of protectiveness towards him.

This was more than just physical admiration, she realized in horror. She had never thought she would feel this way—this attraction—towards anyone ever again. She *liked* him, and not in a way that was confined to mere friendship.

Shame swept over her. She swatted away the traitorous thought which suggested that four months might be a halfway adequate mourning period. Emmett had had his whole life before him, and it could only be a fair exchange if she gave the rest of hers in mourning.

It wasn't right that she should feel this way towards some handsome stranger who had swept into her life, saved it, and now implored her to come on a journey with him to faraway lands she had always longed to see.

Velda closed her eyes against the silvery light of the moon. She would feel differently in the morning, she told herself. Once dreary day had lit the world again, her fancies would melt like so much snow on the northern cliffsides, and the man sleeping beside her would be nothing more than a chance-met acquaintance.

Chapter XI
Mist and Shadow

FISH CROUCHED OVER THE CAMPFIRE, not trusting the foggy wilderness around him.

There was sleep still in his eyes; Nico had shaken him awake without ceremony, then disappeared into the fog to tend to his ablutions. Fish had crawled out of the tent, blanket still around his shoulders, to find himself alone in a sea of fog.

The fire Nico had built during the night smouldered low, providing Fish with something solid to look at. He inched closer, concentrating on the boiling coffee pot that sat in the ashes. The way the fog billowed made him uneasy. It was so *thick*, so seemingly solid, but anything could force its way through there; anything could be waiting just beyond his severely limited field of vision. And out here in the wilds, on the tracks of a slave caravan, the thought of "anything" was a troubling one.

They had left civilization five days ago, when they had taken their leave of the town of Von Dharen. The journey there had been easy; the search for slave-traders had been moderately difficult. No-one in the town wanted to talk to a pair of strangers, and every one of the contacts they had been given to follow up had been impossible to track down. In the taverns, there were whispers of wrong-doings, of murders, of men who came ashore in the night and cloaked themselves in darkness before disappearing. They had languished in the town for more than a week before turning up a single hint: a nearby cove, once frequented by smugglers. The smugglers of Von Dharen had all vanished, no-one knew why nor where to, but the cove remained the safest landing for ships outside of the actual harbour.

Against the warnings of the townsfolk, Nico and Fish had visited the cove. Luck had been with them, and they had found exactly what they sought without running into danger. There were footprints in the cove, above the high-tide mark and leading due east; an entire caravan had disembarked here less than a week ago. There were about a dozen captives, according to Nico, all of them women and children. Their heavy-booted guards numbered at least twice as many. Up above the surf, out of reach from the wild windy sea, they had turned up more in the sand: a discarded shoe, child-size; a chunk of tangled black hair; a wrought-iron collar, rusted through and still attached to a link of disintegrating chain.

The slave caravan had made for the nearby forest to the south of

Von Dharen, and by fear and force had driven their captives to make it under the tree cover within eight hours of their arrival on the beach. Then, they had taken the quickest and steepest possible path into the mountains. The slavers were travelling by night, so the assassins were travelling by day, and keeping watch all night. Fish always took the first watch, and once Nico awoke smartly at midnight, he took over. Every day, the weather and the wilderness reminded them that they were no longer in Ülhard. They were in the wilds, and nature was against them.

Daily they clawed their way up jagged boulders residing in steep ravines, slipped down partially frozen banks of mud, and drew their fur hoods up against the persistent sleet and rain. The tangled vegetation of the lower forests quickly gave way to heather-clad cliffs of basalt and sandstone, making the way easier, but detection more likely. They had left their horses behind in Von Dharen, taking only two sturdy donkeys to carry their gear. Fish's sense of unease increased daily, although he could not have said why. This was not his first foray into wilderness nor danger, and he had always had complete trust in Nico before.

But now, the fog. It had been threatening to come down last night, but Fish would never have guessed how quickly and completely it had subsumed everything. There was no sign of the sun, only a sinister kind of ghost-dawn palely wavering through the white. Fish's ears ached with the silence, as if dampers had been placed over them. He reached for a dagger that Nico had left next to the fire, feeling some comfort in holding it.

He was all alone in the midst of this white wilderness, and yet he felt so strongly that someone was nearby that he had to restrain himself from whipping around. Only muffled noises came to him, but he caught their edge: a twig snapping, a bush shaking, padding footsteps just outside his little circle of solitude. The whiteness of the fog made his eyes ache, and he imagined sights in the corner of his eye: long, whipping hair, fleeting sandals over last year's leaves, a pair of dark eyes watching . . .

A twig snapped, just behind him. Fish was on his feet instantly, lunging with the silvered dagger towards his unseen enemy.

The blade of the dagger halted just below Nico's unprotected chin, who slowly raised his hands, his eyes fixed on his partner. "What . . ."

Fish gave a loud curse and lowered the dagger. "What are you thinking, sneaking around like that?"

"By the sly eyes of Vermayn, Fish, I only went for a . . ." Nico hesitated. "Fish, did something happen?"

"No." Fish slumped back down, running his hands through his hair. His eyes felt weary, dry from staring. "Nico, I'm not used to this. I didn't grow up in this land like you did."

Nico took a seat beside him. "We had more trees around where I grew up," he said brusquely. "Give me some coffee, will you?"

Fish began to feel calmer, now that his partner was here to distract him. "How are we going to get anywhere in this fog?" he asked.

Nico shrugged. "I'm not sure we can. We might be better served waiting up for a day. Give me that map." Fish passed the wax-paper map to him, and he scrutinized it.

"Here's the way we've come," he said, taking a square of paper from the pocket of his jerkin and comparing it to the map. "We've started to turn south. We crossed this stream yesterday, see?"

"Where's that mountain pass?"

Nico pointed out the Peak of Beerstana. "Around this peak. It's the only way back to the lowland. If we keep heading south, we'll run into this range over here. These peaks are impassable; the only way to get around them is to head east towards the pass."

"What if they turn back towards the coast?"

Nico shook his head. "They might reach the sea, but there is no place to moor a ship. The mountains continue almost into the sea; see the cliffs here?"

"Then they have got to be bribing someone to let them through the pass." Fish gulped down a mouthful of coffee. "It's the only way."

"You're probably right," Nico said. "We can be reasonably certain they're making for the pass, which means that we might be able to head them off before they get there."

"Are you sure that's a good idea?"

"Oh, I don't mean to fight them; only to find out for sure how many there are, and in what state the captives are. There's a chance we can free the captives, if we have a safehold for them to take refuge in."

Fish furrowed his brows. "And we have such a safehold?"

"Here." Nico tapped the map, indicating a nearby valley. "There's a settlement here, according to this. It must be a tiny hamlet, but it's likely to have enough defenders to keep the captives safe at least. Depending exactly how many those slavers are, we could even get the villagers to help us hunt them."

"They might be willing," Fish agreed. "But what if we can't get to the pass in time?"

"If we go down to the village, we can loop around this peak here. It's a high road, but it'll get us to the pass faster. The slavers have been slowing down, too. They can't afford to walk their captives to death, and there's no reason for them to believe they need to hurry."

"One thing, though," Fish said, as Nico rolled up the map. "How are we going to move anywhere in this fog?"

"We'll just have to be careful," Nico replied. "We can't stay here long anyway; it's getting colder. We'll be going in the opposite direction from the slave caravan, so we won't have to be as cautious." He reached for his coffee. "How about you pack up the tent, and I'll get the donkeys ready?"

They packed up their campsite quickly, eager to move from that cold spot on the edge of the mountain. It was indeed getting colder as they worked, and the fog, against all expectation, seemed to be thickening. Even the donkeys were more subdued than usual.

They flipped a coin to determine who would take the lead, and

Fish lost. Quietly hoping that his sanity would last, he put a rope around his waist and tied himself to his partner, who attached himself in turn to the lead donkey. They were to move in single file, all tied together to prevent anyone or anything disappearing in the fog. Fish carried a long stick. Nico, as the rearguard, was responsible for marking their path as they went.

It proved to be a long morning. They had intended to head directly to the northeast, but they had not gone far when they came to a sheer cliff. They might have walked straight off into thin air were it not for their precautions; they had no warning of the drop except when Fish suddenly faltered, his stick giving way right in front of his feet. Luckily Nico was able to pull him back before he fell. They threw a rock into the fog, and the length of time that passed before they heard a faint thud at the cliff's bottom made both of them fidget uneasily.

They soon discovered that there was only one way down: southeast. It was steep, muddy, icy and slippery. Fish lost his footing and fell into the mud more times than he could count. Nico saved himself every time by leaning on the donkey's neck for support. But when at last they reached the bottom, a reward was waiting for all their effort. There was a path.

"This'll lead us to the hamlet," Nico said with conviction. "They've rolled logs down here. Recently. See how the edges are all scuffed up?"

The muddy road led them north up a low bluff, turned east to round a sheer cliff, and then headed north again, leading them sharply downhill. Though Fish knew that this must be the valley in which the hamlet resided, he felt further away from civilization than ever. The fog seemed heavier in the valley, and every strange muffled sound inside it made him prickly with unease. Fish wondered if the sun was setting; he could hardly remember how much time had passed. It felt as though they had been walking forever, and would continue to do so for all eternity, swallowed up by the endless fog. When at last he found his path blocked by a high wooden wall, he stopped so suddenly that Nico walked right into him.

"We're here," Fish announced with relief.

"Thank the gods," Nico muttered. Drawing one of his daggers, he strode forward and thumped its hilt upon the sturdy gate.

There was dead silence for a moment, and then a sudden muttering from the other side of the gate. A peephole opened in the wood, and the face of a middle-aged man, lit up by a guttering oil lantern, peered through.

"Strangers," he said to someone beside him, then squinted at Nico and Fish. "What brings you here?"

"We seek shelter," Fish said. "Is there an inn in your village? We will pay well."

"Is that so?" The man's tone was suspicious. "And how would we be knowing that you won't murder us all in our beds whilst we sleep, eh?"

Nico took a folded piece of paper from his pocket. "This is the crest of the Trade Guilds," he said, passing it through the peephole.

"We mean no harm; in fact, we will help if we may," Fish said.

There was much back-and-forth over the scrap of paper on the other side. Fish folded his cloak around himself, shivering. A thin rain had begun to fall, showering them both with the icy kisses of the snow goddess. Fish turned his face up to the rain, seeing nothing but greyness, and hoped that they were not in her bad books.

"Alright," someone finally announced, and there came the sound of the gate-bolts being drawn back. Two men pushed on the gate to open it just wide enough to admit the two assassins and their donkeys. There was a wooden guardhouse to the left, with several men gathered around near the doorway.

A burly man with a grey beard came forward. In one hand he held an enormous axe; in the other, Nico's Guild letter. He was cloaked and hooded in a great bearskin, with stiff deerhide boots on his feet.

"This here letter," he announced to the rest of the men, "says that the bearer is to be treated as a Guild representative, given all the luxuries and respects due to them." He folded the paper carefully and handed it back to Nico. "We have no Guild here," he continued, but not rudely, Fish noted. "You'll have to pay your way here, like any-one else."

"Not a problem," Nico said, stepping forward. He was actually taller than the bear-skin man, Fish noticed absent-mindedly, but Nico would need about thirty more years of eating and drinking and fighting to equal the bear-skin man's bulk.

"*Is* there an inn here?" Nico was asking. "Or someone who could put us up?"

"I will take you to the house of Friedma Smit," the bear-skin man said. "In the summer, she provides housing for young wood-cutters who come up here to assist us, but the season has not yet begun. I am Harold Velman, the elder of this village." He shook both Nico and then Fish's hands as they introduced themselves.

"One moment," one of the assembled men said, a red-faced fellow with even redder bushy whiskers under his woollen cap. "What do them Guilds want here? And what did you mean when you said, *you will help if you may?*"

Nico drew himself up and glanced around. "We are hunting slavers," he said proudly.

There was an animated whispering around the circle of men, and one called out: "Ain't no slavers here! You're wasting your time, ain't you?"

"Are you sure?" Nico retorted. "No strangers hanging around here the past winter? None of your people suddenly going missing?"

At that, the whispering intensified and several men shuffled their feet, looking uncomfortable.

"We don't like to talk of it," Harold said in a low voice, stepping forward again, "but this has been a strange winter. Two young girls've disappeared, and some of the men who went to find them too."

"Monsters took 'em, not slavers," a younger man spoke up. "I saw one of 'em with my own eyes, I swear. A grey creature with the limbs of a man and the savage teeth of a wolf."

"A goblin, I told you," an old greybeard said, as the men around him scoffed.

"Well, I can't speak for whatever you saw," Nico said levelly, "but I do know that there is a band of slave-traders not two days away from this village, and that my partner and I are bound to destroy them. With a little help from you, we could ambush them at the Peak of Beerstana, and get rid of them for good."

It seemed that everyone suddenly had something to say, until Harold stepped forward to stand beside Nico. "Our guests are tired and hungry," he announced. "We will speak no more of this until the morning. Come on." He beckoned for them to follow, and Nico and Fish did so gratefully.

Harold led them down the rutted, potholed track that passed for a village road. "You'll get the lads to go with you to the Peak of Beerstana," he said in a low voice. "I don't believe in monsters or dark creatures, any more than what I believe in the goblins the old wives tell stories about. Give me this night, and I'll have you thirty ready fighters in the morning. Including a few of our women, if I don't mistake myself."

"That's good!" Nico said in surprise.

"Very good!" Fish echoed him. "With thirty behind us, those slavers won't stand a chance."

Harold led them to the far end of the village, where a large log house loomed up out of the fog. The front door was raised off the ground, reached by a flight of wooden steps almost as high as Nico's head. Harold ascended these steps to knock on the door, which was opened by a young woman with brown hair.

"Liezl," he said, making a short bow. "Where is your mother?"

Fish turned his head. To the right of the wooden house, there was a bit of scrub forest, stunted chestnut and poison oak brooding silently in the gloom of the fog. The uneasiness that had been with him all day intensified when he stared into the trees. Movement flickered on the edge of his vision, but he turned sharply to see nothing.

"What's wrong?" Nico asked. Harold was still talking with Liezl and a young man who had come up to the door.

"Nothing," Fish forced himself to say.

It was impossible to dwell on whatever the feeling was, for Friedma Smit, a short middle-aged woman, came bustling out of the house then, introducing herself, her daughter and her son Rudolf.

"Now, usually I put the young men in the cabin out there," she said, pointing somewhere into the woods, "but I've not been up there all winter, and only the gods know what might've made its home in there since. I can't in good conscience ask anyone to sleep up there in the damp, not until I've gone and aired it out, so you'll have a room in the house. I trust you don't mind sharing a bedroom?" She paused no longer than it took to briefly acknowledge their shaken heads, and continued. "We'll put your donkeys up in the stable with my mules." She eyed the obvious swords and other weaponry attached to their packs. "I'll ask you not to take weapons into my house, please."

"Not a problem," Nico said amiably.

"Liezl, take their donkeys to the stable. Rudolf, go and fetch more firewood."

"I'll go with Liezl and take care of our packs," Fish said, thinking that he would rather not take the chance of some unaware country girl poking through any of their gear.

"I'll show you to your room," Friedma said to Nico.

The girl chattered freely as Fish followed her to the stables and helped her groom and feed the little donkeys. His mind was elsewhere. There was a patch of mud near the stables, nothing but mud as far as he could see, that kept catching his eye. Fish's uneasiness intensified sharply, and there was a sudden tingling in his fingertips, making him clench his fist in response.

And with that, Fish suddenly knew what he had been sensing all along, all day, and why it made his blood run cold as ice.

It was magic. Magic he had not felt in years. The sorcery taught to him by his father. The power he had sworn to give up when he had run away, and which he had hoped to never feel again. Shadows of the past, of another life. The long reach of his father. The hand of that dark tyrant, Arran Sylvaissen.

IT WAS MANY HOURS BEFORE Fish could be alone with Nico. The old woman and her children were eager to hear news of the outside world, stories from Ülhard; she cooked a generous meal that night, with boar stew and freshly-baked bread; and at the end of it all there was haggling over the cost of their meal and board, which was eventually settled for the price of a bag of ground coffee and a few boxes of certain medicinal herbs they had brought along.

By the time they retired to their room for the night, Fish had settled it in his mind that he would not tell Nico about the magic. There was no reason to believe that it had anything to do with his father; Arran Sylvaissen was not the only Mage-Gifted person in the world. And telling Nico would only invite questions that Fish was not prepared to answer. For all that he had idly imagined sharing his deepest secrets with his partner, Fish did not know how to even start that conversation.

Better, Fish told himself, to investigate the source of the magic first. There was a possibility that it meant no harm to them, and that all his fears were unfounded. He could but hope.

Nico seated himself on the low bed with a sigh, stretching out his long legs. The bed was the same kind they had shared back in Ülhard. There was a crackling fire in the room, and the lulling patter of rain upon the eaves outside. Fish was halfway through undressing when he saw his partner give a wince and a grimace of pain, clutching his right arm with the other.

"What happened?" he asked, coming over towards Nico

solicitously.

"I think I must've wrenched it sometime today." Nico looked up at him. "Maybe the last time I fell. I half landed on the donkey." Slowly, he picked at the lacings of his leather vambrace, and began to remove his jerkin.

Fish rummaged in his pack, looking for the ointment they used to numb sprains and muscle aches. By the time he found it, Nico had removed vambrace, jerkin, blouse and woollen undershirts, and was trying to assess the extent of the injury for himself. His shoulder was swollen bright red, and Fish winced internally in sympathy.

"You should've said something earlier," he said to Nico.

"There wasn't any time, and besides, it was so cold it didn't hurt."

"Well, all right. Give me your hand, and I'll help you up. The *other* hand, Nic." Fish helped his partner to his feet, led him over to the fire, and helped him down again. "The heat will help. Sit."

Obediently, Nico eased himself into a sitting position on the straw-covered floor, his long legs stretched out in front of him and his left shoulder leaning against the stone pillar of their wash-basin. Fish dropped down cross-legged beside him and began to rub the ointment gently into his shoulder. For a long time neither of them moved nor spoke, Nico seemingly mesmerized by the glowing logs in the fireplace and Fish fascinated by his partner's well-muscled arms and the way the firelight reflected in his eyes.

"You know what I'd really like now?" Nico murmured, closing

his eyes. "A smoke."

"Or some chocolate," Fish said longingly.

"Didn't we bring any?"

"We finished it, remember?"

Nico groaned. Fish chuckled at him. "Don't tell me you've gone all city-soft," he teased.

Nico smiled for a moment, then his face turned serious again. "It's a long time since I've been out this far into the sticks," he said softly.

Fish said nothing, reaching for his partner's shoulder again. Nico caught his hand.

The solid ground seemed to shift underneath him as Nico moved closer, his eyes like pools of dark water Fish could drown in, his lips slightly parted and only a very short distance away. If only he could bridge that gap, Fish thought desperately, but he was frozen. He could hear no sound but his own heart, which had begun to beat very loudly.

Then just as suddenly as he had approached, Nico drew back, clearing his throat and letting go of Fish's hand, his gaze receding towards the floor. Fish sat back, feeling the blood rush to his cheeks, beset with a sudden panic, barely knowing why. He had always wanted to be close to Nico, a desire that went beyond the simple, secret physical attraction he felt towards his partner. He wanted to know Nico better, to be known himself. He wanted to bring him back to where they had been only a moment ago. He asked the first question that came into his mind.

"Nic—what happened in the mountains, in the place where you grew up? Why did you leave?"

His partner looked up, and all the warmth in his eyes was absent. Nico's icy glare turned Fish's stomach, and he sat frozen, pinned to the floor.

"Remember, if you will, what makes us work so well together," Nico said quietly, dangerously.

"W-what?"

"We *don't ask questions*," Nico said with emphasis, "about each other's past."

He got to his feet, pulling himself up by the basin with his good arm, and turned his back on his partner.

Fish could have bitten off his stupid tongue. Wordlessly, he did up the lid on the tin of ointment and waited until Nico was in bed before moving from the fire.

It can never be the way you want it to be, he told himself angrily. *People like us don't have love stories. What if you did—that—with Nico, what then? You'd go right back to being partners in the morning? He's been too long without a woman to chase, that's why he looked at you that way. Don't imagine reasons that aren't there.*

Fish swallowed his own rebuke like the bitterest of medicines and put himself quietly to bed.

CHAPTER XII
NECROMES

ALTHOUGH NICO APPEARED TO HAVE completely forgotten anything uncomfortable he'd said the previous night, Fish couldn't bring himself to act normally around him in the morning. When Nico pressed him, he complained of a non-existent headache, and went outside before Nico had finished breakfast. He wandered over to the stables with the vague idea of seeing how the donkeys were getting on. That patch of mud caught his eye again, but this time, there was someone there.

Fish ducked behind the stable door, keeping out of sight. There was no doubt that the waifish girl sitting cross-legged in the dirt was the source of the magical energy that lay like cobwebs over the whole village. She was no older than fifteen, if Fish was any judge, and the clothes she wore were little more than rags, topped off with a musty-looking fox fur. Tangled black hair obscured most of her face, but she was darker than anyone in the village, similar in colouring to Fish himself, who had always stuck out in this land like a bay horse in a herd of palominos.

With her back turned to Fish, she was throwing a stick to a puppy. Alternately she caressed and played tug-of-war with it. She seemed to be absorbed in the game, but then abruptly she turned around and looked straight in Fish's direction. He tried to duck out of sight, but it was too late. Leaping to her feet, she ran behind a neighbouring house, vanishing from his view. The puppy stayed where it was, happily chewing on the stick. Fish followed the girl, trying to see where she had gone, but she had vanished seemingly into thin air.

Walking back towards the house, trailed by the puppy still carrying its stick, he came across Liezl doing her chores. The puppy nosed happily about her feet.

"Liezl," Fish said, "there was a young girl here."

"The girl dressed in rags? With the long black hair?" Fish nodded, and Liezl grinned. "Don't worry about her. She's harmless. Turned up last year in the autumn." She hefted the basket she carried against her hip.

"Let me help you with that," Fish offered, and she relinquished the basket.

"It's for the chickens," she said, and showed him to a barn where two dozen fat fowl were pecking around in the warmth. She began to shovel out the muck, after showing him where to scatter the feed.

"The girl," Fish said above the animated clucking, "does she have a name?"

"She doesn't seem to understand much of the common speech," Liezl replied, "but she answers to the name of Bree." She shook brown hair from her forehead, and turned to Fish with a stern look. "She ain't no trouble, honest. She does odd chores in the village, and gets food for it. She doesn't steal."

"I only think we may be able to help her," Fish said cryptically. He had his suspicions about how a young girl with the Mage-Gift could have fetched up here. "And she may be able to help us."

As Harold Velman had promised, all the men and half the women of the village were suddenly eager to help them—or at least, to have their say in what was happening. They all gathered in what was evidently the village's only meeting hall, a low wooden building with tables and benches smoke-darkened and stained with age. One of the village men had started a fire in the central pit, and started heating an enormous basin of sour red wine, to which he was now adding dried fruit and spices. Harold and about half a dozen other men sat with Nico, poring over the maps he had brought with him. Fish looked on for a while, only half-listening to Nico's battle plans. He himself had never had much interest in strategy and planning, and the thought of co-ordinating this lot into a viable fighting force made his head ache. Nico was beginning to look like the kind of man that other men might follow into battle, but this was not something Fish had ever wanted for himself.

Does Nico want it? he wondered. *Would he someday want to sit where Harold now sits, to sway the hearts of the men who follow him?* They were a long way from Ülhard now, with no reason to ever return. If Nico wanted, he could remain here for ever. It would be a great deal less glamorous than the life they had led as hired knives in the city, but perhaps Nico would like that. Fish tried to imagine if Nico spent ten years here, married one of those stout brown-haired girls who were already giggling over him, had seven sons and twice as many dogs, and directed wood-cutting operations every day. It was surprisingly easy to imagine.

The heat inside the hall was stifling, the conversation far too loud. Fish took a cup of spiced wine out to the porch, where rain was drizzling miserably from the eaves. The fog had parted slightly since yesterday, and he could see all the way down the hamlet's main road, rutted with cart tracks and muddied with the hooves of mountain mules.

As he stood there, warming his hands on the cup of wine rather than drinking it, he noticed that a lone figure had crept out from the gap between two houses, and now stood watching him in the rain.

Fish started. The overwhelming feeling of magic was back. Less sinister now that he had identified it, but still crawling around in the recesses of his mind like the ghost of a slug, raising the hairs on the back of his neck and sending shivers of cold-heat down his spine. The girl watched him steadfastly. Her long black hair was plastered to the side of her face and down her back, sopping wet and heavy with the rain.

She turned, and Fish started forward, spilling half the wine over his hands. Impatiently, he set the cup down on the ground and stepped into the rain. "Wait!" he yelled. She had already fled, disappearing behind the log house on Fish's left. Cursing, Fish ran after her. He was just in time to see her disappear into the stretch of brushwood that grew beside Friedma's homestead.

He was about to follow her when he heard a shout behind him. Turning, he saw Nico striding up. Although his right arm was still functionally useless, bound in a sling against his body to give his shoulder time to heal, his sword was buckled to his belt, albeit on the wrong side. Nico claimed to be ambidextrous, Fish knew, but he had never seen his partner actually try to fight with his left hand before.

"What are you doing?" Nico demanded.

Fish hesitated. "There's a stray girl in the village," he began slowly, aware of how questionable he sounded. "I think she's from Qwu'Mallorn." When Nico looked blank, he explained, "The Forest of the Morning."

"One of the magic folk?"

"Yes," Fish said. "She's obviously foreign—she has no family here. The villagers don't know where she came from." He looked urgently at Nico. "She must have escaped from the slavers. She may know if they have a hideout nearby. She might be able to tell us how many there are, or where they're hiding out in the mountains."

Nico gave his partner a curious look. "And this girl is the reason you've been so distracted?"

"We've got to follow her," Fish said, turning and darting into the forest. There was a path of sorts, and he could see the slight prints of the girl's thin shoes in the mud. He heard Nico following him. The light rain stirred with his breath as he strode past trees festooned with delicate shoots of green. The ground gradually led uphill, and Fish sensed that they were leaving the village behind. The girl's footsteps were easy to track, leading straight on until they ran dead into the face of a sheer cliff.

Fish looked up. The cliff was rocky, with jutting angles everywhere. It towered a few feet over the top of Nico's head. "She must have climbed," he said.

"You're right," Nico said, examining the mess of prints in the mud. "Looks like she comes up here often. Maybe she doesn't sleep in the village. I wonder why." The tone of his voice made it clear that Nico did not think it could be for any good reason. "Let's go back," he said impatiently. "We won't find her this way."

There was magic still stuffing up all of Fish's senses, so thick on the ground it was choking him. "No, she'll be easy to find," he insisted. He could see the route she had taken up the wet rocks, the way the mud had been scuffed at the top of the cliff. It would be easy enough for him to follow her.

Nico stood looking on in silence as Fish made his way up the face of the cliff, using the same rocks the girl had done. It was as easy as he had thought it would be; the rocks were only slightly slippery, and Fish was not much heavier than the girl herself. Soon he was wriggling his way over the edge, regaining his footing in the mud at the top of the cliffside.

There were no trees up here; he could very well have convinced himself that he had crossed over into a different world. There had been no wind down in the village, but here it persistently blew icy drops of rain into his face. Fish thought of Bree's thin rags, and shivered in sympathy.

In front of him, the mountains seemed to open up, peaks upon sparsely-grassed peaks, with the bare bulwarks of Svanlyn's black buttresses far in the background. Even the lower peaks were topped with snow, and the faraway ones looked like nothing so much as long white fangs ready to crunch up the sky. Out here, the wind was clearing the clouds from those high sharp peaks, and the sun was no longer just a memory.

He could not see where the girl had gone; her fresh prints were obscured by old ones, and they seemed to go off into a dozen different directions. There was a sandstone cliff face a few hundred yards away that seemed as if it might have caves, but the ground rose steeply from where Fish was standing, and he could see that it would be a long climb just to get to the foot of the cliff.

Fish was about to turn around and call off the search, when he heard a loud grunt behind him and turned to see Nico emerging over the rocks. Horrified, he went to help him to his feet. "What are you thinking?" he scolded. "Your shoulder needs time to heal, Nic."

Nico had loosened the sling. "It isn't as bad as you think," he said shortly, but the catch in his breath as he leaned his weight against Fish belied his words. "I had to see what was keeping you up here. Ah." Nico scowled at his partner, gesturing around at the peaks and canyons in their view. "The perfect spot for an ambush."

"A scenic spot for an ambush," Fish retorted, countering Nico's sarcasm with his own.

Nico rolled his eyes. "Well, as long as we're here now, I might as well make some sense of these tracks." He bent over the muddle of prints in the mud. "Well, not all of these are hers. Look. Hobnailed boots, like yours and mine." He pointed at the very old outline of a boot. It was rapidly sinking away with the rain, but it was clear that it had frozen in place in the mud for several weeks.

Fish frowned over the print, then wandered some distance towards the rising hills. The ground he walked on was half frozen, and he left clear prints of his own. There seemed to be a path of sorts leading to a nearby rise, but he found no more prints. Turning to go back to Nico, he thought he saw movement in the corner of his eye, and froze.

There was no warning, just a miasma of dark magic suddenly washing over him, sending him almost to his knees. At the top of the rise, five black shapes materialized in his vision.

Fish took a horrified step backwards as the creatures came streaming over the ridge. "Nico!" he screamed, his partner's name ripping from his throat. "Run!"

As Fish raced towards him, Nico planted his feet in the mud and drew his sword with his left hand, the metal sheath making an icy ringing sound. Fish reached the edge of the cliff. There was nowhere to run, but they could still make it down. He looked desperately back at Nico, who clearly had no intention of running.

"There's only five of them," he growled, hefting his sword as the grey-skinned creatures rushed towards them.

"Nico," Fish began, "you don't understand—"

His words were cut off as Nico sprang forward, sword in hand. The foremost creature rushed at him and ran straight into the sword, which Nico had angled for its neck. There was a loud *thwack*, and it sank into the mud, head nearly severed from its body. Nico pivoted, but there was no time for him to recover. His rush had brought him within reach of the other four. One of them leapt at him, teeth bared in a snarl, a growl ripping from deep within its throat. It collided with his right shoulder, long nails clawing at him. Nico gave a scream of shock and pain and fell back. The footing was poor, ice mixed with mud on top of slick wet grass. And Nico, who was always stalwart and firm-standing, Nico who never seemed to feel any weariness nor pain, who had never misstepped for as long as Fish had known him, slipped in the mud and went down like a fallen stone.

Everything happened so fast, and yet the split second when Nico fell seemed to last an eternity. Flashes of memory from years before played in front of Fish's eyes, as clearly as though he were that frightened eleven-year-old boy all over again. The way their prisoner had screamed when his father strung him up. The way the man's blood had spattered across Fish's face when his father cut his throat. The glowing energy that had spilled from the man, visible only to those who had given themselves to the goddess of blood magic, and how his father had shown him how to seize that energy, take mastery of it, and send it back into the lifeless cadaver to make one more for his army of dead men.

Fish had not used his magic in eight years. He had placed mental blocks around his own mind in order to not touch that part of himself. He had never once fed that power, never allowed it to even rattle the fetters he had placed on it, and with it he had locked all the tormented memories of his childhood away. But in that brief moment when he saw Nico fall, saw the hands of darkness reaching for him, ready to rip and kill, there was no time for mental blocks and conscious thought, only raw instinct. His father had trained that instinct well when Fish was only a boy, drilled him for hours and hours on end until the reflex became more natural than breathing, and now, when his body stood frozen in horror, his mind paralyzed with fear, the magic broke free of its restraints and lashed out to save the life of the one he could not lose.

The red-hot cloud of power broke free from his body and streaked towards the necromes, shimmering the air with its intensity.

Nico only escaped that cloud because he had already hit the ground. There was an impact as if the hills had shifted, and the air around the dark creatures heated in a blinding flash of energy, causing their bodies to burst into flame.

Fish had only the barest of moments to react to what he had done. Nico's silver-edged sword and the silver medallion he always wore were providing him with a measure of protection from the magic, but it was not long before the physical heat of the power would reach him. Clumsily, Fish took hold of the magic, the heat, and flung it away from Nico. There was an impact on the hillside, and a cloud of dust went flying as the muddy ground was baked dry all in a single moment. Shaking, Fish stumbled over to Nico's side. He was still on the ground, holding his sword with a grip gone white, his face a mask of confusion. The sky was raining baked clay and burned body parts.

"W-w-w-what," Nico began. It was the first time Fish had ever heard him stammer.

"We've got to get out of here!" Fish cried, and grabbed at Nico's shirt, trying to haul him to his feet.

Nico's gaze locked onto his, and Fish flinched. Nico had a quick temper sometimes, was prone to bouts of sharpness and sarcasm, but his partner had never looked at him quite like this before. It was as though Nico was seeing him for the first time, and did not love whatever it was he saw. Fish faltered, falling down on one knee, both fists still buried in Nico's shirt.

A ringing voice pierced the air. "What have we here?"

Fish whipped his head up to see one of the many nightmares he had hoped never to come across again. The past had collided with him, he was still reeling from the impact, and now, there was even more.

A few yards away stood a young man, flanked by necromes on either side, dressed in shining armour from open-faced helm to silvered boots. He was eight years Fish's senior, and it was possible to tell that he was half of Morgein blood, half nonmage Vailanan. His skin was tanned to a deep golden hue, and yet his shock of straight hair had both blond and ash in it. Even his eyes were a mixed colour, golden-brown and green together. He had inherited the height and bulk of his nonmage father; he wielded the kind of long sword that would never balance in Fish's hand, which he now brandished in front of him. But he had inherited the magic from his Morgein mother, and was as formidable an opponent as Fish at his best.

Fish was not at his best just then, and well aware of it. Still, defiance carried him to his feet, facing the man, shielding Nico as best he could. He raised a hand to scrape his sweat-sodden hair from his forehead, and the man gave a gasp, taking a half step backwards.

"Surely not!" he said in genuine shock, as if to himself, but he recovered quickly. "*You*. Deryck."

Fish's fist clenched as his heart hammered halfway up into his throat. "Taunus," he managed in return. There was little point in pretending he did not remember. There was already a broad grin on

Taunus's face, and Fish remembered, with a chill in his gut, things that would follow the appearance of that grin . . .

"My long-lost little brother!" Taunus laughed nastily. "What Father would not give to be standing here now. He swore, once, that if ever he saw you again he'd flay you alive and let the magic slowly leak from your body." He gave a mirthless laugh. "But as it is only me, only Taunus here, you need not fear." His eyes became as hard as stones. "It is for others to punish you, not me."

There was a whisper of wind at Fish's shoulder, and he half-turned to see Nico, now on his feet again, still holding his sword in the wrong hand.

Taunus turned to his necromes. "Take them alive."

With incredible speed the creatures pounced, coming towards them in a frantic rush. Fish could not easily tell how many there were, but this was an army in truth.

He reached for his long-dormant power again, this time directing the energy consciously, choosing his targets selectively, sending lashes of fire from his hands to stop the first surge. It was the only thing he could think to do, the only power that might spare them from Taunus. He could not see Nico's face, had no idea what his partner was thinking, but there was no time to spare on speculation. The necromes kept coming on, streaming past him towards Nico, and Fish half-saw, half-felt Nico engage in battle, laying about him with his sword.

From the corner of his eye, Fish saw Taunus move.

In only a few moments he was upon Fish, who just managed to fumble for his own sword before he was engaged. Blades clashed together, and Fish had to retreat before his brother's advance. He was weary from unwonted usage of power long kept dormant, and Taunus was taking full advantage of that, coming on forcefully whilst Fish kept backing away, looking desperately for an opening that never came.

It was inevitable, in a protracted sword fight, that a weary opponent would leave himself open to attack, and that moment came for Fish as he knew it would. Taunus's sword smacked into his unguarded side, robbing him of breath and sending him stumbling backwards. Fish's leather armour saved him from serious injury, but now he was half-sprawled upon the ground, at his brother's mercy.

Frantically Fish racked his brain, trying to find something to say that might halt Taunus in his tracks. But he was too late. All was lost; he could no longer hear the sounds of battle from Nico's side, and he was desperately afraid for his partner.

A gauntleted hand struck him across the face, and for the next few moments, all Fish saw was stars.

When he finally fumbled himself back to his knees, head spinning with nausea, a hand seized him by the hair and pulled his head up. Taunus's face blurred before him, as cruel and cold as ever he remembered, his mocking smile just as Fish had seen it in nightmares past.

"This moment was always going to come, Deryck," he said

softly. "You could never have escaped us."

Fish's head swam, and he stayed silent. As Taunus stood back up, letting go of his hair, he saw a slight, tangle-haired figure come up behind his brother, and the flash of a ragged fox fur.

So you led me into this after all, waif, he thought to himself. *Mystery solved. You belong to Taunus.*

"Chain them and take them to the underground," Taunus declared, and Fish felt a momentary pang of relief to realize that Nico was still alive. But the world fogged in front of his eyes, and all he knew was the stench of death and dark sorcery.

Chapter XIII
Windfall

S PEECHLESSLY DANNINE WALKED AMONGST THE BODIES in the mist of early dawn.

She had never seen anything like this, and until now, she never would have believed it possible. Spells of undoing simply *could not* be this powerful! It went against everything she had learned, all she had experienced in her many years of practising magic.

Going out to the mountains was one of the duties Dannine usually relished. Her father had instructed her to help Taunus build up his army, and so Dannine had established a breeding ground for her own necromes in a warren of caves conveniently located on the north-eastern side of the mountain range. It was not a strenuous job. She simply made a comfortable camp for herself, gave the existing necromes her instructions, and they did the rest. Always, before, they had returned to the caves with their ranks swelled. Arran did not wish to declare himself openly in Svanfeld yet, so they had to be careful, but in this wild country, there were always stragglers and wanderers, and even a very isolated hamlet or two.

Dannine clenched a gauntleted fist against her thigh, and the scar across her palm throbbed dully. *Why* hadn't she been scrying for these necromes? Why had she been blind?

She could answer that for herself well enough. Dannine had three companies of necromes in her caves already, and she had to send them on different ranging courses lest they be seen, or tracked. She could only follow one company at a time, so she chose to conserve her resources and only scry for each company once during the night. She had followed *this* company up towards the remote farmhouses, then severed the link to check on the others. When they failed to come back in the morning, she had tried to scry again, but to her horror, had discovered that she could not. The necromes did not exist any more, and she shuddered to think of what kind of adversary faced her now. To undo the necrome-magic in such a way that she, their creator, did not even notice that the spell had been undone!

The corpses were just corpses; there was nothing more to discover here. There was some evidence that other magic had been done; baked earth attested to a fireball, and she could sense spell-residue. She cast around for tracks, but the morning was misty and a light rain had fallen during the night. Everything was mud and confusion for yards around.

She cast around with her magical senses, and found a slight presence some way off to the east. From what she could tell, not nearly powerful enough to have done this, but perhaps they were exhausted, or conserving their power. She turned her face towards the presence, wondering why it felt familiar. Was it another soldier, a scout from Qwu'Mallorn? Surely not. They had never sent their spies into Svanfeld, and not a single Morgein soldier whom Dannine had ever faced had been powerful enough to frighten her.

She would follow that presence, of course. There was no question of that. For a moment Dannine allowed herself to feel the anguish that burned in her heart. Someone more powerful than she was. Someone who could defeat her. Who could kill her.

What am I, if not my father's faithful daughter? Dannine would do anything for her father, even if it was to pay the ultimate price. She turned towards her quetzal; it stood ready to ride.

Just as she was rearranging the flying-saddle to suit her for a long journey, Dannine felt a tell-tale prickling at the edge of her magical senses, a tentative probe that spoke of a minor spell being performed just under her nose. She knew each of her siblings' magical signatures as well as she knew her father's laboratory, and Dannine detected the overtones of Taunus's clumsy magic.

She fumbled at the saddle-bags, undid a leather clasp and drew out a small, leather-bound notebook. Every vellum page within was quite blank, but Dannine could clearly feel the residue of magic on each. She flicked through until she found the last used page, somewhere in the middle of the book. Hastily scribbled letters appeared, glowing with the magic that had just engendered them.

The words vanished as soon as she read them, rendering the book completely empty to mundane eyes, but the message was branded into Dannine's mind as though she were seeing it over and over again.

Deryck. She had never expected this message to come. She had always thought that if anyone discovered the whereabouts of their erstwhile brother, it would be herself. For a moment she could not even comprehend what had happened, could not understand that her once-brother had stumbled right into Taunus's grasp, that he was being held, waiting for her.

Then realization flowed through her, and the anger began.

Deryck. Taunus was holding him, for *her* to deal with. She would see him again, after eight long years apart, eight years of agony. She could do to him whatever she pleased. Rage flared in Dannine's mind, and reason flew at the very thought.

I should tell Father. I should send the message on to him. But Taunus had not sent this message to Arran. Instead he had contacted her directly, knowing full well that she wanted to deal with Deryck in her own way . . .

Why should Father know? she asked herself fiercely. *Why? All he needs to know is that we caught Deryck . . . he doesn't need to know that we caught him alive.* She trembled at the thought of deceiving her father, but the rage and the temptation were too strong to rescind now. *We will present him with Deryck's corpse at the end . . .*

The quetzal squawked, and Dannine started as if brought out of a trance. What of her current task? What of the sorcerer who was strong enough to reduce her necromes down to nothing? Duty remonstrated hopelessly against anger in her heart. She had made up her mind the moment the fiery message had appeared. She would not, *could* not forsake this windfall. Dannine had always done her duty, what her father expected of her, and nothing more. Until today.

I will send the necromes after the sorcerer, she decided. *I can scry all the way and send them orders down the link.* That would be a lot of effort, but there was no other way. And the business with Deryck ought not to take too long . . .

She looked around, at the hanging mist and brooding clouds. *Bad weather to fly.* The temperature was dropping rapidly, telling of a storm brewing somewhere along the great mountain range. *But that's just too bad.*

Without further ado, she swung into the quetzal's saddle. There was much work ahead of her. She would have to persuade the necromes to remain a safe distance away from their quarry, and that was always difficult. The instinct to kill was always uppermost in their simple minds; they hated the living with every fibre of their cold hearts. *But this sorcerer can undo the binding magic.* Dannine wasn't risking that happening again, and she knew that the necromes would obey. Her will was well honed, and she was practised in exercising it.

She would decide what became of Deryck, this time. Her father could have everything: he could have his kingdom, the world, her life and devotion, but he could not have the life of the boy she had once called her brother.

Deryck is not my brother anymore. Once, he could have stood at Father's right hand, and spared me that place. But he thought only of himself. Only thought of how he *could get away. I stayed. I was loyal. I did everything Father asked. When Deryck left, he didn't betray Father. He betrayed* me.

A cold rage sped Dannine's wings as she set her sights towards the southwest, the way ahead barricaded by fangs of white rising into the distance.

CHAPTER XIV
BLIGHT

SOMEONE WAS SHAKING HER. Velda turned around in bed, confusedly, and murmured, "Em, what's the matter?" Her bed was so hard, almost like the shelf of a tomb, and she was so cold—

Memory flooded back as she opened her eyes and saw the rocky interior of the cave where she had bedded down for the night with a handsome stranger who was certainly not her husband. Albryan was crouching over her, shaking her shoulder to wake her in semi-darkness.

"We need to go now," he said earnestly.

"What?" Velda could discern a thin line of light entering the cave at a low angle. It must be the very break of dawn. "Why?"

"She is nearby," Albryan answered cryptically. "We need to find

Hiram and leave."

Before she could ask any more questions, Albryan had left the cave. Not wanting to stay there alone, Velda followed him out. The shoulder of the mountain was swathed in fog. Velda squinted into the east. The sun was barely visible, a wavering line of brightness driving the fog before it. She gave a sigh of relief. It would be easy to get back to her house.

"Which way do we go?" Albryan's voice had a queer note of panic in it, and he turned round and round in place as if trying to see through the whiteness of the fog.

Despite the grave situation, despite her hunger and exhaustion and everything that had happened the previous day, Velda smiled.

BY THE TIME THEY GOT BACK to the farmhouse, the fog was lifting, and landmarks could be seen yards ahead. They found Hiram on the doorstep, anxiously scanning the fields as he waited. When they emerged out of the fog, he stood up and a sudden smile transformed his face, creasing all weariness from his brow.

Over a hasty breakfast of the things Velda had sitting around in the kitchen, they explained to the old man what had happened the previous evening. Albryan did most of the talking, with Velda answering a question here and there. Hiram took all of it in with remarkable composure.

"We are leaving today, then?" he asked at last, when Albryan finished talking.

"We have to." Albryan cleared his plate and leaned his elbows on the little table. He looked over at Velda, who was sitting next to him. She took a last bite of her toast and set it down, no more appetite.

"The necromes are gone," Albryan continued, looking directly at her now, "but there is still danger, for me and for you as well, Velda. The sorcerer who controls them is somewhere out there, too close for my liking, and she can track me quite effectively through the magic. Whether she can find you that way—" Albryan broke off, and shrugged. "But you would be safe in Qwu'Mallorn," he continued. "Safe—and what's more, this ability of yours—I think that you might be able to bring the war against Arran Sylvaissen to an end."

"The war?" she repeated, confused. "How?"

"I don't know yet," Albryan admitted. "But the key to all this must be in Qwu'Mallorn. I've never heard of anything like this ability you have." He looked over at Hiram, who shook his head gravely, his sharp eyes fixed on Velda.

"You were preparing to leave Lynborder, were you not?" Hiram asked quietly. "Where are you planning to go?"

"Armour City," Velda replied. "To—"

"To see if you could find any trace of family," Hiram completed quietly, and Velda remembered, all at once, that the old man himself had come *here* searching for the same thing, and was the first clue of any kind she'd ever had that perhaps her family was out there after all . . .

"And you—you're going with Albryan?" she queried. "To the Forest of the Morning?"

He nodded. "There are few places where one such as me can find refuge."

"One such as you?"

"An enemy of the Vailanan king," Hiram clarified. His voice was still soft, and he hesitated for a moment before starting to speak again.

"With all that you two have just told me—with your gift, Velda," he began, "going to Armour City with our king on the throne would be like sailing full-mast into a storm. I do not know what your ability portends, yet it is unique, and bound to attract attention at some point. As for your birth family"—he glanced quickly away and back towards her again—"that trail is nineteen years cold. You are unlikely to find more than *I* have found here."

Hiram held her gaze for a long moment, until Albryan touched her arm and she turned to look at him. The question still lay naked in his eyes.

"I'll come with you," Velda said, hiding her lingering doubts behind a genuine smile. "To the Forest of the Morning."

The smile that Albryan gave her in return seemed to light up the whole room without any aid needed from the absent sun.

THEY LEFT THAT SAME DAY, collecting Hiram's mule in town and loading it up with sackfuls of travelling supplies. Velda left a few notes at the monastery: where she was headed; that her pigs had escaped and could be kept by anyone who happened to catch them. Free bacon, she knew, would be a marvellous distraction from whatever they happened to discover in her wake. She was not sure what anyone would make of the heap of necromes—now freshly reduced to human corpses—that she had left in old Stein's fields. "Best say nothing and get away quickly," Albryan advised when she asked him, and Velda could have sworn she saw a sudden amusement dance in Hiram's eyes as he looked on.

Velda had spent all her life in the same corner of the map, the eastern extremity of the Svanlyn mountains just before the range broke off into the Sea of Calms. The furthest she had ever been from home was the town of Palace, fifty miles away, slightly higher into the mountains, and half the size of Lynborder. She had never even been to Sulshome, the mid-sized mercantile town from which ships set sail to faraway destinations.

The Forest of the Morning was in truth not much further away than Palace, though it was a winding route from Lynborder down to the lowlands. At the foot of the mountain lay a wide, shallow canyon of land populated by Vailanan farmers. Known as the "land of the delta-valley," it was well-watered, with tributaries from the mountains flowing into the mighty River Granite, densely wooded, and host to many acres of fertile farmland. The shortest way to

Qwu'Mallorn was to cross the delta-valley—an easy, scenic journey, as Albryan and Hiram both described it—and then climb into the flint hills that formed the western border. The Morgei had erected some sort of magical barrier all along the border, to prevent invaders from penetrating into their sacred lands.

"We won't be safe until we've crossed the Border," Albryan warned them, more than once, along the way. "We'll be in Vailana, on Arran Sylvaissen's lands. We have to reach Qwu'Mallorn before he realizes we're there." A heavy shadow would cross Albryan's eyes whenever he spoke thus, and Velda would think of the savage creatures she had somehow overcome, and of the people in the town she was leaving behind, and wonder whether she was making the right choice. But there was something about Albryan which drew her irresistibly to him, and despite his obvious burdens he was never anything but soft-spoken and courteous towards her.

The road down from Lynborder was a well-travelled one, yet according to Hiram it was very lonely, these days, compared to what it would have been twenty years ago. They only met one other travelling party on the mountain road, a small caravan of traders and fortune-seekers bound for Sulshome. It was late evening when they came face-to-face with the caravan's wagons slogging up the winding road, and the three of them gratefully accepted the guard captain's offer to camp with them for the night and trade news.

The news from Vailana did not sound hopeful. "Whole land's going to shit," said one of the fortune-seekers, a lad no older than sixteen who had apparently joined the caravan in Asmyth. He was one of a knot of boys from small villages and farms, seeing no future in the place they had been born. Most of them were hoping to become sailors, or somehow set themselves up in Sulshome as labourers. There were a few girls in the group as well, and a young couple with a small child.

"Watch your language, Bert," the young father cautioned. "There's ladies present."

The young man scowled. "I can't tell the truth about what *our king's* doing to the country? No-one comes through Asmyth anymore except for *his* armies. There was a big group come marching through two weeks ago, heading for the delta-valley. Couple o' idiots from Asmyth even joined up with them." He shook his head. "I wanted nought to do with it. So much for our king." He turned and spat into the campfire.

Albryan stirred. "Why were they going to the delta-valley?"

Bert shrugged. "Mother Thäle only knows. None of it makes a lick o' sense to me."

"There were rumours, in Armour City," spoke up the young mother, restraining her child as it gazed covetously at the bright coals in the fire. "Sedition and rebellion. It seems some of the folk in the delta-valley were harbouring those with the Mage-Gift."

The others muttered a little at this, and Albryan exchanged an unreadable glance with Hiram.

"Can't they just agree on a truce?" one of the girls said quietly.

"Mages stay in their land, like they always have, and they leave Vailana to us?"

"You forget," Bert spoke up again, "the bastard who sits the throne of Vailana is as much a mage as *they* are. Their war has nought to do with us, but we're the ones suffering for it."

"Better not to speak of such things," the father said quietly. His wife nodded vigorously, and that was the end of the conversation.

"Why *has* there been such a long war?" Velda asked Albryan the next day when they were back on the road, only the three of them, the caravan making its slow way up towards Lynborder. Velda was taking her turn to ride on the mule, which Hiram had named Santie. Albryan loped beside her, tireless as always, seemingly driven on by something no-one else could discern.

"Arran Sylvaissen wants Qwu'Mallorn as part of Vailana." The answer came quickly, and Albryan's expression turned even more grim than usual as he turned to look back at her. "With his . . . particular *creed*, however, it is anyone's guess what he will do with us once he has it."

"Our king was not the first to propose that mage and nonmage should live separately," Hiram remarked from the other side of the mule, "but he was the first Mage-Gifted ever to espouse such ideals. When he appeared and started talking of driving the Morgei back into Qwu'Mallorn, extremists in the southern regions of Vailana were happy to join him."

"But why does he want Qwu'Mallorn in the first place? Isn't

Vailana enough?"

"For people such as him," Albryan interjected, "nothing will ever be enough."

"Qwu'Mallorn has always been part of Vailana," Hiram replied. "Twenty years ago, there was no magical barrier, no reason to distrust outsiders. The Morgei always had some degree of independent rule over the forest, but they had to abide by the laws of the Council in Armour City."

"When it became clear that the people of Vailana were siding with Arran," Albryan said, "the matriarchs in the ruling Councils of our nine regions took control."

"Not all the people of Vailana sided with Arran," Hiram rebutted softly, and Albryan made an apologetic face.

"Of course not. But folk in the south—Zarath, Cythece, Cygnath—they have always been strange."

"Very few Mage-Gifted ever lived in those regions," Hiram said. "People fear what they have never seen for themselves. Exotic magic, strange abilities. Our king was always cautious to keep his abilities private, and let his nonmage followers do most of the polemicking for him."

The day wore on as Hiram continued to talk, of how Vailana had been in the past, a peaceful refuge for folk of all colours and creeds. He spoke of groups Velda had only heard of in history books: the monotheistic Zammùk, fair-haired Novlayans and Arvenians, the Sang people from the eastern jungles, who shared the gift of magic with the Morgei. The old man was a vast repository of knowledge, and yet Velda had, thus far, found none of the answers she sought most. Hiram was not easy to query regarding the events of his own past. Sometimes a question or simple remark would trigger a sudden silence and stare into the middle distance, a state from which the old man recovered only when prodded. It proved impossible to sustain any kind of conversation with him on topics that were apt to trigger this. Velda had already given up, telling herself that perhaps he would be more forthcoming once they had settled down, or when he got to know her a little better.

At last, on the fourth morning of travel, they reached a small bridge over a foaming stream which leapt with boundless energy down on its way to the foot of the mountain. Albryan smiled for what seemed to Velda like the first time since she had agreed to go with him.

They turned off the trade road, not crossing the bridge, and followed the stream downhill for the rest of that morning. It was a steep and narrow road, leading between great grey, shadowy boulders. In the afternoon, the footpath finally rounded the edge of a cliff that overlooked the surrounding lands. They walked from the shadow of the mountain into the bright sunlight, and stood dazzled, with a majestic view of the way they were bound to travel.

The world seemed suddenly new-made to Velda, who all her life had been surrounded by pine-and-broadleaf forest under soaring black peaks. Far below, the ground flattened and rounded into grassland glowing a green so bright it seemed ethereal. The mountain stream cascaded right over the edge of the cliff, falling into a lazy river which wound its way through the meadow. All was peaceful, the grassland basking in the warm spring sunshine. The only sounds were the rush of the waterfall as it thundered down the rocks, the lazy hum of bees foraging in flowers nearby, the excitable chatter of long-tailed mousebirds in the berry bushes that dotted the cliff's edge.

Albryan shaded his eyes as they stood looking down, propping his foot on a rock, much as if he were trying to see somehow beyond the distance. Finally he turned.

"We can see Qwu'Mallorn on the horizon," he announced. Velda squinted into the east. There was a dark green blur framing the broad meadowland. Albryan gazed at it with a peculiar, longing yet almost fearful, look upon his face.

"The river below us is called the Dreaming Water," Hiram said to Velda. "We are seeing it at an auspicious time, swelled by the mountain snowmelt. Usually it runs brown, not blue." He turned towards Albryan. "Two days' travel, by my estimation, until we reach the River Granite."

Albryan nodded. Velda had grown used to the range of grim and sulky expressions he had worn since their journey begun, but his face seemed touched by a particularly deep shadow at the moment. "We'll have to camp out tonight," he said. "We should stop early. Crossing the river will be easier in the morning." He looked as though he might have wanted to say more, but turned away from the view and back towards the boulder-strewn path.

They descended the steep hill-shoulder in single file. The narrow path would not allow it any other way, winding round and round towards the foot of the mountain. The air grew steadily more humid as they went. By the time they reached the bottom, they were all sticky, and the mule was switching her tail against the midges, laying her ears flat against her head.

They did not go far before Albryan called a halt. There was scrub forest and shrubland where they stopped, beside a brook which presumably also flowed into the Dreaming Water somewhere ahead. It sang through the shady trees, and the water was clear and cold as ice. They left Santie grazing happily on the soft grass beside it. Albryan found an enormous thorn-tree, probably the biggest one in those woods, and built a campfire just outside the reach of its spiky branches.

With the glow of the fire on her face and the trunk of the great tree shielding her from the intermittent breeze, Velda felt reasonably cosy, even though she was unused to sleeping outside. As darkness began to fall, she undid her hair from its bun and combed it out with her fingers in the light of the fire. She was thinking about putting it in braids, when suddenly she looked up and saw Albryan in front of her, standing uncertainly, his arms crossed over his chest and his face clouded with worry.

"Velda," he said softly. She felt a sudden pang of anxiety, and looked around for Hiram. He was nestled in a hollow nearby, wrapped securely in his cloak and bedroll, but his eyes were still open.

"Could I have a word with you?"

Velda nodded and moved to make a space for him to sit down, but Albryan shook his head.

"Alone." His voice was barely audible.

Something in his face made Velda forget all about her hair, and she stood up. She glanced back towards Hiram as they made their way into the woods, away from the campsite. He made no motion to indicate that he had seen them. Velda wondered if Albryan had asked him to keep his distance. *For what?* she wondered, and could not shake a sense of unease.

They were about a furlong away from the camp before Albryan sank down upon a fallen log, motioning for Velda to sit beside him. He glanced briefly around as she took her seat, knotting his fingers together in a way that betrayed tension. Velda wondered what on earth he wanted.

But the young man seemed in no hurry to explain himself. He sat silently for a long moment in the dusk, not looking at her. Velda grew impatient, but didn't try to push him.

"We are not far from my homeland now," Albryan finally said, folding his arms as if he were trying to stop himself fidgeting. "I have tried to bring you there as fast as I can possibly manage." He drew his shoulders up, crouching forward. "I suppose I have seemed out of sorts all day," he said. Velda's mouth quirked, but she let him continue without interruption.

"Your ability," he said abruptly, and turned towards her. "You truly had no idea what you were capable of?"

"Absolutely none."

"And you'd never seen magic ever before? Never had anyone perform magic on you, near you?"

Velda shook her head. "Magic is unknown in Lynborder."

Albryan's eyes, shadowed grey-green in the dusk, betrayed a strange expression. It seemed almost like fear.

"And you can't explain how the power works? What you felt when you undid that dark magic?"

Velda hesitated. "It didn't feel . . . quite like me," she finally admitted. "It was more as if there was something—something else, beside me. I can't explain it. But I wanted to defend you—and the other *thing*, whatever it was, it wanted to help me. I know that sounds nuts," she ended lamely.

Albryan gave her a long, measuring look, his eyes both seeing and not-seeing her for a brief moment. "Well, I confirm that you're alone in there right now," he said softly. He put a hand on the back of his neck, then quickly drew it away in the same movement, as if he had touched something that pained him. "I owe you a lot already," he continued, dropping his voice even lower. "But I . . . I have to ask you to help me. Yet again." He sounded so stricken that Velda's breath caught in her throat.

"What's the matter?" she whispered.

"Hiram and I explained to you how we met in the dungeons of

Armour City." She nodded briefly. Albryan took a deep breath and continued, "But I haven't told you—haven't told anyone—that when I was captured, they *did* something to me." Velda searched his face, not understanding, as he continued to speak. "I don't know how much you understand about magic, but it—" He broke off, seemingly searching for the right words. "For those of us who are born with the Gift, it lies at the core of our being, entwined with everything that makes us who we are. Arran Sylvaissen has put something in there, somehow, that is not me. That is *wrong*." He shook his head. "Subtle, yet I have felt it grow every day since leaving his dungeon. I don't know what he intends to do with it, whether perhaps it will grow into something dark and terrible, or somehow give him control over me, and I *cannot* return to Qwu'Mallorn with it still there."

He looked like he would have continued to speak, to try to make her understand, but Velda moved forward. She reached for his hands, clasping them in both of hers. At the first mention of Arran Sylvaissen's name, something had surged up inside her, and she had immediately recognized what it was.

Standing outside of her, the power helped her to read Albryan's feelings in their physical contact. Strongest of all, the twin emotions of shame and fear, underwritten by a complicated nest of longings which she instinctively shied from. There was the feeling of guilt, for being captured in the first place; self-blame, for the mistake that had led him to fall into the hands of the blood sorcerer. And overlying everything, radiating from him, the strong sense of violation, wrongness, something within the self that *should not be*.

She leaned towards him, willing herself to go deeper, to find the source of that wrongness. Albryan's eyes widened and flicked over her as if seeing her for the first time. His breathing came faster than usual, as she began to discern something new about him. The golden substance which flowed through him, ebbing and rising with the beating of his heart, more visible now that he was agitated, shining from within him like the natural luminescence in the heart of deep caves. She was struck by the sheer beauty of it for a moment, until she saw the blight.

Black and fragmented, swelling and pulsating like an abscess with its own blood supply, it skulked in the shadow of that golden light, sending out spiderweb-lines that reached towards his limbs, towards his lungs and heart, all from its base where it sat just below his head. Close to the source of the golden substance, too close.

Velda was suddenly transported into memory, five years back when she had still been living at the monastery. A wood-cutter had accidentally chopped off half his own hand in a remote part of the forest. It had taken his companions two days to get him to the monastery. The wound had gone a similar colour, an abscess seeping angry pus in a way that resembled what she now beheld.

At fourteen, Velda had already been well-versed in the healing arts, having learned almost everything the monks had to teach her. She was particularly gifted at stitching, with small hands and a sharp eye. But she had never seen an infection like that before. It had seemed to her to be almost alive, drawing the strength from the man as he weakened, seeking to steal his life for itself. Despite all their efforts, the man had died from the wound, and the memory, of the pus and the stench, turned Velda's stomach even now.

She was suddenly afraid, but the outside power propped her up, fed her strength, whispered to her. She felt it calm her, infusing her with a sense of purpose as cool and calm as the mountain breeze.

We must heal him, she told the will that moved in tandem with her own.

We will heal him. She could not tell whether the reply originated in her own mind, or whether there really was someone else there with her, lending her confidence and strength, guiding her hands as she prepared to go to work.

Velda took a deep breath, and reached for the evil knot of dark sorcery.

SHE COULD NOT TELL HOW LONG it had been before she finally emerged, to find that somehow Albryan had collapsed to the ground and she had fallen across him. It seemed as though many hours had passed, yet the night was as she remembered it just before becoming immersed in his golden light. Frogs sang in the brook nearby, and moonlight shimmered between the new leaves of the thorn-bushes.

For one dazed moment, Velda allowed herself to feel everything just as it was. She felt Albryan's warmth through his shirt, smelled the sweat of the day's exertion on him. He stirred, opening his eyes to find her close to him, so near she could feel the whisper of his breath on her cheek.

The blood rushed to her face, and she began to draw away, but Albryan reached out and found the soft shadow of her hair beside her cheek, sliding his hand into it. Their eyes met, and suddenly she felt dizzy. The fear in Albryan's eyes had been replaced by something else. He was looking at her as though she were a lifeline in the storm.

That moment, when she realized what lay in his eyes, was too much for Velda. She drew back, trembling. Albryan seemed to sense the refusal behind the movement, and set her away from him as slowly he drew himself into a sitting position on the ground. It was a long time before either of them broke the silence.

"Velda . . ." He seemed to be searching for the right words to say. "I . . . thank you."

She remembered, then, what she had just done, and a sweet sense of accomplishment flowed through her. She remembered the way the dreadful tumour had disintegrated and turned to silver, dispersing in the golden glow. She remembered how it had resisted, and how she had fought back with determination until she found it . . . found the key to undoing the dark spell. It had been difficult. The spell had been intricate, woven in a far more complex way than the magic that gave being to the necromes, but she remembered the lingering thought, *if there is ever a next time, it will go faster.*

She was able to give him a genuine smile, then. "Please don't mention it. I would have done it for anyone." She hesitated. "That thing . . . it was like a disease. What kind of person would think of doing something like that to another?"

If Albryan found the question childish, he gave no sign of it. "The kind that practices blood magic," he replied quietly. "This is why we have been at war for so many years."

Chapter XV
Brialise Grenova

FISH AWOKE IN A DIM CAVE, not certain whether it was night or day. He closed his eyes against disorientation and nausea, clenched his stomach against the bile that rose up in his throat. He managed to move himself from a curled-up position to a sitting one upon the cold, damp rock beneath him. The silver chains were long enough to allow that, at least. He shivered violently, searching his mind for the thing that had been so important.

Then he remembered, and the shock of it jolted him, rattling the chains. He tried to look around, but his eyes were not working properly. He could make out some kind of phosphorescent blur above him: was that the roof of the cave? Or had he somehow become turned around, and it was the floor? He tried to search for something, anything, that would ground him, stop his head from spinning and his insides from heaving so much. He could not find Nico. Without him, Fish was lost, not even sure which way he was facing.

"Easy," came a harsh voice from the corner. "I think you have a concussion. Try to settle down."

Fish froze. Wide-eyed, he turned his whole body towards the voice, searching until he spotted a murky outline.

"Nico?" he breathed, even though he would have known its timbres anywhere.

"The same, Deryck."

Silence settled in the cave, apart from the chains rattling and Fish's heart beating somewhere in his throat. Either his eyes getting used to the dark, or perhaps the phosphorescence was getting brighter, because he could see more clearly now. It was a large, airy cave they had been chained in, the roof towering nearly fifty feet above them. A guttering oil lantern set somewhere near the entrance did very little to illuminate the shadow. The cave floor was composed of rounded boulders, many of which had been fitted with stakes and chains. Only two of these were occupied at present. Fish was staked in the middle of the cave, with Nico sitting roughly ten feet away from him. Somewhere, water trickled with a soft chittering, and when he leaned far to the side, he could see a thin stream flowing between the boulders to his right.

By the light of the phosphorescence, he could also see Nico's scowl, as ugly an expression as the blond assassin had ever worn in

Fish's presence. It was not only the look on Nico's face that disquieted him, though. His partner looked much the worse for wear. His face was scuffed and bruised, his shirtsleeve torn, and he huddled over his sprained arm, maintaining a tense, unnatural position to keep it cradled in his lap.

What had happened to him? Fish tried to remember their journey into the mountains, carted along by the necromes, but only flashes returned to him. He had struggled, and the creature holding him had thrown him against the cliff, cracking his head on a rock. Things were hazy after that. Taunus's dry chuckle. Nico's voice, threatening something. The descent into the caves. The grunting of the necromes and their overarching stench.

"What a pass we have come to, Deryck," Nico remarked dryly, and Fish raised up his head.

"Why do you keep calling me that?"

His voice fell harshly amongst vague echoes. Nico's eyes met his, from across the chasm between them.

"That's your real name." Nico's eyes bored into him. "Isn't it?"

Fish snorted softly.

"What else is there that you haven't told me?"

Fish's head snapped up. "We *don't ask questions about each other's past.* Remember?"

He glared across the gap, and for a moment Nico seemed abashed. Then he rallied.

"*My* past contains nothing that could ever endanger you."

"And how was I to know that any of this would happen?" Fish snapped. "Why did you stand and fight, Nico, when I *screamed* for you not to? Why wouldn't you listen to me?"

"If we hadn't been captured, would you ever have told me your story?" Nico snapped back, not missing a beat.

Fish was halfway through answering in the affirmative, when the word stuck in his throat. Nico's breath hissed through his teeth.

"You're so used to lying that you can't even answer that."

Fish glared at him and subsided into silence. But Nico was not ready to let it go.

"That—what you did," he began. "That was magic."

Fish saw no point in denying it. "Yes."

"You're Mage-Gifted." Fish didn't answer. "You're from the Forest of the Morning."

"No," Fish whispered. "I'm from Vailana, as I've always told you."

"I can't deduce much," Nico said, "but it seems that someone's been after you all along. This sorcerer—this Taunus—he's been hunting you."

Fish did not reply.

"Did you know he was after you?"

"Does it make any difference what I say?" Fish demanded.

An even darker shadow passed across Nico's face, and Fish saw his good hand clench as if he would have liked to wrap it around Fish's neck. For some reason, he felt a dark glee at the thought.

Another beat passed in silence. Then Nico turned to him again.

"I trusted you with my life, Fish!" he burst out. "Personal history is one thing, but you've had hunters on your tail all this time! And now we're in a worse spot than we've ever been, surrounded by magickers and mutant creatures and only gods know what else!" He paused for a moment. Fish's heart was beating so loudly that he hardly heard Nico's next words, which were almost whispered.

"I don't suppose you can . . . do the magic again? Try and get us out?"

Seething with frustration, Fish held up his cuffed hands. "These are plated with silver. Silver will not tolerate a magical field within its vicinity. I can do nothing unless I get out of these cuffs."

He continued to stare at Nico, his breath coming heavily. "You don't understand," he shot bitterly at his partner. "You don't understand how much—what our friendship meant to me. What I would have done just to stay by your side."

His heart felt as heavy as lead, and he was nauseous. It felt as if something had shattered between him and Nico. It was the vision of himself he had tried so hard to maintain. A pretence of someone who had no past, who was always cheerful and casual and ready to take on any fight. A vision of someone Nico would like. Would love.

"And now you know," Fish threw into the silence that had fallen. "Now you know what I am."

"Fish." Nico's voice, though still strained, was calmer. "Fish, please tell me the truth."

"You know enough, don't you?" Fish fought the urge to hide his face. Instead he crouched lower on his rock to avoid Nico's eyes. "You know I—the magic—my father—" A spell of dizziness and attendant nausea struck him, and he leaned over, touching his aching head to the cold rock, trying to orient himself once again.

He had no idea how much time had passed, but when he was finally able to lift his head and take in his surroundings once more, all he could hear was Nico shouting for him. It sounded so stupid that he might have laughed, if his head hadn't hurt so much. That nickname . . . he'd always been ridiculously attached to it. The first name he'd had that didn't connect back to his father. *Fish* had come before the alias of Benjamin Fisher, the full name he'd dreamed up as an explanation for what the old woman in Zarath had called him.

Cautiously and slowly, he brought himself upright. Nico subsided, but Fish could still feel the tension and desperation practically emanating from where he sat.

"You have a concussion," Nico said again. His chains rattled as he leaned forward. "Damn all of this to the realm of Thrombolis! Do you have anything on you that might help?"

Fish shook his head weakly. He lowered his head, and curled up again. It was uncomfortable, as were all positions on this flattened rock with the slight length of chain afforded to him. He stared up at the roof of the cave, where the glow was definitely much brighter than it had been before. Perhaps the strange organisms which produced the light in these underground places had a daily cycle.

He could hear Nico breathing heavily, a catch of pain in the sound. Fish furrowed his brows as resentment burned acid in his gut. How many times had he saved Nico's life, now? They had been getting into dangerous situations together for more than a year, and Fish was not too bashful to say that it was his own skill and cunning which had usually extricated them. And what was his reward for all of it? Indifference and fury. Blame for something he could not control. Shock and horror at the monstrous magic that his father had bequeathed him . . .

But as he lay, a memory unbidden stretched out before his mind's eye. A pirate with an axe. A direct hit against his ribcage, cutting right through his leather armour. Blood everywhere, much more blood than what he thought there ought to be. Exhaustion, falling, and then a sudden waking. Nico carrying him like a child, the warm, safe feeling of knowing that his partner was with him. Nico tightening the linen bandages across him, muttering soothing and meaningless words. Nico's hand on his cheek, slapping him to keep him awake.

Wake up, partner. We're going to get you patched up good and proper.

Another flash of memory, this one totally different, yet related. Nico's arm around his shoulders, singing a drinking song at the top of his voice as they wandered back from the pub, in a surprisingly impressive baritone. Nico supporting him as he retched in the street, even smoothing his hair away from his sweaty forehead. The slight shock and thrill as Nico lifted him bodily, carrying him the rest of the way home.

Gods only knew what would have happened on that particular night if Fish had been in control of his reactions. As it was, he had been far too drunk to do or say any of the things he'd dreamed he would.

But that wasn't Nico's fault, he had to admit to himself. *He will never be your lover, but have you ever had a friend who cared this much about you? Bar the old woman, of course. But she's dead.*

Tears stung Fish's eyes, and he resolutely wiped them away. He knew that Nico cared for him, maybe even loved him. Like a brother. They ate together, worked together, spent the best part of each day together, looked out for each other. The only things that had ever come between them were their secrets.

Nico, never afraid to set a boundary, had said this out loud. *We don't ask questions about the past.* But Fish had never come so far as to admit that he even *had* a past. He had been so stupid. He had thought that Arran would never find him, grown complacent over the years, started to believe that maybe they had forgotten all about him.

Started to believe that the magic would leave me eventually. That I would never use it again.

He wasn't sure, in the end, how long he lay there, drifting. But it must have been for hours at the very least, for when he woke, the glow from the roof was dimming and Nico was snoring softly in his chains.

His throat was parched. Fish perched on the very edge of his boulder and contemplated the babbling little stream below. With some manoeuvring, he managed to get his feet over the rock so they dangled in the water, but his arms would not reach. He climbed back up and tried again.

Eventually, he found a position where he could dangle his hands in the water and bring them carefully to his mouth. He did not feel much the worse for wear from hanging upside down, and with some relief, he realized that his concussion must have taken care of itself.

Nico had awoken with the noise of Fish's chains rattling about with all the repositioning, and was now perched upon his own rock, enviously looking on. Fish's mind was starting to clear at last, and he had an idea.

"Nico," he called, "throw me your boot."

His partner's face lit up, realizing what he had in mind. Nico threw one of his boots over and Fish caught it deftly, then hung back upside down to fill it in the stream. He wound the bootlaces round and round the top to keep it closed, then threw it back.

Nico made a face at the taste, but didn't complain. "Your head feels better, then?" he asked, and Fish nodded.

Fish waited for a moment, listening to the insistent drip and clink of water falling over the stones. Then he gathered his courage.

"Nic, the reason I never told you about—about my past." He took a deep breath. "I was too ashamed."

"Ashamed?" Nico repeated the word back to him with no inflection.

Fish sighed. "I simply wanted to escape my father." He didn't wait for Nico to ask. "Arran Sylvaissen. The dark sorcerer of Armour City."

Nico stared at him for a long moment. Finally he spoke.

"Your father is the king of Vailana?" He wrinkled his brow. "So . . . does that make you a prince?"

"That was the rank they gave us," Fish acknowledged quietly. "Five of us there were, all adopted. Father couldn't have children of his own, the dark magic prevented that." He stared at his boots, seeking to avoid Nico's intent gaze. "He kidnapped us, bought us . . . in my case, he gave a handful of silver pawns to some passing slavers who had captured me. I was just a babe—unlike the others, I don't even remember my real parents."

Nico's face was troubled. "Fish," he said quietly, "you're not making all this up, are you?"

Fish felt like laughing hysterically. Instead he schooled his face to calm. "I'm not." He didn't offer any platitudes, swear on anything he held dear, plead for Nico to believe him. Nico would just have to decide for himself.

To Fish's faint surprise, Nico seemed to accept that. "And then what happened?" he asked quietly.

"Then I was a child," Fish replied, "in the care of a succession of nurses and teachers. Arran didn't try and teach me much magic until

I was older. I was as normal a child as you can imagine, save that I didn't see my father very often. But I never knew, back then—I didn't see the things—" He broke off. "I didn't . . . didn't know what he did when he wasn't with me."

"I understand," Nico said quietly.

"I was a nobleman's son no different from any other, I suppose." Despite himself, Fish glanced briefly over at his partner, and saw the ironic amusement flicker briefly over Nico's face as well. "My nurses taught me my letters, history and geography and languages, even helped me exercise some minor magicks." Fish looked down at his right hand, lying caged now in shackles of silver. He almost imagined he could see the path that the lightning-quick outpouring of magic had traced through his veins, leaving a dull ache behind, faint patterns stirring under his skin. "My abilities came on me early. My father was so pleased and proud. I quickly became his favourite child, and my brothers hated me for it."

Nico didn't say anything. Fish became aware that his body was trembling, whether from the chill in the cave or because of something else, he could not say.

"My father began training me around my eighth year. It was then that I discovered my true purpose." Fish flexed his fingers, rattling the cuff of the chain. "Arran wanted us as war leaders. Five magically gifted children, we would be his generals in the war to come. We would carry out his orders, help him with his dark magic—"

He hesitated, and shook his head, wishing he could shake the memories away. "Nico, you can't—you can't imagine the things that must be done in order to invoke my father's magic." He rubbed his arms reflexively, feeling the shame crawl across his skin. "The things I was forced to do." He glanced at Nico, who sat grim and silent, his beard hiding whatever expression was passing across his face. "Take those mutant creatures, for example. The necromes. You kill a man and seize his life-energy, which spills out of him at the moment of death. Then you use it to make him come back to life again—the corpse you just killed, creating a thing that obeys orders, does not tire, and hates the living with every ounce of its will."

He looked away from Nico's stricken face. "Anyway, there's not much to tell after that. I ran away from him when I was eleven. I didn't know they were still hunting me, though I should—I should have suspected. I stopped using my magic entirely." He directed a pleading glance at Nico. "I hid from him—successfully, until now. I never thought I would have a reason to tell you all of this."

Nico sighed. "That's a lot to take in, Fish."

Fish tried to keep his cool, but the burning question simply could not be halted.

"Do you hate me because of my magic?" he asked softly, scanning Nico's face.

Nico frowned. "Fish—you keep talking of dark magic, but I remember we were taught that it was an inborn trait. The Morgei were born that way, the monks told me when I asked. And no history ever tells of the people of the Forest of the Morning using such a thing as *dark* magic."

Fish shrugged expansively. "Be that as it may. I wasn't born in the Forest of the Morning, and the dark side is all I know. What my father taught me."

"You were a child," Nico said. "You weren't to blame."

"Nico, when I was a child, do you know how many people I killed?"

"And do you know how many *I* did?"

Fish fell silent, staring at his partner.

"Perhaps not so young as eleven," Nico conceded, looking away and masking his own past once again. "But you can't carry that guilt, Fish. It's what got us captured, and it's what will prevent us escaping. You were a child. And you still had the courage to escape from him."

Fish didn't answer. Nico curled up on his rock, sighing loudly.

"Been a few times when a bit of magic could've come in handy," he remarked. "Imagine those Guild buggers' faces if you'd sent a fireball at 'em . . ."

Fish chuckled softly, mostly from relief. "Still partners?" he whispered across the space between them, half afraid to even ask the question.

Nico gave a grunt as he lay down and stretched his arm across his forehead. "Still partners."

Fish woke again, how long afterwards he could not say. The glow in the roof of the cave was still dim.

Had he imagined that sound? The patter of a pair of feet coming across the rocks?

Fish turned himself to look around and gave a start, nearly falling off his boulder. There was a shadow standing in front of him, a slight figure with long straggly hair.

"What do you want?" he demanded of the girl, whose large dark eyes seemed to pierce the gloom to meet his.

She did not answer, but proffered something wrapped in a rag. Fish took it and wound the rag open. There were strips of dried meat, some very old bread, and a leather skin of fresh water.

Fish was taken aback. "Thank you."

She said nothing, leaving him to wind her way around towards Nico's rock. Once she had delivered him his ration, she turned her back on both of them and headed towards the mouth of the cave.

"Wait!" Fish called. "Bree!"

She paused and turned around uncertainly. Fish held up the bundle of food.

"Why don't you stay and eat with us?"

Warily, Bree came closer. She was raggedy, and there were old bruises on her face, but for the first time Fish noticed that she was not starved. There was something strange about her, about the way she held herself . . .

When Fish offered her some of the dried meat, she shook her

head.

"Not hungry?"

She shook her head again. "I have food," she said in a low voice. Even the short sentence was melodious, her intonation almost like a song. She would have stuck out in Svanfeld for that accent alone. Fish knew that his own manner of speaking was mixed all together from all the places he'd lived, from Armour City to Zarath to the ship that had plied the western ocean until he'd disembarked in Ülhard. It was a powerful advantage, from his point of view, because he could easily slip into someone else's style of speaking, putting them at their ease.

"How do you get food?" he asked, shifting now from the intonations he had always used with Nico.

She shrugged. "There are soldiers."

"Human soldiers?" Fish asked quietly. She nodded.

Fish wanted to ask *why* they fed her, but stopped himself in time, since it was something he thought he already knew the answer to. Instead he changed the subject.

"My name is Fish," he said, "and this is Nico."

She frowned. "I heard Master Taunus say that your name was Deryck."

"Not anymore," Fish said decisively.

She looked at him quizzically. "If I call you Fish, you must call me Brialise."

"That's a beautiful name," Fish said without missing a beat. "Is that what your parents called you?"

She looked down and nodded.

"What were their names?"

She took a moment to answer, and Fish waited patiently until she did. "Analise Grenova, she was my mother. Fiolon was her husband and my father."

"They lived in Qwu'Mallorn, did they not?"

"Yes." She looked back at him. "And your parents?"

"I never knew them," Fish answered simply. "Slavers took me when I was very young, and sold me to an evil man."

"Master Taunus calls you brother."

Fish grimaced. "Our father was the evil man."

She gave a sudden giggle, startling Fish again. She really was no older than fifteen.

"Do you want to come and sit down?" he offered, moving slightly to one side.

Brialise tilted her head sideways, as if she were considering. She was in full possession of her magic, yet Fish knew that not all magical ability was created equal. The majority of Gifted children would never be able to throw a fireball nor spin a black web. Arran had taken particular care to select adoptive children who seemed to show an ability beyond the usual. The least powerful of the five of them had been Taunus, and even he could probably outmatch most of the peasants who lived in the Forest of the Morning.

The waif climbed up the rock to sit beside him.

Had Fish been a different brand of felon, she would have regretted that decision the moment she came within arm's length. But he had no intention of hurting the girl, especially when she dropped down cross-legged beside him, inadvertently revealing the reason why she moved so awkwardly.

The threadbare dress and cloak she wore were too big for her and had kept her covered up, so far. But as she sat, briefly cradling her belly, it was all too obvious.

Fifteen, family dead, abducted from home, heavily pregnant. No wonder she doesn't seem to care if I strangle her to death. Nico and I aren't the most desperate ones in this cave, not by a long shot.

THE GIRL RETURNED SOONER than Nico had expected, slipping into the cave to sit next to Fish again. Nico could not help but be impressed by the charm Fish had worked on her in such a short time. He had long known that his associate was personable and persuasive, but the friendship Fish had struck with the little war orphan had been something to watch. He had played it perfectly, being sympathetic and funny and even a little dangerous at times, convincing Brialise that he was capable of protecting her from a tribe of rampaging goblins, or necromes, if only his chains were struck off. Nico rather hoped that the girl was not more devious than what she seemed, but what other choice did they have?

He leaned forward just far enough to overhear their whispered conversation. Brialise appeared to have forgotten his very presence, which as far as Nico was concerned was all to the better.

"There is a storm approaching from the north," she was saying. "They say it will be a heavy one, a last winter storm. Master Taunus was expecting a visitor, but she will not come if it snows. She will have to wait for it to clear."

"A visitor?" Fish inquired.

"His sister," Brialise replied, and Nico saw Fish's brows come together above his slightly-slanted oval eyes in a way that betrayed concern. "She has long golden hair, and is very beautiful. It was"—she seemed to choke for a moment on the words—"it was she who attacked our homestead, and took me. I saw her. She killed—so many."

"The storm will give us cover," Fish said. "We cannot wait until my . . . until Taunus's sister gets here. We must be safely away before she can lay eyes on us." He paused. "Did Taunus send for anyone else?"

Brialise shook her head. "I don't think so. I have not heard, but it could be secret."

Fish leaned forward and touched her cheek. "Be brave, now. Lie low. When the storm breaks, that is when you must come to us."

She obeyed him and left, lingering with a last trusting look.

Nico waited several long moments, listening to the chattering of the little stream that flowed through their cave, before speaking.

"Fish, are you sure this is a wise plan?"

"My magic is sufficient to get us back to the village," Fish replied, clenching and unclenching one hand. Some of Nico's frustration must have showed on his face, for Fish took one glance at him and continued, "Truly, Nic, Taunus is not the greatest threat here. I know him. I know how he thinks. He will not anticipate our escape, and his response will be too slow. We have a chance, if we are willing to take it—escape him now, before . . ." He trailed off.

"Before what?" Nico prompted. There was something strange and dark behind Fish's eyes, something that unsettled him. He knew what it was to be haunted by the past, by things that had been done to him, and until now he had never fully grasped that it was a darkness Fish shared as well. He shivered internally. Fish might be a good liar, but Nico knew him well enough to know that there was more beneath the smooth exterior that Fish had quickly painted on after their last conversation. More about his family, his adoptive siblings whose power Nico could not begin to fathom. The revelations Fish had shared had stunned him, and yet he felt as though he had still barely scratched the surface.

Fish clenched his hands together. "Before my sister gets here," he said in a low voice.

"Your sister?"

"Dannine," Fish whispered. "My sister. She was the only one who loved me . . . once. Undoubtedly she hates me now. Dannine was never the forgiving sort . . . and I abandoned her." Fish glanced up. "I am much, much more afraid of what *she* might do. Taunus was cruel, but never had her drive and determination. Truth be told,

I would rather be facing my father." He looked towards the cave roof, where glow-worms gave off a dreary radiance. "I will protect us, Nico. I have enough magic to ward against the storm."

I hope you're right, Fish. By the sly eyes of Vermayn and all the rest of the gods, I hope so. Nico said nothing aloud. There was, after all, no choice but to trust in his partner. To trust that this wild-eyed magician was the same person underneath, the boy who had won Nico's trust and become his best friend. Because the assassin had no idea what he'd do without him.

Gods damn me, Fish, but it's true. I couldn't imagine life without you as my partner.

CHAPTER XVI

LAND OF THE DELTA-VALLEY

ALBRYAN SAT AS SILENT and poised as a forest cat in the tree as the troop of soldiers passed beneath him. There were not many—around twenty or so—but he did not like this at all. They had the look of common brigands, but were better armed and armoured than such rogues had any right to be. And then there were the captives . . .

Behind the soldiers, at least thirty ragged prisoners trailed miserably, their feet bound in chains linking their ankles, fastened each to the next in line. Most of them were women. A few were young children, and even fewer were men who had the look of farmers, poor farmers at that. There were no babes in arms. Albryan saw the way a young girl flinched from a soldier who walked too near, and had to clench his fists against the branch he was straddling. *You can do noth-*

ing for them, he told himself harshly. *Your first duty is to Qwu'Mallorn. To your own people, your homeland.*

Foliage shielded him above and below; Albryan needed no magic to hide himself from sight. The farmlands of the delta-valley lay behind them, and here the first ironwoods appeared in the forest. The one Albryan sat in was a true giant of the breed, with branches wide enough for a man to fall asleep on. It was almost like being back home, except that brigands such as this had never been able to pass beyond the magical barrier for long.

He was so close to home, and yet to get there, he would have to figure out some way to cross this land that was suddenly crawling with hostile armed forces. The only mercy was that apparently Arran had not seen fit to equip these with guns and cannons. But if they were merely attacking farmsteads and taking common farm-folk as captives, they certainly needed little more than sword and bow, and carrying gunpowder would only slow them down.

The few days since Albryan had camped beside the Dreaming Water with his two charges had passed in a blur. The land of the delta-valley was beautiful, dappled in broadleaf forest, sweet with native grasses and wildflowers, with lazy streams meandering through the fields in threads of blue as clear as the sky above. The mountain breezes off the high peaks now grey in the far distance kept the air fresh and cool, and every morning was crisp and new, brimming with the yet unknown.

They had forded the River Granite, which in these lowlands ran shallow and slow across a heavily silted floodplain. The river had been practically stationary at the point where they had crossed, foamy brown water sloshing over a wide pavement of the dusty pink rock for which it was named. Hills of that granite rose in the far southern distance for those who cared to look, but Albryan's focus had been only for the east bank of the river, where a staid ironwood rose above scrubby thorn-bushes like a sentinel standing watch. It had been the last lap, he remembered thinking. Albryan was too old a campaigner to imagine that nothing could befall them in the two days it would take to reach the top of the flint hills where the magical Border began. But even he was dismayed by the speed at which everything had started to go wrong.

They had met no-one else that day. That alone had struck Albryan as passing strange, since they were travelling through the most fertile part of the valley, where rich river silt supported a thriving agriculture. But the fields beside the road had been wild and grassy, unploughed, unplanted, no labourers working the soil. Velda had noticed, he knew, being of farmer stock herself: he remembered how the sinister mood had gradually grown on the three of them. And then they had seen the smoke, smelled the foulness on the air.

Albryan swallowed bile, remembering. They had cautiously approached the ruined farmstead, his hand on the hilt of his sword all the while. There had been new furrows in the fallow meadows, mud on the rutted road. They had passed the carcass of a milch cow, half-charred and bloated, left to lie, and half a dozen dead goats. And then

Velda had stumbled over the corpse of a young boy, no older than twelve, his rough tunic scarlet with blood that was still wet.

They had made a hasty retreat; the ruined farmhouse was smouldering, too hot to approach, and the thick black smoke had set them all to coughing. They had sheltered in the woods just beyond the farm. Soon enough, Albryan, scouting alone whilst the other two holed up in a cluster of thorn bushes, had detected the roving bands of brigands with their captives in tow.

It was now the third day since they had crossed the River Granite, and still they had not reached the flint hills. Albryan had not dared to go more than a few miles every night, each time directing them to move only when he was quite sure that the soldiers had made camp for the evening. They were running low on food, only bread and cheese left to sustain them, but Albryan did not dare take the time to try and hunt. And doubly, he did not dare to use any magic . . .

He thought of Velda, and was assailed by a flood of emotion he only barely understood. She had cried the night after the ruined farm, as might be expected of anyone who had never witnessed true warfare. Hiram had been unsettled too, Albryan knew, though the old man was more used to atrocity, having lived through the siege of Armour City.

Things were not supposed to have gone this way. He had been taking her to safety. He had not realized . . .

He had not realized so many things. The thought of the young woman he had found in the mountains confused Albryan so much that he had tried to put her at arm's length whenever possible. But on that night, he had taken her in his arms to comfort her. And all the emotion from that evening beside the Dreaming Water had come flooding back, the things he had felt when she'd healed him, the way their eyes had met and he'd been unable to look away.

She was unremarkable, common-born, no special talent but for the incredible power that moved through her in defiance of all natural laws. *She can undo magic.* That alone made Albryan caution himself against her, knowing that this diminutive woman could not be touched by any measure of his Mage-Gift. She could take him apart simply by existing. Albryan felt an instinctive revulsion against this, even as he was undeniably attracted to *her*. He had never thought that anything like it could possibly exist, and could only guess at what it portended.

Albryan could match any Morgein woman in magical prowess, could match any nonmage mercenary with his sword. He would even have welcomed a rematch against Dannine Sylvaissen, preferably after a long rest and a chance to recover from the ordeal he had endured. Velda's power, however, was something he had no defence for. And no matter how well he liked the girl, how attractive she was, with strong Vailanan features and dark enough to have sprung from the jungles of Sanghui, how much her vulnerable side awakened his protective instincts—he must remember his duty. He had to bring her to Qwu'Mallorn, bring her quickly and quietly, contain her, contain any possibility of danger. The girl had within her the power to end the war. Had she not agreed to come with him, Albryan would have had to take her by force, and as much as his heart constricted in shame at that thought, he would have done it without hesitation.

You need to focus, soldier, he told himself, as he was often doing these days. *She cannot understand what the sacred forest means to you—to all who dwell within it. She cannot know what truly lies in your heart.*

Because you've never shared that with her, stupid lout, he argued back with himself. Secrecy was a hard habit to break, and he had not wanted to scare the girl off. She had to come with him; he could sort out the rest later. *An orphan from some borderland town in Svanfeld. That's all she is. How could she ever understand?*

She had saved him three times, given freely without expecting anything from him in return. The very thought riddled him with guilt, and yet he knew that all of it had been necessary. He had gone to the Svanlyn mountains on a whim, and she had crossed his path in a meeting that Albryan could only believe was predestined. She was *meant* to come with him. She was meant to help him. And if he had already ruined whatever was growing between them, if she ended up hating him, that was too bad. Albryan had survived worse.

The war is the only thing that matters, he told himself, perched on the wide branch watching the brigands lead their lines of shackled slaves by. He could not make a true friend of Velda, and he could not help these people.

Albryan had heard reports of fighting in this region, but he had never realized how bad the situation truly was. He knew that Dannine had occasionally broken through the magical barrier of Qwu'Mallorn and attacked a few isolated farmsteads on the very western fringe of the mother forest, but he had never considered what Arran might be doing to those who had no magical barrier to protect them, the simple nonmage farm-folk who dwelled here.

Yet the question nagged at him: *why?* These people were Arran's own subjects, ruled from the stronghold of Armour City, answering to Arran's own laws. Not to mention, some percentage of Armour City's food stores were grown in this very area. Why would the sorcerer-king indiscriminately terrorize his own people like this? The soldiers passing beneath were human, not necrome, and they wore the blood sorcerer's own insignia, the silver-and-white that was Arran's uniform and standard.

More than once, Albryan had observed that Arran Sylvaissen did not really seem to care how much he spent in war or how the people of his land loathed him. He ruled by fear, yes, but some things he did simply defied logic.

Albryan had once witnessed one of Arran's public displays of punishment in Armour City. His job had been simply to observe and report back to Thinas, so he had not intervened in what it pleased Arran to call justice. He had not intervened even when small children far too young to know anything of treason were strung up and gutted beside their parents. Albryan had remained calm when the spectators began to turn against their king, when the crowd had heaved and tried to storm the blood sorcerer and his children, and he had quietly slipped away as Arran's soldiers began cutting into the crowd.

And he would do nothing now, when Arran was terrorizing his own people, slaughtering the innocent and raping the land, because an end to the war, the slightest chance to bring an end to the blood sorcerer and all his cruelty, was more important. Velda was more important, because somehow, Albryan knew, she held the key to all of this.

IN A SHELTERED CAVE-HOLLOW at the edge of a low cliff where Albryan had left them, Velda lay apparently asleep whilst Hiram kept watch from the narrow cave opening. Through half-slitted lids, she could see his ragged outline, narrow face poised towards the outside, thin hands working idly as he carved an indistinct shape from a twig he had found on the ground. He had been working at this for a while now, claiming that he had been proficient at carving animals and flowers in his youth, but the skill seemed to be slow in returning.

Velda closed her eyes and pressed her face to her bedroll, moving into a kind of half-sleep where impressions floated across her mind, only lightly touching her with wisps of memory. Foremost was the thing she could not forget, the burned homestead and the dead boy.

Velda could not even remember, now, when she had first seen death. The monks of Lynborder kept herds of sheep and goats, and at some point she had even helped butcher lambs for the table. Emmett had had his pigs, and Velda was no stranger to the process that turned farm animals into chops and roasts. That had never drawn any strong reaction from her.

Worse had been the people she had watched die over the years. She had been nine or ten when she first began learning basic wound-care. She had tended minor injuries and illnesses at first, the cut on the hand from a kitchen knife or butcher's cleaver, ankles sprained or broken from people who misstepped in the mountains, babies with coughs and colics. Some of the oldest brothers at the monastery had died throughout the years, and she had attended their corpses and even helped prepare one or two for their last rites before burial.

She had been twelve the first time she had seen death by injury, though. A farmer had fallen from his horse and gotten trampled by his own cows before he could get up. Brother Henck Smelter had gone to attend the injured man in his homestead, taking Velda and an older boy along to assist him. She remembered that day very clearly, the monk turning pale as snow when he lifted the blanket from the injured man, the way the man's gaze had been almost totally blank, gone already though breath somehow remained in his body. How Brother Henck had spent much longer comforting the wife and children than he had attending the dying man, for as he said later, he could see at one glance that there was nothing to be done.

Farming was dangerous, sometimes, and so were the mountains, where cliff and scree and snow-covered slopes waited for the unwary to look upon them with overconfidence. But Velda knew that com-

monplace accidents, things no-one would ever think to be dangerous, claimed more lives by far. Infection was the single biggest killer
in Lynborder, from the blades of axes and kitchen knives, and once a
pitchfork some old man had put through his foot digging furrows
for his tomatoes. The monks' remedy for infection was the holy
word *prevention*, but often by the time people came to seek their aid,
it was too late for that.

Then there was the violent death of childbirth, one Velda was
intimately familiar with. For a day or two, she had believed she might
die after delivering her son. Her labour had taken longer than a day,
and afterwards she had languished in a deep sleep, bleeding more
than she should have. She had flitted in and out of consciousness,
sometimes half aware of the child's crying and Emmett holding her
hand, other times halfway towards her unknown ancestors. But the
danger had passed at last; no infection had come, and she had lived
to see her son buried before she ever was. Other women had not
pulled through. Old Stein's sister Lissy, diminutive Kess, her friend
Elna . . .

It had all come upon her in a rush, that moment she had stumbled over the dead child and turned him to see the face, half believing
that maybe the corpse was only sleeping. It could have been her own
son lying there, dark-haired and brown-eyed, perhaps from some bi-
zarre alternative future where Ricard had lived another ten years only
to be cut down by warmongering mercenaries.

That was what she found so hard to accept, that in this world of diseases and mischance someone had made the cold decision to side with death, taken a whole life without reason and thought so little of it that they left the corpse where it had fallen in the despoiled fields. Albryan had comforted her afterwards, smoothing her hair and murmuring soothing nothings as one might to an frightened horse, but he could not know that anger, far more than fear, was the cause of her tears. Even in the face of sudden danger, Albryan's quiet competence assuaged her fear. She need not panic until he did, she knew, and so far the young soldier had shown no sign of anything more than an even grimmer determination to get back to his homeland.

Strangely, that event had helped clear Velda's head, even as it dried up the easy conversation she had shared with her travelling companions. She felt more comfortable in silence during times of stress, and the two men had not said much to each other either. And in that silent calm, reminded how fragile was the very thing she called life, Velda had looked across the space between them to the clear eyes and stubborn lips of Albryan Lana, and suddenly realized that if he made any move close to kissing her again, she would embrace him back without hesitation.

If he ever did. If they were ever alone together again. If he even wanted to. Velda thought she had seen attraction in his eyes that night when she had pulled the blight from him, but it could just as well have been gratitude.

But that wasn't the most important part, she knew. The point was that her heart was suddenly free to fly again. She seemed to have freed it, somehow, in her flight from the mountains. The spring sun had come out and shone upon her, and the pain of loss had retreated into the distance, no longer all-consuming.

When she thought of her husband now, her first image of him was not of the day he had died, the pallid wasted face which had haunted her for so many months afterwards. No, she saw him as he had been when they'd first met, both of them all of sixteen, wild hearts with no planned future and no duty but to live. Emmett had just found work as a common labourer on the Lester farm, and had spent all of that day digging trenches for drainage of the carrot and turnip fields. She had been running a few errands in town and was headed back towards the monastery when she saw him for the first time, straw-headed, sun-tanned, crooked-toothed and crusted with tilth, sneaking a lone cigarillo where the edge of the field met the little stream and the rutted farm road, under a drooping willow tree. She could not quite remember how that first conversation had gone, but she did remember his north-country burr when he introduced him-self, holding out one dirt-encrusted hand to shake, and how she had taken it before he remembered that it was bad manners to get dirt on girls. She remembered how he had blushed and stammered then, and to cover his embarrassment suddenly blurted out, "You're real pretty." She had waited for the qualifier—*if it weren't for your nose*—as she had heard all her life, but from Emmett it had never come.

As confusing as this new power of hers was—this *undoing*—she thought she could recognize in it something she had always worked for. *Healing.* If nothing else, the power seemed to closely correspond to her desire to heal and fix. If only it had come in time for Ric and Em, but it had come with Albryan, and for that alone she felt grateful towards him. Perhaps the gods had finally smiled upon Velda, despite a lifetime of misgivings. She knew little of the mother goddess the Morgei were said to worship, though from Albryan she had learned the name: Qwu'Kiya.

The religion Velda had been brought up to held that there were no false gods. Minor deities governed the earth and all human affairs, and the Great Father and Mother, Vezzat and Thäle, smiled down upon all. It would not be a contradiction for the goddess of the sacred forest to have brought a blessing along with her young soldier. The monks spoke often of heroes in the past who had received just such gifts, like the silver armour of Prince Edwin or the prophetic dreams of Saint Aric. The idea scared Velda a little, but more than that, it thrilled her, making her truly feel like a heroine in a song.

She must have drifted off to sleep in the end, for the next thing she knew was the gentle pressure of Hiram's hand, shaking at her shoulder. She sat up and blinked sleep from her eyes, tucking stray hairs away from her face into her bun. The orange glow of sunset beamed through the narrow entrance of the cave, and Albryan had returned, crouching on the sandy floor and making a hasty snack of some spare bread and cheese. Hiram wordlessly handed the same to Velda to break her fast after the afternoon sleep.

"I followed the men all afternoon," Albryan said in a low voice.

"There are fewer soldiers than I thought. No more than twenty in this band. They're Arran's, no doubt about it." He flicked a meaningful look at Hiram, who nodded grimly. "Silver-and-white insignia. I followed them until they made camp for the night. They have at least thirty prisoners, need to guard them. They won't be doing any patrols tonight." He looked between Hiram and Velda. "We have to get past them. Tonight, in the dark. We may not see such an opportunity again."

Velda stirred. "What of the prisoners?"

For a moment Albryan looked lost. "The prisoners?"

"The folk of this land, aren't they?" Velda pressed. "The survivors. What are the soldiers planning to do with them?"

Albryan fidgeted a little. "From what I could see—" He hesitated. "They were chained together. Indicates perhaps they're planning to sell the captives as slaves."

Velda swallowed, remembering. *A handful of silver pawns.* If the people of Lynborder had not intervened, where would she be now? Somewhere in the Dark Empire, perhaps? Or serving some pirate in a secret lair on the Sea of Calms?

"We should help them." She was surprised that the words had escaped her lips, and yet as she raised defiant eyes to Albryan's troubled blue-green ones, she was glad they had. Hiram, to her surprise, nodded vehemently.

"We should," he said softly. "They do not—no-one deserves this."

Albryan stared at both of them in turn, aghast. "Velda," he finally said, "I'm not sure you know what you are saying. "There are twenty of these men, armed and armoured better than I am, and neither of you two even knows one end of a sword from the other. And there may well be more of them within hailing distance. Arran's armies are numerous, and only the Goddess knows what else may be out there."

"We are very close to Qwu'Mallorn," Hiram said, again unexpectedly. "Two hours' stiff walk at the most, if I can trust my estimation."

"We could use magic against them," Velda suggested. "Bryan, you could do something like—like that fireball I saw you use."

"*No.*"

"Why not?" Velda realized that she and Hiram had said the words together. Albryan glared at them both.

"As I've said, we are very close," Hiram said. "With a little magic, you could wipe out this troop of bandits, not having to worry about leaving them in our rear, and it would not be long before we were in Qwu'Mallorn and behind the protection of the barrier."

Albryan's colour deepened slightly against the sunset light, freckles standing out on his nose. "I haven't told you this," he finally said, haltingly, "but these soldiers are not our only problem. We are still being tracked by necromes."

Velda heard a sharp intake of breath from Hiram. "How is that possible?" she demanded. "And why haven't you told us before?"

"I knew they would not catch up with us," Albryan said shortly. "They have no intelligence of their own, and it seems their master is not with them. But with the delay on this side of the river, they passed us a few days ago, and now they are between us and the border of Qwu'Mallorn, roaming, as far as I can tell, slightly to the southwest. The soldiers are in our path, and the only way to get to the Border is to veer north." He gestured with his hand. "This is a longer way, yet we have no choice. Not if we want to avoid the necromes."

Velda gave him a defiant look. "I dealt with them once. I can do it again."

Albryan seized her hand. "No," he said, in the kind of tone that did not entertain defiance. Velda wondered momentarily whether he used that voice for his soldiers. "We do not know for sure what would happen, Velda. You are too precious to risk in such a way." He let her hand fall, and turned to Hiram. "As for you—do you truly want to be captured by Dannine? As I was?" His eyes blazed lightning-blue. "You would return to that dungeon in Armour City, or worse." He began to get to his feet, nearly bumping his head on the cave roof. "I expect you both to obey me. In this, at least."

Velda said nothing. She did not want to look at him. Beside her, Hiram stirred.

"You speak to us as you would to a pair of recruits, Albryan," he finally said, "but I don't recall that either Velda or I ever swore an oath to you."

"My first duty is to my homeland." The voice was cold, and

Velda's heart hammered defiance in her chest. She could understand fear, could tolerate caution. Yet she could not stop thinking about the boy, the dead boy she had fancied looked like her own dead son. Tears pricked at her eyes, but she blinked them away.

"Velda," Albryan said, and his tone was suddenly a lot softer. "You must understand. If the war is won—"

"I understand," she said shortly, and stood up herself. She did not have to bow her head to stand upright in the cave. "I understand what you believe, Albryan."

CHAPTER XVII
ROOF OF THE WORLD

DANNINE STOOD UPON THE roof of the world, watching the storm approach, and felt like shrieking into the howling wind.

I knew the weather was too bad to fly. I knew, and I came anyway. Cold tears tracked down her cheeks. She stilled their source as soon as she noticed, but the fear and anguish remained.

She retreated further into the gap between two bare cliffs, the only place she had been able to find for shelter. The quetzals flew high, and this was the highest part of Svanlyn, the roof above all other things, the great temples of craggy black rock where nothing grew and no men lived. Farther down the mountain, there were sandstone caverns, hollows carved out by the elements, offering dry ground for a fire and protection from the scouring wind. But all around her now there was nothing but black basalt, cliff edges carved into serrated blades and shelves of bare rock. Before Dannine's feet, a sad covering of yellow grass stood as the only living thing for miles about; not even the stunted mountain bushes grew up here. Behind her, in the gap, the quetzal lay heaving, trembling in the teeth of the wind, which was now blowing flurries of snowflakes before it. The storm was nigh.

The quetzals were not made for this kind of weather. Arran had discovered them long ago on an island he named as Wyndlis, a place that was windswept and barren yet warm all year round. Somewhere there upon the Sea of Calms, Dannine knew, her father had had his first home. She did not know much of his past beyond that.

Arran had quickly learned how to control the quetzals, had flown the great lizard-birds from island to island upon the Sea of Calms, and over time he had bound them to him, breeding them selectively for flight and endurance and culling those that were too weak, or too independent of will to be controlled. Yet nothing could change their basic nature: they were made for flights over the warm salt sea and desert isles, eaters of fish and gulls. Their large, flexible-shelled eggs needed some amount of moisture in the air to hatch and thrive, and the females would return every year to the marshy islands, building secret nests in the bogs and watching over their hatchlings.

Dannine cast an eye towards the shivering quetzal that had carried her to this forsaken place, a young female. She wondered whether it felt that pull even now, the urge to surrender herself to the wild mating ritual on some forsaken desert rock, then the long flight to the nesting grounds, draining her reserves as she bore a clutch of eggs. Whether it felt the strange pull of motherhood. Dannine never had; the blood sorcery had rendered her barren for the rest of her life, but it was never something she would regret. No matter what other hurts were inflicted upon her body, she would never know the humiliation of pregnancy, the danger of childbirth. That much was a relief.

The quetzals had no experience of frost and snow, and would die if they lost too much heat. Dannine had not been able to fly all the way to Taunus's stronghold because of that. With the temperature rapidly dropping as she flew, her quetzal had slowed and slowed until they were tracking across the landscape barely faster than a leaf blown aloft by a lazy wind. No matter how she cajoled and threatened and tormented, the creature could not fly faster. It simply was not possible. At last its reactions had slackened to reptilian sluggishness even as Dannine could smell the snow, and she had allowed it to land just before they fell from the sky.

Now she had to use precious stores of magic just to keep the creature alive. She had managed to persuade it to crawl inside a narrow chimney of rock, just big enough for it to lie with wings folded, protected from the worst of the wind, but still it needed protection from the cold. There was no brushwood up here, no way for her to start a fire nor keep it going, so the only thing she could do was to weave her magic into a dense cocoon around the creature, sealing it off from the weather. The quetzal was unable to retain its own stores of body heat, and so she had to keep on feeding energy from her own reserves into the cocoon.

She knew, watching the billowing snowflakes, that soon she would have to retreat into the cocoon herself, for even the native, fur-enveloped creatures would soon freeze to death in the onslaught that was approaching. For now, however, she paced up and down before the cliffs, fidgeting, cursing silently, resisting the temptation to give the quetzal a few well-placed mental jabs. It would do her no good; tormenting the creature would accomplish nothing but to drain her own energy, and if it froze to death, Dannine had no illusions of how long *she* would last up here, alone, with nothing but a ten-thousand-foot walk back down to the plains of Vailana.

She worried about her reserves; they had not been high to start with. She had been tired, barely sleeping, and cold. She was supposed to be scrying on the necromes she had left behind, but didn't dare. She didn't have the energy to spare. Fear rose up in her throat again, and she pushed it back down. *Survive this,* she told herself. *Survive this, and then we will see about those necromes, and Deryck, and Father. Survive this.* She was tired, though. She had been surviving for the better part of her twenty-two years. Surviving *alone.*

Unbidden, a memory came to her mind. Dannine did not like to dwell on memories, but the ultimate loneliness of this place left her no choice. She was eleven again, her little brother Deryck no older than eight. He was quick and strong and the palace armsmaster often paired them against each other, since Dannine was small for her age and light on her feet. There was one training day when she was particularly desperate to show her skill, the progress she had made. But she lost her footing at a critical time, and the wooden practise-sword instinctively came up and cracked Deryck right across the face.

Dannine fidgeted. She did not want to remember this. Even though it was just a broken nose, the thought of hurting Deryck had filled her with such horror that she had sobbed for days afterwards. Why had she been so upset? By that age, neither she nor Deryck were strangers to bloodshed. He had been half a soldier already, his magical abilities had developed so early.

Yet all Dannine's being congealed in that memory, the *crack* of the practice-sword as it hit his face, the way he had fallen backwards, crying in pain, blood spurting from between his fingers as he clutched at his nose.

She had never wanted to hurt her brother, and yet the pain when he ran away, three years later, had been worse than any anguish Dannine had ever experienced on his behalf. He had hurt her far more than she had ever hurt him, accidentally or otherwise.

The wind blew ice into Dannine's face, and she wound her scarf around her head, covering everything except her eyes. The barren cliffside was a freezing black hole in a maelstrom of white. She could not see the further peaks anymore; the whole landscape appeared to be swathed in wool. The wind was shrieking through the rocky chimneys and hurling itself from the ice-slick cliffs like an animal that wanted to die.

Dannine kept the heat of her inner fire going, feeding it with thoughts of revenge, stoking it with anger. *I am stronger than this,* she told herself. *I am stronger than my weakness. Stronger than these feelings. I flinched from hurting Deryck when I loved him, but now I would find his torment more pleasurable than the sensation of flying. I am no longer the sweet, weak girl I was then. How many have died at my hand? How many Morgein soldiers have died in pain, screaming for their mothers? I have made them fear me, and I need not fear the coming of the storm!*

She spread her arms wide, tasted snow melting through her scarf, felt her spirit soar on the violence of the winds. And for just a moment, facing the righteous rage of the gods of Svanlyn, Dannine Sylvaissen forgot about fear and revenge and regret, and wished only to live.

CHAPTER XVIII
STORM

BRIALISE ARRIVED LATER THAN NICO would have liked, holding no keys and glancing anxiously over her shoulder every now and then. She had a silver-edged dagger in one hand that Nico recognized: it was one of his own. Before he and Fish had been thrown into this cave, Taunus had frisked them both thoroughly, removing all their concealed weapons. Fish had been half unconscious, suffering from that crack against his head. Nico remembered Taunus's leer, the intimate way he had slid a hand into Fish's hair to shake him awake after finding every one of his hidden daggers, and felt his skin crawl. No, the sooner they were away from here, the better. This was no job they should ever have accepted. There was still a way out, however. Take Fish and run. What he should have done in the first place.

"No keys?" Fish asked, and the girl shook her head miserably.

"Master Taunus is keeping them. He—he speaks of coming down here soon, said something about his sister being delayed, said he needs to check on you himself." She glanced fearfully over her shoulder. "I managed to snatch this without them noticing. Can you open the locks with it?" She proffered the dagger to Fish.

"Nico's much better with that than I am. Better take it to him."

The girl was much warier around Nico; she stepped delicately over the rocks and handed the dagger to him, wordlessly, at arm's length.

Nico had long been familiar with the arts of burglary; when he'd first arrived in Ülhard, there had not been many opportunities for honest paid work. He had been too big to make a successful burglar himself, but he'd made an excellent look-out, and before long they had begun to hire him for other things.

The lock between his ankles clicked open and Nico rose to his feet, cursing as pins and needles erupted in his calves. He climbed down unsteadily, finding it difficult to balance with his arm bound in its sling, and made his way towards his partner.

After so many days of sitting yards apart, Nico was uncomfortably aware of the boy's proximity and impatience as he worked the blade of the dagger into the lock between Fish's wrists, then between his ankles. When he was done, Fish climbed down using the expedient method of putting his hands on Nico's shoulders and swinging to the ground.

"We had better go fast," Brialise said, and there was no more time for Nico to dwell on whatever it was that he was suddenly feeling, lust or love or fear. He tucked his cloak tightly around himself, keeping his injured arm close to his chest. He could feel the pain of the overstretched tendon keeping pace with him, twinging a little every time he took a step.

The cave had numerous exits, at least six that Nico had counted in the dim light whilst sitting in his chains. He knew which way they had come when they'd been put here: off to the left, through the entry Brialise normally used. The tunnel leading from that entrance ran uphill towards a desolate valley where wind continually screeched through imposing black rocks. But that way led past Taunus's men, the captains who commanded over the necromes, and past Taunus himself. It did not therefore surprise him that the girl took the opposite entryway, down a narrow tunnel dark as night, with water trickling from numerous gaps to pool upon the worn rocky floor.

Brialise produced a single torch from somewhere in her furs, along with a steel-and-flint striker. Nico had to help her glean sparks from it. He wondered how long the route to safety under the mountain was, and whether this one torch would have to last them all the way.

They went single file up the narrow passageway, Brialise in front with the torch, Nico bringing up the rear. The footing was uneven, and they could go only slowly. Nico looked up and saw the roof far above, narrowing to a crack somewhere in the darkness. A thin spray of water seeped from that crack and misted their faces as they went.

"Does Taunus know this way?" Fish's voice was low, yet echoes still magnified the sound and sent the words bouncing off the walls. Nico saw Brialise shake her head.

"We had better not talk until later," she warned, and Fish fell silent. Nico could sense the urgency emanating from his partner, and knew that Fish would rather have talked away his tension, all the way to the surface. There were few things that could make Fish shut up, necessity and sometimes drunkenness and—Nico felt a twinge of something like regret—his own disapproval.

The narrow tunnel seemed to stretch on forever, hundreds and hundreds of paces. All three of them were damp from the continuous spray of water by the time it widened and led out into a straight, spacious tunnel that looked suspiciously like a walkway. Brialise halted at the exit and handed the torch to Fish, peered both ways into the darkness, then seized the torch again and crept to a crevice in the tunnel wall opposite, motioning for the two men to follow her.

Nico and Fish sheltered beside her as best they could, and Brialise explained in a low voice: "This is where the necromes usually go. When Master Taunus sends them to hunt. This leads down—all the way down—to the valleys." She paused. "I know another way, a safer way. It is longer, but unbeknownst to them." She peered at their faces in the shadows, as they nodded their agreement. "We will have to go some ways down this tunnel." She pointed in the direction where the tunnel began to slope ever-so-slightly downwards. "We will . . . we will have to go past some dead prisoners. They will not bother us."

"*Dead* prisoners?" Nico repeated. Fish touched his arm, gripping him.

"Corpses that are being turned," he whispered, and Nico saw Brialise nod in affirmation. "Into necromes."

"Can't—can't we do something to help them?" Nico asked lamely, even as somehow he knew the answer would be negative.

"They're difficult to kill, even in the larval stage," Fish explained, looking away from him. "There is no true suffering in them, Nico. They're already dead."

Nico shuddered. "Well, you're the expert."

"We should go quickly," Brialise said.

They nodded their assent, and set off. The floor was flat, compacted earth remarkably like a road, and the tunnel was wide enough for them to have walked at least five abreast. Nico disliked the openness, and wished he had a sword on him. His own had been taken by Taunus, and he supposed there was no chance of getting it back.

The plan was simply to get back to the hamlet, and then figure out what came next. Perhaps the whole village would have to help them fight off Taunus when he came looking for them, or everyone would have to flee. Nico found himself wondering how the villagers had reacted to their disappearance. He had liked and respected Harold Velman, and had been mildly surprised to find how easily the others, even the younger men of the village, had accepted him and drawn him into their company. It had been a little like going home.

Nico had never known a true family; he had been raised as a foundling in a monastery further north, in the shadow of the mighty mountain he now crept under, and this was the only thing that Fish knew about his past. What had happened to Nico after he left the monastery, at sixteen, was something he would never tell another soul.

The closest monastery to where they now were lay south, near Lake Mountaindale, where Nico had never been. Perhaps he would end up seeing it in passing. All roads from here led down the mountain: back to Von Dharen, which had too much of a Guild presence; north past Pine, where Nico would never return; or down the other way, around the famed high pass of Beerstana Peak and south towards the great lake and the plains of Vailana beyond. It would not do to pass too close to Armour City, not with what he now knew of Fish, but there was a highway along the southern slopes of Svanlyn, leading across the mountain from Greensland to Palace to Lynborder and Wolverton, crossing the lowest part of the mountains to end up in Sulshome with its famous port on the Sea of Calms. A lonely road, said to be infested with bandits, but a better hope than any other. They could take ship at Sulshome, sign on with a crew, become pirates perhaps. Or sail to Arven, that land of isles north of Svanfeld, where supposedly bands of marauders regularly made the crossing to old Novlaya and the faraway Zemlyan Empire, gathering riches and having adventures untold.

Or if they sailed the other way, they could find some sort of employment in the Eastern Empire, perhaps as caravan guards. Nico had heard all his life about the perilous trade routes that led in and out of the Eastern Continent, the savages who lived in the rainforest, the pirates who prowled the oceans. A dangerous life that would be, for sure, but it sounded a deal better than getting roasted by a vengeful dark sorcerer hell-bent on conquering the whole of his homeland.

Fish had not told him the reason for his brother's presence here in Svanfeld, but Nico could make an educated guess. Arran Sylvaissen, the famed sorcerer tyrant, had conquered Vailana pretty handily and was probably going to overrun the Forest of the Morning any day now, if half of what was reported in Ülhard was true. It only seemed natural that he would turn his attention to the northern country across the mountains as well.

It seemed to Nico that it might be a good idea to not be here when the sorcerer-king finally came across the mountains. Doubly so since apparently Fish had betrayed him. For the past four years, Nico had been a constant companion to danger, but only fools invited it near.

Fools and the mad and those bent on vengeance, he corrected himself, covertly studying Fish's angular features by the light of the flickering torch. The boy's face showed nothing but calm determination. It was a ways away from the expression Nico had seen on his face when Fish had suddenly caused the whole world to burst into flame, that anguish, that near madness. It had frightened Nico more than the magic itself, if truth be told.

There were soft and strange sounds ahead, the source too far to see in the small circle of torchlight that clung to Brialise as if it were afraid of the yawning darkness beyond. Grunting, perhaps—or snarling? Gnawing? Nico shivered despite himself, and tried to touch a sword hilt that was not there.

A few more steps, and the first of the figures came into view. Nico started, for all that he had been trying to prepare himself for whatever foul sight awaited. A narrow cage of wire had been strung along each side of the tunnel, wide enough only for a person to stand upright in. He could not tell whether the figure facing him now had been man or woman. It was still half dressed, rags of what could have been trousers or skirt hanging from the waist. The skin was not yet completely grey. Welts of pinkish red flamed over the heaving hide; a shimmering ichor covered it like a sheen of sweat. The ends of long, lank hair dripped with it as the creature shuddered and heaved. Nico could not see its eyes, but the end of the jaw hung slack. The lips were cracked and crusted in dried blood, yet mouthed the soft noises that had carried up the tunnel, a kind of animal mewling that set his hair on end.

Nico would have been the first to say that he had certainly seen more grisly sights than this. But he could not let go of the miasma of horror and fear that overtook him, especially when Brialise lifted the torch and illumined the path ahead, showing just how *many* there were straining against that wire cage. The noises they made were like nothing human, yet something in them was just familiar enough to creep inside him and chill his blood. He wanted to help them. He wanted to kill them. He wanted to run far away from this place and never come back.

The other two seemed to be holding up far better than he was. Nico sought for strength inside himself and, for the first time in a long time, found himself mouthing a prayer to the gods he'd known as a child. The god who watched over travellers and adventurers, Run, had failed Nico so badly that he would probably never utter the name again, but he drew his silver medallion out from beneath his leather jerkin and thought of Nursala, the god of foresters, Ynsa, the cold implacable spirit of the mountains, and Mother Thäle. Her above all. Nico had never known a mother of his own, but Thäle's name had been taught to him since before he could walk. She stood for peace and mercy, two things he felt he sorely needed at this moment.

They slowly walked between the rows and rows of mewling corpses, Brialise holding the torch steadily aloft. Fish looked troubled, and Nico gripped his medallion and tried not to look too hard at any faces, somehow fearing what he might see. A few of the creatures snuffled towards them as they approached. Others shrank away from the light. One attempted to leap at them, snarling deep in the back of its throat, but was held back by the cage.

Fish stopped, so abruptly that he was nearly outside the circle of light before Brialise noticed. She stopped, too, and Nico turned to see his partner staring intently at one of the motionless, wretched cadavers, a grim and unreadable expression on his face.

"Brialise," he said quietly, "bring me the torch."

Frowning, she handed it over, and Fish thrust the light forward. The corpse he gazed at was a big one. It had probably been a strong man in life, but now it had been reduced just like all the others, whimpering softly as it changed slowly into something that was not human anymore.

"Nico," Fish said softly. "Tell me I'm wrong."

Nico started forward. "What have you seen?" Apprehensively, he stared at the big corpse, and suddenly a chill washed over him.

It was hard to recognize individual features on the wasted face, to see in the slack jaw what he might have looked like in life. But the colour of the still-bushy beard was right. The height, the size. And he remembered that bearskin well . . .

Fish shifted the torch, and Nico recognized more and more of the muttering figures. The men and boys of the village. The very people he had found sanctuary with. The village where they hoped to go, to escape from here . . .

Nico rounded upon Brialise. "What happened?"

"These—they came looking for you," she quavered. Nico felt the words as a blow to his heart.

The torchlight danced red in Fish's eyes. "And you didn't think to tell us?"

She didn't answer, but Fish wasn't done. "You agreed to this plan," he snarled. "You agreed to take us back to that village. Pray tell me, how do we go back there when half their people are gone? How do we answer their questions? How do we convince them that we're still on their side?"

Tears filled Brialise's eyes, and she took a step backwards. "I—I don't know."

Something seemed to have come over Fish, something more than just shock. The hand that held the torch was shaking. "Why didn't you tell us?" he repeated loudly. She still didn't answer, only shook her head in tears. "I'll answer for you! Because you only care about yourself and your own safety! Isn't that right? Who cares what becomes of *us*, as long as we've served our purpose on your behalf?"

"No," the girl whispered. "I—"

Fish took a step towards her, and she recoiled. Nico moved forward, reaching for his partner's arm.

"Fish, calm yourself."

"That's rich coming from you!" Fish snapped as he whirled round. To Nico's dismay, he saw that the boy was glowing.

"She meant no harm," Nico remonstrated. Fish only glared at him. There was something unhinged in his eyes, something which matched the fiery magic he'd done on the mountainside.

"We can't go back there," he whispered to Nico, and gave a mirthless laugh. Turning away, he strode down the passage towards the very end of the cages. Nico caught Brialise's arm and kept pace, half-dragging her along behind him.

Fish reached the end and turned, facing the cages, holding the torch aloft before him. Propelled by some instinct, Nico edged back until he and Brialise were both well behind him.

Fish threw the torch overhand, flames outlined in a red welt as the torch spun, and moved both of his hands in a quick, simple gesture. The flames expanded, reverberated from the walls, filled the whole passageway and swallowed everything. Nico could no longer hear the soft squalling of the would-be necromes; the fire roared like a living thing, and he felt a sickening heat rush up the tunnel towards them.

Brialise screamed and Nico stepped in front of her, shielding her from the blast of heat as best he could, keeping his own face turned away as the blaze rolled over him. Fish stood in the roiling light of his own destruction, apparently not feeling any ill effect. Nico wanted to yell to him, but didn't dare turn his face towards the fire. He could feel the heat scorching the back of his cloak.

Then the radiance of the fires and the searing heat dimmed, and Nico dared to turn around. There was nothing but ash and red-hot metal and the charred stink of the burned dead. Fish was breathing heavily, his eyes glazed, his curls stirring in a hot dry wind. Nico reached out to him, grabbed his arm, and recoiled with a cry. His hand burned as if he had dared to touch a red-hot sword straight out of the forge.

"Now," Fish said, ignoring Nico and facing the girl, "take me to Taunus."

"What?" Nico resisted the urge to grab the boy. "Fish, *no*! Are you mad?"

"As mad as ever I have been," Fish replied without looking at him. His hands were still shaking, Nico saw. "I have just enough left in me to make an end of this. Do the job that we came here to do. To wipe these slavers—my brother—from the face of the earth. I understand if you want to leave, Nico."

"Fish—" Nico's voice almost failed him. "I don't understand. We should run. Get away from here together. Come with me."

"No." He turned to Brialise, and seized her by the wrist. Nico gasped, but the girl seemed to be immune to whatever it was that had burned Nico. She faced Fish steadfastly. "To Taunus. Now."

Wordlessly, Brialise turned and took a path into the darkness, leaving Nico behind. He hesitated, cursed, sent up yet another prayer to his gods, and followed in Fish's wake. Leaving the boy had never been an option.

OUTSIDE, THE WORLD WAS WHITE. Brialise had not lied about the storm. It raged and howled before them as they stood a few paces away from the cave opening. Fish was still glowing with some kind of eerie power, and Brialise's outline was grey and slumped beside him.

This high in the mountains, it was worse than any winter storm Nico had ever seen. The cold blew in with the wind, setting his arm to throbbing and frosting the very breath that blew through his nostrils. Nothing could be seen from the mouth of the cave, only a screen of white. Supposedly they were facing Taunus's valley, but for all Nico knew, they could be on the other side of the world.

Fish stared out into the snow, but there was no sign of dismay or remorse on his face. "I can feel him," he said. "And he knows what I've done. Must have felt a surge like that."

"Fish." Nico came up beside him, stepping closer to the cold. He did not dare to touch his partner as he normally would have, and tried to put all of his meaning into his eyes. "It's not too late. We can still run."

For the first time since they had escaped their bonds, Fish looked directly at him. He lifted his hands, and gave a grin that seemed empty of all sanity. "And where would we run to, Nico?"

Nico would have liked to answer that, to tell him of the high road that led past Lynborder and the ships at Sulshome and the adventures that they could have together, but his words failed him. The wailing of the wind in the valley drowned out his very thoughts.

Fish furrowed his brows together as if in concentration, and the glow around him receded somewhat. He moved closer to Nico, and touched the silver medallion that hung around his neck, caressing the embossed symbols with his thumb, looking at it and not at Nico's face. "You go, Nico," he finally said. "Anywhere you want. Escape from here. You deserve that much."

"You're my partner," Nico said. "Remember? I'm not leaving without you. Wherever we go, we go together."

Fish looked up at him. There was a queer light in his golden eyes. "Together," he repeated. "Then let's finish this together." And without hesitating, he turned towards the storm. He spread his arms wide, glowed for a moment so brightly that Nico had to shield his eyes. When he looked again, he gave a gasp of fright and disbelief.

The sky had cleared. The ground beneath was carpeted with snow, but a thin and pale sun shone from heavens that had opened blue over the valley. It must be around midday, Nico thought absently. Even as he watched, the rage of the winds was dying in the distance. Fish had walked out into the snow and stood in a pose of acute concentration, face turned up to the clear sky.

Nico ventured towards him and spun round, trying to make sense of the kind of power he wielded. There was a vortex in the valley, a blue hole in the midst of the grey storm. The winds had been set at a distance, blowing in a circle around the valley, and where they stood was enveloped in utter calm.

Nico could now see that the valley was teardrop-shaped, hedged in by high cliffs that rose to the front and sides. He shaded his eyes against the sudden snowglare and looked around. The only approach to the valley seemed to be at a point behind him, where a narrow passage sloped between two peaks. Everything was covered with fresh, wet snow. Nico felt the weight of it when he moved his feet. The air was sharp, the watery sun doing little to warm it.

Fish's focus had shifted, and he stood as if at attention, facing towards the end of the valley where it was swallowed up by the cliffsides. The storm raged there beyond the restraints of his power, a wall of grey that disoriented Nico. He turned, trying to see what had become of Brialise. She had disappeared. *Probably gone further inside the cave*, he thought. The girl wore shoes with paper-thin soles, was singularly under-equipped for this kind of cold. She would be safer under the mountain, in the tunnels she seemed to know so well.

Could she get herself out? Nico wondered. If she were inclined to flee, this would probably be a good opportunity. Let Fish distract the sorcerer, and run whilst his attention was focused elsewhere.

She was, most likely, gone. But Nico had pledged to stay, and he hovered a dozen paces or so behind his partner, wishing he had some better weapon than a single silvered dagger. His heart seemed to be beating very loudly, and he could hear his own breath as it frosted in the air. All was still.

As it had always been just before all hell broke loose, the assassin felt no fear. There was a calm that lay just beyond, after one made the decision to walk into danger, and he was there now, wading into the waters of battle-madness. He tested the weight and balance of the dagger in his hand, made a disgusted face. He was comfortable writing and eating with his left hand, but he'd favoured his right from the beginning when it came to holding a blade. That had cost him dear, during the battle with the necromes. He had never learned the motions of fighting with his left hand alone, and had been off-balance, unsteady.

Something to learn, if I survive this. Nico stowed the thought away, and knew that he could not risk that unsteadiness again. He cut the sling that bound his right arm, stretched it out and flexed the fingers, flinched in pain as a spasm shot through him. The arm was still tender, hot to the touch, but the balance of the dagger felt *right* in a way that reassured him. He could endure the pain.

Something stirred at the end of the valley. Nico shielded his eyes from the white-hot glare of the sun on the distant snowdrifts. *Five figures.* The one in the middle could only be Taunus, a bulky man with a reach to match Nico's. The other four must be his lieutenants, the human soldiers who kept the necromes in line. Nico watched their movements carefully. Their swords were unsheathed, held in ready hands. Taunus alone had left his sword in its scabbard by his side, and all his attention was focused on Fish.

Closer they moved, and Nico readied himself, trusting Fish as he always had. It was different now, yet the same. Nico had never guessed that his partner could call up sorcery, but he now trusted Fish to handle the magic Taunus threw at them, and readied himself to deal with the physical attack.

They were within range of hearing, now, and Taunus halted, the four flanking him stopping just behind. He raised his voice and said something to Fish; Nico did not even register the words, so intent he was upon the four guardsmen. They threw lazy glances at him, seemingly secure in their numerical superiority. Fish did not answer his brother.

There seemed to be something humming in the air, something

Nico could not place. It was difficult to look at Fish now, and Nico turned his full attention to Taunus's guards. The sorcerer barked an order, and the four swarmed *around* Fish, going wide as if to avoid something Nico could not see.

They made straight for him, spreading out in a circle, grins on their faces, swords out and ready. Nico gripped his dagger and stood his ground. The boldest, closer than the other three, came up with a swagger. Five paces away. Nico counted. Four, three, two—

Quick as a snake, he struck the man in the face with the same hand that was holding the dagger, laying open his cheek and sending him down with a scream. No time to recover; Nico swung past a glancing swordstroke and seized the second swordsman's free arm, pulling him sideways with his greater weight. He collided hard with the third man, grabbed his wrist.

Nico wrested the guardsman's sword away, passing his dagger quickly to his left hand as he raised the purloined weapon in his right. The fourth had come up behind him; Nico met his stroke on the backspin, came up inside his guard, whacked him on the side of the helm. His world narrowed to the action before him; he barely noticed the abrupt growl of thunder, the eldritch green streak that flashed across a sky suddenly grown grey as lead. He fought in a tight circle, desperately staving away blows that came for his unprotected head, ignoring the strokes that bit into his leather armour. His dagger found purchase, more than once, slashing at wrists and faces. One of the guards lost his helm, and the other could not see through a face dripping with blood.

Then something in the world shifted, the ground suddenly sloping away from his feet where it had been level before, and Nico gasped as a disorienting sensation filled him, a feeling of being struck like a gong and having the vibrations run all through his being.

Nico stumbled, but kept his footing. The four around him fell to their knees, and for the first time in this fight, he looked for Fish.

There was not much to see. Fish and his brother stood ten feet apart, Fish looking tired and windswept. Taunus had lost his helm, and nursed some kind of hand injury. The sky above had changed, leaden clouds swathed across it thick as a woollen blanket, and forked green lighting swept across the clouds as Nico watched. The clear vortex, which had so sharply separated the storm from the valley, seemed to have blurred. The winds were still howling around the crag, nearby the snow still fell on the mountains, but it all seemed closer than before, the valley smaller.

Fish raised his hand, and Nico saw something like a flicker of desperation in Taunus's eyes. His own spirit answered that fleeting moment, and he went for the stumbling guard nearest to him, swatting the uncertain sword away, then swiftly opening the man's throat with his dagger. Taunus's guards seemed a lot more disoriented than Nico was, and he ruthlessly capitalized on that advantage. They had abandoned their coordinated attack, and came at him one by one, sluggishly.

Nico finished them one by one, batting aside their swords to bury his dagger in their throats. He stood for a moment, catching his breath, and his arm gave a wrench that caught the breath in his throat. The pain blinded him, and he felt the sword in his hand drop from nerveless fingers.

He started as he felt a flake of snow settle on his head. He looked up into a sky that was still tinged with green, snowflakes spiralling lazily down towards the world. There was no wind, but the storm was no longer barred from the valley.

Fish was twenty feet away, swaying slightly as the snow fell. Taunus still stood opposite him. The two seemed to be grappling with some invisible force that lay between them. Fish's curly hair was soaked through, sweat dripping from his face, and his brother's features were strained with exertion.

Then Taunus, with an effort as if he were wrenching a great weight from himself, made a cutting gesture with his right hand. There was an audible *snap*, a smell of brimstone in the air, and Fish cried out in real, physical pain and fell to his knees.

Nico gazed at him desperately. *Get up, Fish!* His own limbs seemed to have turned to ice where he stood. *Get up! You can't fail us now!*

Taunus began to laugh. Nico started. The sorcerer paced forward, made for Fish. The boy seemed to be in too much pain even to move, yet Nico could see no wound.

Taunus stopped in front of Fish, grinned, put a hand to the sword at his side.

At last, Nico moved. There was no real plan; he simply rushed forward and attacked the sorcerer as if he were a tough in a street-fight, brandishing his dagger and yelling at the top of his voice. Taunus started at first, surprised, as if he had completely forgotten Nico's very existence. But his mailed arm came up and engaged Nico's stroke, swatting him away.

Nico came around again, met another blow. The sorcerer was skilled even at hand-to-hand fighting. The dagger flashed again and again, but Nico could not find the opening he sought. From the corner of his eye, he saw Fish slump down in the snow.

The sight gave him pause, and a mailed fist struck the side of his head. He reeled backwards, felt himself lose the dagger, spat out blood. The sorcerer came forward, pressing his advantage. Nico fell, crawled to hands and knees. A steel-tipped boot hit him in the chest, came in again to meet his chin. Nico had just enough presence of mind left to grab it and pull.

Taunus came down on top of him, obviously no stranger to grappling, steel gauntlet meeting Nico's face in a blur of pain and blood.

So this is what it comes to, Nico thought dully, as he fought back in desperation. *Two men grappling in the mud, winner takes all.* And they were not free yet. Nico could not imagine why Taunus had not brought his necromes to the fight, yet they were nowhere to be seen. Was it his own hubris, as Fish had implied? Or were they waiting in the wings even now, ready to move in and end this farce of a battle?

And what of Taunus's magic? He half expected to feel the searing blaze of fire at any moment, to find himself roasted before he even knew he had lost the fight. But Nico had noticed, already, that both Fish and his brother appeared to need at least a moment to *think* before actually managing to cast a spell, and he did not intend to give Taunus that moment if he could help it.

Taunus managed to get the upper hand, and he slammed Nico hard against the ground. But in doing so, he had left an opening. Nico's fist found his jaw, connecting so hard that his head snapped backwards. Nico felt something in his own hand shatter. With grim amusement he remembered the pair of trusty knuckledusters he'd once owned, useful things when engaging in street fights.

Despite the force of that blow, Taunus was nowhere near done for. He recovered quickly, still pinning Nico to the ground with his armoured weight, and Nico saw the flash of silver and iron in his hand.

He could do nothing but throw up his hands to defend himself, and he felt the blade of the knife cut deep into his palms. Madness overtook him, and he closed his hand on the blade, feeling the bite and not caring, grappling for his life against Taunus's grip. Somehow their faces were close together now, and years of practice at dirty fighting distilled in Nico. He brought himself forward in a rush, smashing his head into Taunus's face. There was the *crunch* of something breaking, and more importantly, the feel of Taunus's grip loosening on the dagger. Quickly Nico yanked it out of his hands, and with his last strength, defying the pain and the fatigue and the thought of *what's happened to Fish*, buried the blade in the sorcerer's throat.

Blood burbled, last breath rasped, and Nico found himself crouching over a corpse. Not the first time this had transpired, but usually, he had been in much better shape afterwards. A wave of disorientation shook him, and he edged away, wanting to vomit. He could not feel his own face. It hurt to breathe, whether from the cold or some injury in his ribcage, he could not tell. There was fire and ice all along his right arm, and he found that he could not put his weight on it as he crawled through the snow. The flakes were falling fast now, the storm had caught up with them. Fish lay all in a heap, face turned downwards, no way to tell whether he was still breathing.

Nico left a red trail as he crawled through the snow towards his partner, no thought in his mind but to reach him. He turned the boy's face up, scrabbled clumsily for a pulse but could not find it. Numbly, he gathered Fish into his arms, having no thought but that perhaps the heat of his own body would revive him. The boy was very cold. Nico wrapped his cloak around both of them, closed his eyes against the pain. He could hardly feel anything. Fish was solid beside him, one bulwark of comfort against the howling chaos. Darkness was waiting.

Nico did not want to go into the darkness, but there was no help for it now. Exhaustion overtook him, and even the snow did not feel cold anymore.

CHAPTER XIX
RELEASE

THE NIGHT WAS DARK, the air warm, the forest close. There was no moon.

Velda donned the darkest of the two dresses she had brought with her, wrapped a black ribbon around her hair to keep stray curls from falling into her eyes. They moved through the trees in single file, Velda in front, Albryan bringing up the rear behind Hiram, who led the mule. Occasionally, Albryan would call a halt and scout up ahead, leaving the others waiting in the bushes. From where he went whenever this happened, Velda soon deduced where the enemy camp was. She even thought she could see the glow of their campfires between the trees once, far off. Albryan had warned them that there would be sentries about, but Velda never saw one. They moved quickly, the young captain setting the pace. Start, then stop.

Stop, then start again. And again.

But at last, Albryan seemed satisfied that they were clear, and moved into the lead as they made a brisk pace through the trees. They were around six hours' walk from Qwu'Mallorn, and he hoped to put at least two of those hours between them and the enemy before the night was through.

He had covered about half the distance intended when Velda stumbled hard in the undergrowth and fell flat on her face, biting off a cry of pain.

"It's my ankle," she whispered as the two men crowded around her in the darkness. "Damn and blast! I can't walk on it. Bryan, I'm so sorry."

Albryan gave Velda his arm, and managed to help her to a more sheltered spot, some way off the path he had chosen. It was far too dark for him to see anything, and Velda stripped off her boot and made her own inspection.

"It might not be sprained," she finally said, knowing that she was the authority in this. "If it's not, I could be able to walk again in a few hours." That was perfectly true; sprained and broken ankles were one of the most common injuries in the mountains. Velda had had a bad sprain herself before, and knew exactly how it would present.

"If it *is* sprained, though . . ." Hiram's voice was troubled.

"No way of knowing," Albryan said curtly. He looked very tired, what little she could see of him using only the light of the stars. "Nothing for it but to rest, then. Velda, do you think you could stay up for the first watch?"

"Sure thing," she replied easily. "I had a long nap this afternoon."

Albryan curled himself up in a patch of bracken, Hiram soon following suit. The forest was quiet around them, yet not as quiet as it could be in a mountain winter. The trees Albryan called milkwoods bushed about them, black branches snaking horizontally across the ground.

It was a long moment before Velda moved. First she pulled her boot back on, making just enough noise so that she might know whether Albryan was really asleep. He continued to snore softly, Hiram echoing, and Velda got to her feet.

Her first instinct was to run, but Velda had sneaked around in the rooms back at the Lynborder monastery often enough to know that caution was better than speed in this kind of situation. She placed her feet carefully, desperate to avoid entangling them in something. A *real* twisted ankle would not do.

When she finally reached the antelope-track Albryan had had them following in the dark, she breathed again and began to walk faster. She headed back the way they had come, keeping her bearings by the direction of the cool breeze that was blowing from the mountains. Her heart hammered in fear, fear of Albryan discovering her or fear of what lay ahead she could not say. But it was the right thing to do. She knew it, and Albryan's ire be damned.

AN HOUR LATER, VELDA PRESSED herself back against the great trunk of a silver-barked tree, not daring to breathe. She could hear the sounds of the camp beyond the tree, behind her, the faint crackling of a fire and men's voices. She thought a patrol was passing somewhere in the darkness, but she couldn't be sure. She had been trying to learn the little tricks of woodscraft from Albryan, integrating it into the knowledge she had long ago gleaned from her friend and fellow orphan Klaus whenever he let her go hunting with him, but she feared she was not as silent nor as observant as she should have been.

Velda wondered if she should climb the tree, whether that would give her a view into the camp. She finally decided that she would, and found the nearest branch. She had climbed enough trees back home, running wild in the mountain forests around Lynborder, but that had been before Ricard was born. Her weight shifted at just the wrong moment, and the branch gave a loud *crack* as she slipped, falling to the ground with a scraping noise and loud thud.

She got back to her feet and torchlight shone full in her face, the surprised faces of two sentries illuminated right in front of her. "What have we here?" one of the huge men growled.

Velda turned to flee, and stumbled right into the third sentry, who seized her wrists and held her easily, shrugging off her struggles with little effort.

She wanted to scream. She wanted to be stronger. Velda tried to reach the power inside herself, as had been her plan all along, but it would not come. Even though she was in panic, half-crazed, more afraid than she had been when facing the strange undead necromes, she felt no answer to her call. What if it had left her? The thought made the panic worse, and she could do nothing as she was dragged towards the brigands' camp.

THE BIG OFFICER STUDIED HER. "I don't recall seeing this one before," he said to his men.

"We found her in the forest, sir," one of Velda's captors said, holding her arm securely.

Their captain, a burly straw-haired man in his forties, stepped towards her and tucked a stray strand of hair behind her ear, running his hand along her cheekbone and neck on the way back. It was a gesture remarkably similar to the one Albryan had used before, and it made Velda's skin crawl. Real fear was in her now; she was no innocent maid who believed in the inherent goodness of men. She desperately wished, now, that she had listened to Albryan.

The officer's tent-flaps snapped in the wind behind him, the flames of the great fire dancing in the breeze. Several dozen yards away, the miserable mass of prisoners huddled, away from the light of the fire. Almost the whole horde had come out from sleep when Velda had been dragged in, struggling against her captors, and most were still loitering just beyond the firelight. Velda trembled. She was not struggling now.

"Pretty," the captain remarked, turning away as if he had concluded the sale of a sow. "Well, put her with the others. Not like me to turn away any windfall." He gave a nasty grin. The two who had dragged Velda into camp now dragged her towards the dark mass of prisoners, shackled her wrists and ankles together, fastened her to the long chain that linked all the prisoners in line. Velda was at the end of a chain a dozen long, she saw, one of three such chains. The woman in line next to her was stout, brown-haired and brown-eyed, as were most of the others. Farm folk, Velda knew, not so different from the folks she had known in Lynborder, a bit darker of complexion but remarkably similar-looking all the same. She imagined the people of her little town, dirty-cheeked and tear-eyed and chained together just like this lot. Zelma Friedman in the stout woman's place, the Stein children for that gaggle of urchins just opposite, Liezl and Susie in the place of two curly-headed girls who clung to each other. She swallowed bile.

The stout woman's eyes were upon her, taking her in with a measuring glance. She looked up, and Velda's eyes followed. Two guards strode back and forth between the lines of sleeping prisoners. The others had melted away, even the curious onlookers. It must be past midnight, Velda realized, and the camp was silent save for the measured tread of the pacing guards and the clinking of chains.

Yet all of the chained prisoners were awake now, and no-one showed any sign of wanting to fall asleep again. Heads were alert; gazes swept the camp furtively, lingering on the two night guards and quickly flicking away. She could sense a restlessness, an impatience.

The guards moved away, and the stout woman looked at Velda again. "What's your name?" she heard the woman whisper.

"Velda." The fear was not so bad now; Velda had stopped trembling. She knew she *had* to escape tonight. Or suffer the consequences. She had not liked the look in the officer's eyes at all.

A look that *this* woman, no doubt, had known for days, maybe weeks. Since her home had been burned, her livestock killed and left to lie in the fields, her husband cut down. Most of the captives were women; only a few were boys and older men.

"I'm Daisy," the stout woman said. "You stick with me." She leaned closer. "We try to help each other."

Velda nodded. Daisy's eyes followed the pacing guards without blinking, keeping them in her sights and speaking with as little movement as possible. "They don't want us to talk," she continued. "But—" One of the guards looked her way, and the word was immediately cut off.

"I understand," Velda whispered back, when the sentry's attention had passed again.

Daisy's brown eyes studied her, lingering somewhere on her hair as if the woman was memorizing her profile. She stirred.

"Velda," came the whisper on the guards' next round, "are those pins in your hair?"

She nodded, felt her heart beat louder. The thickness of her hair had always necessitated a little help when styling, but it was not the only reason she wore pins. Velda had taught herself to lockpick, long ago, when she was sixteen and had a curfew and wanted to meet Emmett at night. The window to the room she'd shared with three other girls had been easy enough to get through, the creeping ivy thick enough for one slight girl to descend, but the padlock on the barred gate across the footpath had been another matter.

Daisy's voice came very soft, very close to her ear. "Could you get your own manacles off?"

Velda nodded again, not daring to make a sound. One of the pacing guards lit a cigarillo, flaring suddenly in the gloom. He took a drag, passed it to his comrade. Daisy took the opportunity to whisper in her ear once more.

"We escape. Tonight. Made preparations; been waiting." Daisy's eyes moved beyond her, and Velda followed her gaze to a post nailed into the ground. The ankle-chain which kept all the prisoners together was wound around the post, but Velda's heart leapt when she saw there was no padlock upon it.

Velda would never know what prompted Daisy to trust her, what kind of extra sense told the woman that Velda was willing and able to help. Had come here for just that purpose, even. She mimed unwrapping the chain, and the older woman nodded.

The manacles, as Velda had thought, were old-fashioned and cheaply made, the keyhole big enough to easily admit the heavy pin. Even so, it took much longer to pick them than she would have liked. It had been a long time since she had been sixteen and reckless, over two years since she had married the boy and no longer needed to shroud their relations in secrecy. She worked carefully, trying to avoid the notice of the pacing guards. Most of the prisoners around her carefully and deliberately averted their eyes, but she knew that everyone had seen what she was about. They were all waiting with bated breath.

The manacles clicked loudly, snapping open, and Velda's heart shot into her mouth. But before the guards could register what the sudden noise had been, a teenaged boy from the next line over began a hacking cough that pulled their attention towards him. Velda saw Daisy's gaze flash towards the boy, saw the look of unmistakable maternal pride in her eyes. She leaned down and began to work on the lock of her ankle chains, muffling it this time with the hem of her dress.

It took only a few more minutes, an eternity to Velda, who had to hide what she was doing from the guards and make it look like her hands were still chained up. More of the prisoners were stirring now, unable to even pretend to be sleeping, and the guards seemed to have noticed and looked more alert than before. Velda could simply not see how she was ever going to be able to cross the five yards between where she sat to the chain-post.

"We need a distraction," she mouthed to Daisy. The older woman shot a glance over to her son, who had not taken his eyes from her all the while. He seemed to understand some silent gesture which Daisy gave, and turned away, signalling someone else in the third line of prisoners, furthest from where Velda was.

An old man in that line suddenly stumbled to his feet, chains clanking about him. The attention of the guards was immediately arrested.

Velda did not need Daisy's nod to know that she had to move immediately. There was no time for fear, for hesitation. Even as she kept half an ear turned towards the commotion, as the guards yelled and threatened and the old man bellowed, she sprinted for the post.

She was halfway through unwinding the heavy chain when she heard the shout. They had seen her, but were too far away. The second line roiled like a black metal snake as the prisoners all sprang to their feet. She spared a single glance over her shoulder, and did a double-take. The prisoners of the second line, Daisy's teenage son included, had fallen upon the two guards and entangled them in the ankle chain. Despite the element of surprise being in their favour, though, they had little hope of winning. Velda could see the flash of the guards' steel, and soon enough the rest would hear the commotion and come out of their tents, and that would be the end.

She flung herself at the heavy chain, unwound it. Those at the other end seized the chain and pulled it through with a rattling as loud as thunder. The night was filled with prisoners pulling themselves free, clamour from the fight, curses and cheers. Fully half of the freed prisoners made immediately for the forest, shuffling as fast as they could with their ankles bound. Velda sprinted for the second post, Daisy on her heels. Together they unwrapped the next chain, spilling it on the ground like a coiled snake. Someone seized the loose end and wrapped it around a guard's throat, strangling him. Velda could not tell where the original two guards had gone, nor how many more had arrived. She made for the third post, no thought in her mind but to get everyone free.

Chains clanked to the ground. People were running. There were nowhere near as many guards as she had expected. The old man who had made the distraction for them lay on the ground, his head bloody. Two others attempted to wake him, failed, dragged him between them as they ran. Velda moved through the prisoners, helped those who had gotten entangled in the loose chains, yelled at them all to run.

Suddenly Daisy was there, her son by her side. The boy's nose was bleeding; Velda did not know how that had happened.

"Come with us!" Daisy yelled.

"Not until everyone is out!" Velda replied, and ran towards a girl who had tripped over her ankle chains.

She lost Daisy then. Everyone was on the run now, and Velda followed. She risked one look behind. The camp was boiling with soldiers, black outlines like ants in the light of the blazing fire.

Arrows zipped behind her, and Velda faltered, losing her footing and stumbling. There were yards and yards between her and the last stragglers, she realized. She had waited and struggled to get them all out, and now she was the last one.

An arrow struck into the ground right beside her, and Velda froze and let out a sob of fear. Fear had been arrested, for a little while.

Escape had been more important. She could hear running behind her, could hear the loosing of more arrows. She flattened herself instinctively against the ground.

She felt rough hands grasp her shoulders, allowed herself to be pulled up bonelessly. She had been captured again. She glanced about. *But the others escaped. All the others. Everyone. It was I who made the difference.* There was a furtive kind of pride in that, to be sure. Without magic, she had succeeded in a plan Albryan would not even consider. But now, she knew, she was bound to pay the price.

THE SOLDIERS RISKED NO CHANCE of their one remaining prisoner escaping. The captain took one look at her and ordered his men to strip her, though they left her in her sleeveless underdress, loose hair brushing her shoulders. There was not much that the worn fabric would hide, however, and Velda was horribly aware of the way the men looked at her when they bound her up again. This time she was marched up against a tall post and tied against it so tightly that after a few minutes, she could not feel her fingertips.

Surprisingly enough, no-one paid much attention to her after that; almost every single remaining man was sent out to recapture the escapees. She was left bound to the post with the fire at her back, one remaining soldier standing guard over her, the captain seated nearby, taking the time to sharpen his sword. No-one spoke to her, and she was left with her thoughts and fears and the pain in her bound wrists.

The insistent breeze turned cold, chilling her even in the glow of the fire. She had been bound facing westwards, her face in the teeth of the wind. She wondered if there was a storm on the slopes of Svanlyn, whether the last snow was raging over the faraway peaks even now.

Dawn was not far off; she could smell it on the breeze. She wondered whether Albryan would try to save her. One part of her pictured it, the gallant soldier coming to her rescue in a blaze of fiery magic. Another part thought that perhaps he would be too angry at her disobedience, that he would simply leave her to her fate. But on the other hand, he needed her. It was his job to deliver her to his people to help with the war; he had said so. She trembled. But if her sudden gift had genuinely abandoned her, would he still care?

The minutes crept by. The younger soldier stared at her chest as the cold wind encircled her. Were her hands not bound, Velda would have covered her breasts instinctively, as little as that would help her. None of the others had yet returned. The escaped prisoners were bound hand and foot, most of them young or old or female, all hungry and ill-used and exhausted from tramping in chains for who knew how many days. The soldiers were sure to recapture at least a few of them. The knowledge felt bitter. If Albryan had helped her . . .

She waited, unable to do anything else. It felt as though hours and hours had gone by, and yet the world was still dark. She felt almost too tired to even contemplate the impending threat of rape anymore; terror had run its course, and she was numb from it. The captain stood up and walked towards the other soldier.

"They should have been back by now," she heard him say. His eyes swivelled towards the darkness beyond the glare of the fire. A faint hope, she could not say for whom, flickered in her heart.

More minutes ticked by, and the captain grew restless. He paced up and down, turned to look at Velda, who returned his glare steadfastly.

Out in the forest, there was a sudden shriek, cut off abruptly and horribly. The two men started. Both drew their swords. Velda strained to see into the darkness. She thought that it seemed lighter now, that perhaps dawn was coming to this endless night after all.

"Who's there?" the younger soldier called, and his captain shot him a dirty look.

"Where's your bow?" he demanded. But just as the young guard turned to find it, there was movement in the darkness. A grey, shadowy shape resolved itself, strode forward into the flickering light cast by the fire.

Relief and a warmth that had nothing to do with the fire flowed through her as Albryan strode into view, casually as if he were on a leisure walk, his bloodied sword leaning against his shoulder. Velda had never been so glad to see anyone in her life. She trembled all over, and felt tears come to her eyes.

The captain hefted his sword, adopted a defensive pose. "Who goes there?" he growled.

Albryan grinned, and reflected flames seemed to dance green in his eyes. There was blood spattered halfway up his left sleeve, Velda noticed, and on the side of his face too.

"I could ask the same of you." Albryan's voice was curiously soft. "You have no business here."

"We have the business of justice." The captain made a motion, and the younger soldier lifted a bow that was already strung with a ready arrow. Velda began to cry out in warning, but Albryan raised a hand quicker than she could react.

The wooden bow burst into flame. The young soldier screamed and dropped it, backing away.

"You wear no armour, Morgein scum," the captain hissed, seemingly undaunted by the sudden magic. And without any more preamble, he went for Albryan.

Albryan easily deflected the first few blows, dancing backwards. The younger guard joined the attack, and now Albryan had to defend himself against two. He was faster and lighter on his feet than either of them, dodging cuts and strokes until Velda's heart was in her mouth, landing blows of his own that met only chainmail and leather.

The two bandits worked as a team, trying to get him between them. As he dodged a blow of the captain's from behind, the young soldier charged him, and this time Albryan did not dodge in time. The blade glanced against his unprotected chest, and blood welled from a shallow cut. Yet Albryan did not flinch, and the young soldier was now within his reach. He struck with a deft, powerful stroke, driving the point of his blade up into the armpit where the young soldier's sleeveless chainmail shirt met his pauldrons.

The young soldier screamed and buckled to his knees, and Albryan's sword was withdrawn just in time to meet the captain's retaliatory blow. Albryan danced away, leading the captain.

The young soldier seemed unable to rise. Blood welled from under the hand he clamped into his armpit. His face was white. Albryan grinned in the light of the fire. His own shirt was stained with blood, yet he seemed hardly to notice.

"Had enough?" he asked. The captain did not answer, but charged him. There was a short flurry of blows, then a gasp of pain, and the bandit captain reeled back, bleeding from the wrist. Albryan pressed him backwards, not letting up. The swords clashed once, twice, and then Albryan's blade bit once more into the unprotected wrist. The captain dropped his sword and stumbled back.

Albryan's stroke came back around so fast it seemed surreal, the blade catching the bandit's neck at just the right place, the gap where his chainmail met his helmet, biting halfway into his neck. Blood gushed, coating the already gory blade, and the captain's corpse collapsed silently.

Albryan turned back to the younger soldier, who still knelt, white-faced, on the ground. "Mercy," he began. "Spare me. I surrender."

Albryan was breathing fast, but did not seem winded. The blade of his sword glowed red in the firelight. Light was creeping from the dawning sunrise towards him, showing up the mud on his boots and the blood on his shirt. He stepped forward towards the young bandit.

"Take off your helm," he commanded.

The young soldier shuddered as he released his wound, but did as he was bid. "Please," he said, dropping his helmet to the ground.

"Please," Albryan echoed, and the ghost of a smile quirked his lips. "I bet that's a word you heard a lot, out here."

He raised his sword in both hands, met the other man's eyes, struck fast and true. The force of the blow took the young soldier's head clean off. Albryan stepped away, sheathed the gory blade by his side, and ran to Velda.

"Are you all right?" he demanded. His demeanour was completely altered; he cupped her cheek, turned her head this way and that as if to inspect her. "Did they hurt you?"

"No." She squirmed against her bonds. "Please get me free. You came for me. I'm so glad to see you—Bryan—"

Albryan took a small hunting knife from his belt and carefully sawed through her bonds, releasing Velda's hands at last. He gathered her into his arms, hugging her tightly. She massaged her wrist, gasping as the feeling returned to her hands and arms all in pins and needles.

"The other soldiers?" she asked breathlessly. "They were going after the prisoners—"

"All accounted for," Albryan replied. She stared at him. His lips quirked. "Come now. You got them all free without even needing my help, d'you think I want them captured again?"

He didn't seem in the least angry with her, Velda thought, even seemed to be *pleased* with her somehow. She wasn't sure how to take any of this.

"Can you run?" he asked, and she nodded. "We need to leave here, and quickly. There'll be magical residue. Can't say who might come for it." He led her away from the camp for a little ways, then turned back and faced the fire. "Might as well muddle what happened here, though." He raised his hands.

The fire, which had been smouldering low, suddenly roared back into leaping flame. It expanded, ate the ground before it. The whole site was wreathed in flames; the rough tents went up like so many sticks of kindling. Albryan dropped his hands again, and the fire smouldered low once more, this time reducing the whole campsite to nothing more than smoking ashes and cherry-red cinders. Velda could not say that she was upset to see it that way.

"Come on." Albryan seized her hand, and they moved away as fast as they could.

ALBRYAN SET THE PACE, jogging along a path in the underbrush he seemed to know, but in the end he tired before she did. They came to a halt in a hollow bowl carpeted with lush ferns, some of them near as tall as Velda. A great black-barked tree loomed over them, and the surrounding bushes made murk of the approaching daylight.

Albryan motioned her to sit on a fallen tree trunk, then sank to his knees, shrugging off his shirt. A pang went through her as she saw that the wound on his chest was still bleeding. She would have come forward to offer her help, but he bundled up the shirt and pressed down hard on the cut, and after a few moments she saw with relief that it had been stanched.

The forest was silent around them, save for the soft chirpings of the earliest birds somewhere in branches far away. It had been a long night, and yet Velda was not tired anymore. She still felt the thrill of Albryan's rescue, the relief that had swept over her. Relief—and something else. Whatever it was, he seemed to feel it too, for he leaned towards her until they were almost touching, and met her gaze with eyes that were shadowed green as the ferns surrounding them.

"Velda." He put out a hand and slid it into her hair, apparently unaware of his half nakedness and close proximity, the thrill that ran through her at his touch, at the sound of her name on his lips. His features were twisted with a strange emotion, and he cupped her face hard, the caress of his thumb rough against her cheek. "Velda—I'm sorry. I'm sorry."

His eyes were filled with relief and longing; the hand he held to her face was warm, his stubborn lips slightly parted. And after all, she had decided what she would do ages ago. In the next instant, Velda bridged the distance between their faces, pressing her lips to his.

He started for a moment, pulled away—and his eyes sought hers in the dim light, a myriad of questions behind them. But whatever he saw in her face seemed to answer, for all at once he drew her closer to him, kissed her back so hard their faces seemed to meld together. His beard was prickly and there was a strange metallic taste in his mouth, like flint or copper pennies, but she hardly cared. All that mattered was the closeness and the feel of him, an end to the hunger that had woken inside her. She ran her hand across his lean torso, feeling the heat of him, the hardness of the knots in his shoulders, the coarse hairs that tangled between her fingers.

And then suddenly her back was down on the hard earth and he was on top of her, entangled with her, too close for comfort, and yet she did not, would not ask him to stop. Her body had fallen just the right way, cupping him between her thighs, perhaps out of some residual instinct, a primal response to the loneliness that had been hers such a short time ago. A familiar urgency welled in the bottom of her belly.

Grief and fear and lust welded themselves together inside her, and all she knew was that she was exactly where she wanted to be, that she wanted him more than she could remember wanting anything else in her life. And he did not pull away from her, but held her tighter and closer to the heat of him, his hands trailing everywhere then tightening on the fabric of her flimsy underdress, sliding it up until the hem passed her hips and she was as naked from the waist down as he was from the waist up.

And then she was undoing his belt and struggling with the trouser lacings, pushing away the sword that was still buckled at his side, gasping, taking in breath as he entered her hard and fast, underdress ruched up around her hips and the taste of brimstone in his mouth as he kissed her, pleasure and release as he moved inside her, roughness and blinding heat against her inner core, his hands on the small of her back pulling her close as molten fire woke between their bodies, gripping her hard enough to leave bruises. Each movement, every touch and taste of him, was confirmation that she had made it out, she was still here, *she was still alive.* Her breath came in harsh sobs, the embrace too much and yet not enough, *never enough, kiss me harder, pull me closer, show me how much life there is still to be lived and how much to experience—*

The storm subsided and Albryan was still there, running his hands through her hair, whispering some endearment in a foreign tongue—*Ki'jaya, ki'jaya*—and despite the chill of the air and the hardness of the dirt and the ache in her spent limbs, she would gladly have remained here for as long as he wanted to keep her.

CHAPTER XX
FOREST FIRE

THE FOREST GREW DENSER as Hiram followed the gravelly path into the flint hills, the last geographical barrier that lay between Qwu'Mallorn and the outside world. Soon he would reach the point where the magical barrier lay, a web of power he could not pass on his own. Albryan had explained the workings of the barrier in only very simplistic terms, but the gist of it was that the web recognized all who sheltered under it. A child born in the forest realm would be recognized from the moment of their birth, and would always be able to pass to and fro over the border.

Not so anyone who had been born on the outside, and Albryan had warned Hiram not to test the web. "Hole up near the path and wait for us," he had told Hiram, last night after they had woken to find Velda gone and the dawn fast approaching. "There are hollows there big enough to hide the mule, and you can collect forage. We'll catch up with you by midday."

Santie was surefooted on the winding, overgrown track. Above Hiram's head, trees towered into the clear blue sky. They had left the land of the delta-valley behind, and here grew true forest. Black branches of milkwood and yellowwood and ironwood blocked the face of the sun as well as the path ahead. Hiram could see only that the track led gradually upwards, getting stonier as it climbed into the hills. He needed to stay on this trail until he passed over the first hill, then seek shelter in the forest beyond.

Safety was close, and yet Hiram's heart was pounding. He did not like the idea of splitting the group, but of course Velda had already done that and it was better that he go on alone rather than slow Albryan down.

Not that he blamed Velda for that. He had had half a suspicion of what she was going to do, and felt a queer sort of pride for it. Pride in her.

I am only afraid because it is too much like that night. The night I lost all. Despite nearly twenty years of imprisonment, Hiram found it impossible to dim the memory. The screams and clash of steel behind them, his daughter sobbing in his arms, their scrabbling flight down the ravine that was far too much like the slope of this very hill he now traversed. The last sight of her face haunted him, desperate and tear-streaked, fading away into the darkness as he stayed to face their pursuers.

The thought of the lost Lathea turned his mind towards the girl he had found, the girl who looked so much like his daughter that he still had to catch his breath whenever he looked at her. The last couple of weeks, travelling with Velda had been bittersweet. Yet he would not have made any different choice. Whatever happened, he was grateful to have met her. And he could only chuckle, despite himself, when he thought of the sheer bravery and raw guts it must have taken for her to go directly against Albryan.

It was what Drailin would have done. Forthright and outspoken, Hiram's wife had had little of the aloof bearing of most mage-maidens. She'd not been particularly stunning to look at either, brown-haired and brown-eyed with an angular narrow face, but Hiram had loved her spirit since the day he'd met her along the riverfront of Armour City. She'd been selling her services as a painter of magical portraits—"*Sit for me and I'll show you an image of yourself you could never imagine*" as he remembered her sales pitch—and he'd been a shy young man taking a break from his studies of law, totally unprepared for her sudden appearance in his life.

Yet the unexpected encounters are oft the ones of greatest importance. He knew this well. He had visited the monastery in Lynborder with little hope of finding any trail to Lathea, yet he had come away thinking he'd seen a ghost. A ghost of some possible future, one where his daughter had lived to raise a daughter of her own.

He had not breathed a word of this family resemblance to Velda herself. Yet he, who had known Lathea her whole life, could not gainsay it. From the dubious starting material of her parents, Lathea Remnia had somehow distilled a quiet beauty of her own. That beauty was reflected back in Velda's face, eyes of the same colour and shape, the same crooked smile of mischief, even the same nose, the beak she'd inherited from him. Velda's darker skin tone and black curls, though, that could have been Karat's, who had been his daughter's husband. Half Sang and half Morgein, Karat had been darker than most of the Mage-Gifted who dwelt in Armour City. Hiram well remembered the moment he had first seen Velda; he had been half convinced that he'd hallucinated her, and probably come across as being unforgivably rude that day.

There was a gulf between the evidence of Hiram's eyes and what he actually knew to be true, though, and so he had kept his silence on the subject. Velda had just finished grieving the loss of one family; the burden of a family she had never known would be too cruel a thing to lay on her. Hiram had thought that he would much rather spend this time getting to know who she was, rather than having to dwell upon the painful past. Upon what had happened to Drailin, to Karat, to Lathea and the second child she had been carrying.

Likely Hiram would never know the full truth, never know exactly how the orphan girl had fetched up at the monastery. *A pair of traders sold her for a handful of silver pawns.* What that portended, if Lathea had been her mother, was something Hiram could hardly bear to face.

The trail grew abruptly narrower and steeper, and he dismounted to lead Santie forward. It sounded as though something were moving through the undergrowth nearby, with swift footsteps upon the ground and rustling in the bushes. He told himself that it must be a herd of antelope.

The tree cover was thinning on the way up, and the sky peeked through the branches, blue as periwinkle. Hiram lifted his eyes to look ahead on the path, and stopped dead. The mule shied and pulled her halter from his hand, turned around with a bray of fear, and ran back the way they had come. Hiram, however, found himself unable to move or speak.

A shining silver-armoured figure stood above him, facing him down on the path. He tried to move, tried to flee, and found that he could not. A smile spread over the armoured woman's face as she advanced towards him.

Knowing that she had caught him in a spell, Hiram was afraid, yet resolute. After all, he had lived his life. He knew that this most likely marked his end, yet he also knew that this woman was not after *him*. He was secondary bait, and she wanted something much, much more precious.

Dark shapes materialized from beneath the trees. *Necromes.* Hiram wondered, for a moment, why he was being captured and not outright killed, and then quickly realized the truth.

And, just as quickly, he made his decision. There had never been any question. He would gladly have died for Lathea's sake.

THE SUN HAD FINALLY COME OUT, yet Albryan's mind was in darkness as he refastened his belt and shrugged his shirt back on. He had no idea how to behave now, no inkling of what to say.

Velda sat on the fallen tree a few feet away, the dawning sun in her curly hair and a pensive look in her eyes. The light behind her made them a translucent, warm golden-yellow. Albryan was struck by how much she resembled the little deer that lived in the southernmost part of Qwu'Mallorn, not antelope but true deer, tiny and brown with their trusting golden eyes. There was a spot of blood on her front, on the white shift, where he'd bled on her when the wound on his chest reopened with the intensity of their movements together.

He was about to open his mouth to speak, to say that Hiram was waiting and they had to move on quickly, when the sensation hit him. Fire and blood, copper and steel, and over it all the instinctive nausea he felt at sensing *her* again. *Dannine Sylvaissen.* He cursed loudly, and Velda started.

"What's the matter?"

"We have to go. *Now.* Can you still run?" She nodded wordlessly and stood up. "I'll carry you if I have to," he promised. "Velda—it's the one who controls the necromes, nearby again." He scanned her face to make sure she understood. "Not close, not yet, but she will be on our trail soon." He held out his hand to her. "Will you follow me?"

She nodded and took his hand. Obedient now, with almost no trace of the cervine wildness she had displayed just a moment ago. Yet Albryan was not like to forget anytime soon, the madness that had swept over him, the feel of her in his arms and the sweet taste of her kiss.

He cursed himself for the delay, yet well knew that there was nothing to be done. *Save your strength for the fight, soldier*, he told himself. *Not for worry, or self-blame. Get her to safety. Most important thing. More important than anything you've ever done.* He pulled her closer, and set off into the rays of the dawning sun.

At first they made good time, the dawn forest flashing by as he led the way unerringly along the track he knew was there. Law and custom held that this part of the forest was not claimed by the Morgei, was not counted within the borders of their sacred woods. But trees paid no heed to human custom and law, grew here as surely as they did across the magical Border, and Albryan knew his footing would not fail under the ironwoods of his home.

But soon enough Velda tired, and so did Albryan himself. They sloped off to a trot, then a fast walk. Albryan would not allow them to stop, so they stumbled forward, and all the while the danger was right behind him, the knowledge that Dannine Sylvaissen was after him again. It was hard for Albryan not to turn and look behind, even when he knew exactly how close she was. *Not close enough*, he told himself. *Not yet. We may still make it. We're ahead of her, I can feel it.* His breath rasped in his own ears, counterpoint to Velda's softer breathing behind. Albryan kept her hand in his, even when she strug-gled to match his strides. He would not, could not let her fall behind.

Like any old campaigner, Albryan was a master at creating and revising plans on the fly, and his mind worked continuously as he went. If Dannine found them, he would have to hide Velda some-how. He could let himself be retaken, tortured, killed, it didn't mat-ter. Albryan was used to weighing the importance of his own life against other outcomes. Even if they were separated, Velda had a chance to survive. He recalled the direction the would-be slaves whom she had helped free had taken. Perhaps there was safety in numbers; certainly no-one would think twice of the girl in their group. They'd accepted her as one of their own almost instantly. She seemed to have that kind of talent.

Albryan's heart hammered against his ribs, and the green woods swam before his eyes. He slowed, easing off his pace before he bent his knees. Velda hit the ground before he did, obviously caring about nought but the reprise.

Albryan felt far more light-headed than he should have, by his own estimation. He touched the shallow wound on his chest. His shirt was so filthy, with his blood and the blood of the men he'd killed, that it was impossible to tell how much the wound had bled just from looking at it, but he could feel a warm, sticky wetness against his chest and halfway down to his waist now. He cursed softly.

Velda crouched near him. "Should I—should I take a look at

that, again?"

"Nothing we can do besides hope that it'll stop bleeding," he replied curtly, pressing his shirt into the wound again. He could see the concern in her eyes; the shirt was gory, and it was a risk for infection, but he couldn't afford to worry about that. When he got free—if he got free with her—then they would be in Qwu'Mallorn, and he would easily find treatment for any infection.

He took deep breaths, gulping in replenishing air, willed his magical senses to remain reliable, to serve him. Dannine was no closer than could be expected at this point, if all else had remained the same. Albryan darted a nervous glance around the trees. If the amount of magic she was using had remained constant. He had felt no surges, and assumed that he was sensing her normal background level of magic. If she was damping it somehow, though . . . she could be much closer than what he guessed. And she could feel him, there was no doubt of that, and more than likely knew how depleted he was.

"Velda." Albryan took her hand again. "Listen to me."

She was pallid with fear, but Albryan saw resolve behind the golden eyes she turned towards him. She had amazed him with her resolve already; perhaps it was a good thing that she was made so stubborn. Perhaps it would save her.

"The blood sorcerer," Albryan began. "Arran Sylvaissen. Velda, he cannot win. He must not. If they take you, kill you . . . all is lost." He saw the look on her face, and forestalled her. "I know it, Velda. I feel it. If Arran has you, Qwu'Mallorn will fall. The whole continent will fall to him. We will die, the magic-folk, and blood sorcery—dark magic—will remain. There is no-one who can stand against this on their own." He took both her hands in his. "Only you." He searched her eyes. "Do you understand how important you are?"

She dropped her gaze. "Albryan, if you're wrong about—"

"I am not wrong. Not in this." Albryan reached out and put a hand in her hair, smoothed it down, trying to transmit calm. "Velda, you are the one who must escape. Not me. If I tell you to hide, you must obey me. Please." He waited for her nod. "You promise to obey?"

"I do." Her voice was small. "I'll run, or hide if you tell me to."

"Thank you." He drew her closer. "Keep going east, and you will find the flint hills. Hiram will wait there, at the border of Qwu'Mallorn. Without me, though, you cannot enter. But the people you freed from the soldiers tonight—they are heading towards the coast. There is a small village at the delta where they hunt gems on the beach. If you and Hiram head there, with the farmers, you should be safe until I can find you again."

"You're not going to leave me now, though?" Her voice was high with fear.

"No." He had not planned to kiss her, but suddenly it was the most natural and necessary thing. She was trembling even as she gave him her mouth, clinging to him in what seemed half passion and half fear. Albryan wondered whether this sweet kiss would be his last, whether he'd spent his last seed inside a woman with her, and suddenly, overwhelmingly, he did not want to let her go. Not ever; not even if it was the most logical course of action. They could not, should not be apart; he could not lose her.

Velda broke the kiss and coughed, and in a moment Albryan smelled it too. He got slowly to his feet. Smoke was curling through the branches around them.

"Fire," Velda whispered needlessly. Albryan could hear the crack of splitting branches and the whoosh of flame already, and above the trees bright tongues of yellow and orange were appearing, higher than the tallest yellowwoods. The trees were damp, he knew, the weather had been nowhere near dry enough for a fire that big to develop . . . yet none of that mattered. Not when the fire had obviously been started by magic.

Velda hovered behind him. "How—"

"No time." Albryan fell back, mouth dry, and dragged her alongside him. "We have to get out of here."

It was not the direction they had been heading, but that didn't matter anymore. Albryan wound his way abreast of the smoke as best he could, trying to get ahead of the front of fire. Some patches of woodland had refused to catch even in the magically enhanced blaze, and Albryan steered in that direction, hoping to avoid being drawn too far south.

They were blinded by the smoke and disoriented by the movement of the fire, and worst of all, he could no longer figure out how far Dannine Sylvaissen was. Magic lay thick on the ground with the flames, and he obviously could not hide Velda here. He held on to her hand and hoped for the best, tried to outrun the flames for now, tried to hold on to his bearings.

At last he stumbled onto flint pebbles underfoot, and relief washed through him. He looked ahead. The slope of the hill was afire, blocking the way.

He wondered briefly where Hiram was. Velda clung to his arm, breathing hard in panic. Albryan focused his power. They only needed one clear path. Over the hill which stood in front of them, and then home free.

Dredging up the last of his reserves, he reached for the fire. His own power flowed over the land, cooling, pulling the fire back into the earth. The tall flames dimmed, faltered, shrank back, leaving only ash and smouldering brush behind. By his side, Velda gaped, and Albryan allowed himself the smallest of prideful flickers. It was not something just anyone could have done, for his focus had to be impeccable. It was always easier to direct chaos rather than use magic in an orderly fashion. Chaos came from raw power, whereas order depended on the magician's focus and control.

He led Velda swiftly up the slope. The brush was still smouldering, and he warned her to move quickly. They reached a gravel path, began to climb swiftly. Albryan's heart pounded; he was incoherent with haste. *Just a little further.* Damping the fire had drawn away almost all of his reserves, and the surge of magic was sure to alert Dannine to his position.

They reached the summit of the hill, and Albryan paused for breath. The slope to his left was forested, fire creeping slowly uphill even as he watched. To his right was a steeply falling cliff. He gazed across the gap to the slope of the neighbouring hillock, and his heart turned to stone as sunlight reflected stark from the surface of gleaming silvered armour.

Surrounded by her necromes and smouldering pockets of smoke and flame, she stood proudly, as though she had planned every detail of the trap she would lead them into. Which of course she had. She was cool and collected; even from the distance between, Albryan could see her smile. Even as they watched, she threw another fireball into the forest above them, almost lazily, as if it were no expenditure of energy at all.

Albryan clenched his fist on the hilt of his sword.

"Are you sure you want to fight?" Dannine called. "Fat lot of good it did you last time—oh, and you might want to consider—"

She beckoned two of her necromes forward, and Albryan felt sick. *Hiram.* The old man looked grim in the grip of his captors, but was as yet unhurt.

Albryan felt Velda move beside him, and flung out a hand to intercept her, seizing her by the arm and putting her securely behind him. She started to call to Hiram, but Albryan forestalled her. "Don't!" She subsided at his glare.

"Resist me, and I kill this pathetic old man," Dannine called languorously.

Albryan's mouth was dry. "I'll surrender. I'll come willingly."

"You and the girl both."

Albryan moved another inch in front of Velda. "She's nobody. Neither of them are. They have no Mage-Gift."

Dannine's smile flashed silver. "I'll be the judge of that."

"They're both innocent." Albryan moved sideways, trying to lessen the size of the target they would make. "Let them go, and I won't fight you. You know I can beat you."

Dannine laughed, long and loudly. Albryan's gaze roved across the gap and met Hiram's.

Albryan had not known the former Alderman for a long time, only the few weeks they had journeyed together. But there was something in the hawkish eyes that he thought he recognized—had seen in soldiers' eyes before.

Hiram held his gaze, as if to assure that Albryan understood.

He could only gaze back, not daring to breathe. Flames were crackling around them in all directions now. Even if Dannine bespelled them, there was no guarantee that she would be able to retrieve him and Velda. Hiram must understand that, he knew, and surely he also understood that Velda would never consent to leave without rescuing him.

All at once, as if desperately trying to escape the grip of the necromes that held him, the old man darted forward.

Velda screamed. It was over in a heartbeat. Claws ripped the old man's throat, blood spattered on the ground, and Hiram collapsed.

Albryan grasped Velda's wrist hard enough to bruise even as she cried out, holding her back, pulling her again behind him.

Dannine spared only a sidelong glance for the carnage. "Surrender," she called coolly across the gap between the hills, "or your fates will mirror his."

Albryan drew his sword instead.

Dannine threw a web of power at him. It was so fast even Albryan had trouble following its arc. Velda, who could not see pure magic with the naked eye and had no Sense to show her the lines of magic on the other plane, should not even have known that it existed. Yet she moved as quickly as Dannine had, wrenching her arm from Albryan's grasp and stepping in front of him.

The arc of power struck *something* that encased the air around Velda, reverberated like a gong on the other plane and through his magical senses, sent Albryan reeling back with aftershock. The world seemed to have tilted, and yet Velda had not moved. Dannine fell back, her eyes wide, face stricken with horror. She called to her necromes, and they surged forward.

Velda stood her ground, and Albryan felt an alien force radiating from her body. Not magic, but the opposite of magic. All her being was focused on the necromes, as she sent that miraculous force into their hideous bodies of dark sorcery to break apart the bonds that had been woven of pain and death and evil. She was a tool of light, and yet Albryan was afraid. His spirit cowered from her, a creature of magic instinctively hiding from the clutches of a ravening predator, from the waves of undoing which were dreadful to him in a way even blood sorcery was not. He did not know whether he should run far away or fall to his knees in abject servitude. The power she wielded was beyond him, and as Albryan had before, he seemed to see the shape of the Mother Goddess in her, beautiful yet terrible to mortal eyes, fiercely protective yet a force of pure destruction.

The necromes fell where they stood, mid-stride, the foremost only yards away, black magic sloughing off into the ether, their bodies reverting to mundane humanity.

It was then that Dannine dropped her sword, boots slipping on the flint pebbles, knees buckling, real fear on her face. Velda spared her one last look and turned away.

Bemused, Albryan watched as Santie, their mule, appeared from behind a bush and made straight for her. Velda took the mule's halter, stroked her nose.

The forest fire was blazing all around them now, far too close for Albryan's comfort. Yet Velda turned the mule's head due east, as if she knew exactly where the border of Qwu'Mallorn was, and grabbed hold of Albryan's hand.

"Stay with me." Fearlessly, she stepped onto the path, smoke roiling around her. Albryan sensed more impacts of magic, Dannine flinging bolts wildly, but none of them even came close to striking, dissipating in the blinding radiance of Velda's power. At the last moment Dannine tried to follow them, sprinting down the hill, but her own fires caught up with her and she collapsed, coughing, in the smoke.

Albryan turned away, eyes fixing upon Velda's face. There were streaks of tears across her cheeks, mixed in with smoke from the fire and blood from Albryan's own hands, yet her expression was one of resolution and absolute calm. She was completely focused on something beyond Albryan's ability to discern, some goal he could not see beyond his anguish and the raw fear that burned in him at her display of power.

Velda seemed to follow a path only she knew, twisting and turning to avoid the fires and pockets of roiling smoke, as if guided by a sense from outside of herself. The mule followed her trustingly, never once wavering, and so did Albryan Lana.

Our heroes continue on their journey . . .

"What happened to you?" Elithan looked him up and down, gripped him by the shoulders, inspected his face as carefully as any concerned grandfather. "You've lost weight, but you don't seem nearly as dead as we all thought."

***

She had an accent, Fish realized with some surprise, that was nearly identical to Nico's, flavoured with the ruggedness of the Svanlyn mountains. She was not a mage, either; Fish probed carefully, and found only the same not-presence that someone like Nico gave off in the ether.

***

Dannine was disgraced. She would be lucky to leave here alive, she thought, and there was a certain freedom in that. She did not fear death, not at the hands of the father who had shaped her to become all she was.

Book 2 of the Forest of the Morning trilogy

Maiden of Despair

Coming 2025

Keep updated at www.thepinkhydra.com

Other books by Emmylou Kotzé:

The Broken Knight

Stories of Nico and Fish:

"What Makes a Man . . ." (Cloaked Press, Fall Into
Fantasy 2024)

And more to come . . .

About the Author

 Emmylou Kotzé is a poet and writer from Mangaung, South Africa. The name of her birthplace translates as "The Place of the Cheetah," which may help explain her lifelong fondness for mystic felines. The major artistic influence on her life as a child was the TV show *Xena, Warrior Princess*, which showed the ideal of a woman who can kick ass, solve problems, and break hearts wherever she goes. Since then, Emmylou has had a burning passion to write the lives of unconventional heroes in historical settings in all their passion, power, guts and glory.

"Forest of the Morning" is a narrative that has undergone many branching-offs, retellings, and alterations over the years. Originally a saga titled "Elfmage," about a long-lost elven princess reclaiming her kingdom, it all started in 2006 with Velda and Hiram. Albryan was added in 2008 as the love interest, and Dannine as the principal antagonist. In 2009, when a young assassin named Nico entered the narrative along with his handsome, flippant partner Fish, the story began to gain direction.

About Pink Hydra Press

Founded in 2024 to make a space for new, queer, and weird speculative literature, Pink Hydra Press is the only organization of its kind in Africa. The genre/lit magazine The Pink Hydra has published short stories and poems from dozens of international authors. The book press is just starting out.

If you enjoy stories with a touch of the weird, or if you're an author who loves writing books and poetry infused with weirdness, come visit us at www.thepinkhydra.com.

We publish a variety of genres, but we are particularly interested in queer science fiction and fantasy, stories written by and about women, stories which challenge the current status quo, and spicy romantic and erotic stories.

Many heads. One mission.